UNMASKED!

Following the rules of the masquerade ball, the man wore the costume of a scarlet domino, but Georgina knew who he was. There was no mistaking the strikingly strong figure, arrogant carriage, and burning gaze of David Linwood.

Trembling, Georgina realized she was alone with the one man she feared most to be alone with. She backed against the wall as Linwood followed her step by step, like a panther hunting prey. He reached out and removed her mask. Then his lips came down hard on hers.

"But what is this?" he said, when he released her at last. "I understood you were a widow. What a cold marriage you must have had! Why, any fifteen-year-old maid receives a man with more passion. What a great deal I have to teach you."

And Georgina knew she had been unmasked in more ways than one. . . .

A SURFEIT OF SUITORS

A Surfeit of Suitors

Barbara Hazard

A SIGNET BOOK

NEW AMERICAN LIBRARY

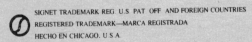

SIGNET, SIGNET CLASSIC, MENTOR, ONYX, PLUME, MERIDIAN
and NAL BOOKS are published by NAL PENGUIN INC.,
1633 Broadway, New York, New York 10019

First Printing, March, 1983

    4   5   6   7   8   9   10   11   12

PRINTED IN THE UNITED STATES OF AMERICA

Of all the torments, all the cares,
With which our lives are cursed;
Of all the plagues a lover bears,
Sure rivals are the worst!

—William Walsh, 1663–1708

1

"Well, if you don't care to ride in the park this afternoon, or go for a fitting on your new ball gown, and you have no interest in accompanying me to dinner with Lord and Lady Chandler, why don't you marry Teddy Waring then?"

The lady who was standing at the window of the elegant town house on Brooks Street, staring out on a mild March day, dropped the brocade drapery she was holding and spun around to gaze at the other occupant of the drawing room in some amazement. "Can I have heard you correctly, aunt?" she asked in an incredulous voice from which she was unable to hide a quiver of amusement. "Marry Lord Waring? Whatever for?"

"It seems the most sensible course for one who is so sunk in listlessness that anything that is suggested not only fails to amuse but also falls on deaf ears. Here I have mentioned any number of unexceptional activities, and your only response has been 'mmm . . . perhaps . . . but I think not.' Perhaps if you were married, you would not have time to be so bored!"

She spoke in an incisive voice, shaking her head in exasperation, but the young woman at the window only broke into peals of laughter as she came to take a seat across from the lady. When she was able to speak at last, she asked, "You don't feel, dear Aunt Bess, the course you propose is too drastic a cure for mere *ennui*? And how very unfair to poor Edward, when I have not the least *tendre* for him!"

Her aunt looked up from the tapestry she was working on. "As if that would matter to the man! He is so mad about you, he will not even notice! And perhaps with a

1

husband, and eventually children, to concern you, you will forget these die-away airs, Georgie!"

The younger lady folded her hands in her lap and lowered her eyelashes in pretended chagrin. "Forgive me, dear aunt. How boring for *you* to have me drooping about, all dreary sighs. I was not aware of my failing."

Miss Hersham looked up over her spectacles, her little blue eyes sharp. "Pooh! You know very well, Georgie, that that is an exaggeration. I did not mean that you have not been everything that is correct; vivacious in company, yet always pleasant and well-bred. But for someone who has known you as long as I have, it is obvious that you no longer find life the adventure you once did. Some might think you are still mourning your husband; of course *I* know that for the whisker it is!"

Her niece leaned forward a little, startled by this intelligence, as Miss Hersham continued, "Married you may have been, but it was only because your father insisted on the alliance and convinced you to consent to it. I wish I had been at Mumford Park then! I would have told Sir George a thing or two . . . the very idea! No better than babies the two of you were, with not even the time to fix your interests, but your father was dazzled by the title and considered that since *he* liked the family so well, naturally you should follow suit. *Men!*" She paused, and seeing her niece in complete amazement, hastened to add, "I know you only thought of John Spalding as a boy you had grown up with, and when he went off to the Peninsular War with Wellington, your relief was obvious, at least to me. Now here you are, a young, beautiful, and bored widow. But, Georgie"—and here she leaned forward in turn and shook her finger at her niece—"if you do not change your ways, you will end up old and wrinkled, and still bored to boot. If you cannot like Lord Waring, at least remain in town for the coming Season now you are out of black gloves, and see who else might appeal to you, for I warn you, there is no sense at all in returning to Somerset to await a Prince Charming come to storm the citadel and win your hand. Such things occur only in novels; in real life a woman must be cleverer than that!"

Lady Spalding stared at her aunt, stunned that she knew so much of what she thought she had concealed so successfully. When at twenty she had married the only son and heir of her father's dearest friend and nearest neighbor, she had been young and completely unsophisticated, with not even a Season in town to lend her confidence, for the year she turned eighteen, her mother had been ill and unable to present her to society. Then Lady Mumford died, and there was no thought of a Season while the family was in mourning, nor could there be one later when her father fell ill himself. Somehow Georgina found herself unable to refuse him when he begged her to marry John Spalding before he died. He told her it was his dearest wish, and the wish of her dead mother as well, and so, with only a mild liking for the young Captain, Georgina became his bride. She was wiser now than she had been then, and when she thought about it at all, it was to admit to herself that she preferred the single state. Her brief marriage had done nothing to encourage her to repeat the performance. The liking she had for Captain Spalding, Marquess of Allyndale, had not deepened into love, and when John went away with his regiment, she had been able to feel only a guilty sense of relief to be free of him. The news of his death at San Sebastian in 1813 had caused her to feel regret, not for herself, but that such a young life had ended so abruptly, and she was hard put to mourn him as he deserved. Certainly she had never felt the wild grief she had when her father died only a few weeks after her wedding day. When her husband's cousin came to claim the title, and Aunt Bess, her mother's spinster sister, offered to live with her in the dower house on the Marquess's estate, Georgina thought her life settled and comfortable, and was content to visit her brother and his family, rent a house in Brighton or Bath, or go to town whenever she wished. She liked country amusements better than those of London; the riding and the hunting, the family celebrations, and the occasional Assembly at Salisbury. Perhaps it was because there had been so many deaths in such a short time in her life that she preferred the peaceful tempo of Somerset to the noise and confusion of town, and she had in fact been making vague plans to remove there in a few weeks so she might enjoy the spring and early summer in the countryside. But now, here was her aunt predicting a dire and solitary future, old and wrinkled and ugly as well. She rose and went to the mirror over the mantelpiece, tucking back an errant curl as she did so.

The face she observed with the thickly lashed green eyes that stared back at her was reassuring. True, she wished she was not so fair that freckles had always been a constant worry, and she thought her cheekbones much too prominent, but she was pleased with her high forehead and aristocratic nose and with her determined round chin. The only thing she really disliked about her looks was her mouth, especially the lower lip, which she felt was much too full for beauty. She had no idea how intriguing a feature this was, nor how many gentlemen had wondered what it would feel like to kiss. She decided her hair was her best asset—thick and curling and a glorious deep chestnut that gleamed in the sunlight with golden lights. Her gaze travelled down her smart afternoon gown of nile-green silk trimmed with matching braid. It was cut narrowly in the latest mode, and since her figure was excellent, became her to perfection. Her waist was as small as anyone could wish, and every modiste she had ever honoured with her custom had exclaimed over the gentle swell of her hips and breasts and over her long, slim legs. Suddenly she smiled and made a face at her reflection before she shrugged and went back to her aunt.

"Come, now, dear, *dear* Aunt Bess! Such a gloomy prophecy! I am not vain, but an old and ugly widow indeed!" She took her seat on the sofa again, laughing the deep, throaty chuckle that had also intrigued many a gentleman. "You know very well I never have to sit out a dance, and I refuse to think it is only because of my wealth and title, for I can see as well as you can what the mirror shows me. Besides, I am only twenty-five!"

Her aunt snipped her thread and smoothed her tapestry, darting a quick glance at her handsome niece. "Pretty is as pretty does, my gel! And if you continue to act so nonchalantly when a gentleman shows any interest in you, before you know it you will be thirty, and then thirty-five and at your last prayers."

Lady Spalding smiled, her eyes twinkling. "A fine one you are to be calling the kettle black, when you yourself have never married! I remember Mama telling me of all the offers you refused, so perhaps it is only that I take after you, aunt."

Miss Hersham put down the scarlet thread she was measuring and said in a quieter voice, "Perhaps that is why I am now such an advocate of connubial bliss, having walked all these years the path you are so determined to embrace."

Lady Spalding thought her eyes seemed sad and faraway and hastened to say, "I must tell you, Aunt Bess, that two years of marriage did not inspire me to rush to the altar again!"

At her aunt's intent look and raised eyebrows, she added in a lighter tone, "Not that John was not a good husband. I would not like you to think that, for he was always most kind and considerate, but . . . but I discovered that marriage was not to my liking. I really do prefer my single state, and you know that as a widow I am allowed more freedom than I have ever known before. It seems to me I have the best of all possible worlds: enough wealth so that I do not have to worry about my future nor force myself to accept some gentleman just so he will support me, and the freedom to do just what I please. Why should I want to marry again, to have to adjust to another's ways, pleasing him and keeping his house, having his children and sharing his bed, and always forced to put my wishes after his? No, no! A second marriage would not suit me at all!"

Miss Hersham sighed. "So, I was right! How sad that you have never been in love! And poor Lord Waring cannot tempt you to matrimony, eh? I only hope I live long enough to see the paragon you finally lose your heart to, Georgie, for no one who looks like you is destined for the single state; 'twould be too cruel a jest of nature! I only hope he does not take too long appearing on the stage, for then you might not have any children, and that, I can tell you, would be a sadness; believe me, I know!"

Lady Georgina came and hugged her. "But you have me, Aunt Bess, as I have all of Roger's children to play at aunt with. If the day should ever come that I regret my decision, I am sure you will be quick to say you told me so, and then we can both bemoan my stubbornness."

What her aunt might have replied was lost, for just then Geering knocked on the drawing-room door and entered to present some calling cards on a silver salver. Afternoon calls were about to begin, and nothing more could be said for the time being, although Lady Spalding was sure her aunt had every intention of returning to the subject again and again. She loved her Aunt Bess in spite of her tendency to fuss over her like a mother hen with one chick, and she had always admired her style. In spite of her completely grey hair, she was still as slim as she had been as a girl, and although at the age of fifty-two she had given up any pretensions to youth, she was always dressed in the first stare of fashion, and she had such a witty turn of phrase, and was so refreshingly outspoken, that wherever she went, she gathered her own little court around her. Now Georgina watched her rise to greet Lord Edward Waring and his tiny mother and younger sister, noticing the special smile she had for this young lady who was about to embark on her first Season and who was almost painfully shy.

For the next hour Lady Spalding was too busy greeting her guests, making sure they were comfortably seated and had been served refreshments, to think more about what her aunt had said. Lord Waring especially seemed determined to monopolize her attention. He was a tall man not much older than she was herself, but his solid, robust form, clad in a severely cut coat from Stultz, made him appear older than his years. Georgina neither disliked him nor cared for him; however, she saw that her aunt was right, and he was trying to fix her interest.

"I have told my sister Emmaline, dear Lady Spalding, that she can have no better model to follow than your own perfect self, and that if she wishes to present a creditable front to society, she should follow your example in dress, manner, and behaviour." He spoke in a whispered aside, for which Georgina was grateful, for his normal speaking voice was a booming, resonant bass. She raised her eyebrows, unable to reply as she stole a glance at the young lady in question, who was now bright red with embarrassment as Mr. Rexton paused by her chair to speak to her. The girl was so gauche, so shy, so . . . so young!

"Lord Waring," she demurred, "surely it would have been better to choose a lady nearer in age to your sister; if she emulates my behaviour, it can only gain her censure! You forget the difference in our ages and stations; what a widow in her twenty-sixth year may do is vastly different from the behaviour required of a seventeen-year-old debutante!"

"Dear lady, you are too modest. How like you to try to turn the compliment," he replied, his eyes never leaving her face. "Everything about you is of the first style of excellence, and your love of gaiety and repartee has never tempted you to go beyond the line of what is pleasing. You are not so very old, dear Lady Spalding . . . I may call you '*dear* lady'? So kind! And now that you have put off your mourning, what a delight for us all, and, as I am sure I need not point out, for one *especially* who worships at your feet."

Georgina wondered why she had never noticed before what a bore Teddy Waring was, but since there did not seem to be anything she could reply to this ponderous compliment, she nodded with composure and excused herself to go and speak to Lady Martin.

"Escaping the wearisome Lord Waring, Georgie?" this lady asked as she took a seat beside her. Georgina smiled. Lady Martin was one of her favorite people, an old friend and confidante of her aunt's and one who never hesitated to speak her mind about any subject that appealed to her. She was in her late fifties, and troubled occasionally with a rheumatic complaint, but she held her head high and was never heard to complain about her condition.

"Dear Lady Martin, what big eyes you have!" Georgina teased her. "Yes, Lord Waring seems determined to bring up heavier artillery today. I had not realized he thought himself my foremost admirer; he was almost proprietary in his manners!" She paused and a little frown appeared between her brows, which Lady Martin was quick to notice.

"Never mind him, Georgie! It can only add to your consequence to have him dancing attendance on you, you know, even if he is a pompous stick, for his family is an old and honorable one, and he himself worth twenty thousand pounds a year. If he becomes too troublesome, I am sure you will know just how to depress his presumptions and cool his ardour!"

Georgina smiled again. "I have certainly never encouraged him, m'lady!" she said earnestly.

"Of course not, but that will not stop him from pursuing you; he thinks so well of himself, he needs no encouragement. In all the years I have watched society, I have never been able to fathom why some men choose the most unsuitable women to fall in love with; women who, if they did agree to matrimony, would drive their bridegrooms crazy in a month!"

She snorted, and Georgina asked in mock melancholy, "What, am I so unsuitable, then? How lowering that it should be so!"

Lady Martin patted her hand. "None of your sarcasm with me, Georgie! But what makes a Teddy Waring think that a vivacious, gay, and intelligent gel like you would want to have to do with the likes of him? He is cut from such a worthy yard of cloth; prosy, opinionated, and above all, so *dull!* No, no, my dear! We shall find you someone much better than that!"

Georgina rose before her temper got the better of her. Lady Martin too; it was too much! "I must speak to my aunt, ma'am. I beg you not to trouble yourself, or encourage Aunt Bess to do so either. I have no intention of marrying again, so there is no necessity for either of you to search for a husband for me, for I would refuse even royalty if asked."

She smiled to remove the sting from her words and went away, and Lady Martin's shrewd eyes followed her across the drawing room. Dear Georgie had been almost tart; perhaps Bess had been speaking to her? Then she chuckled to herself. As if either one of them would have to lift a finger. Where Lady Georgina Spalding was concerned, what would be more to the point was a large watchdog with a very big stick to beat back the hordes of suitors who were sure to appear. She beckoned to Miss Hersham, and in a short time the two old friends had their heads together, deep in conversation.

Lady Spalding went to speak to Emmaline Waring, but it could not be said to be a success. Beyond whispering monosyllabic replies, Emmaline made no contribution to the conversation, and when Georgina saw Lord Waring smiling and nodding his approval, she excused herself, her color a little high as she went to join a group by the fire. She was so charming to Lady Sefton, and flirted so gaily with young Mr. Rexton, who was also about to embark on his first lengthy stay in town, that she quite turned his head. When he went away to fetch her a glass of negus, Maria Sefton tapped her hand. "Naughty of you, Georgie! Leave the poor boy alone, else he will spend the Season in a dream of unrequited love, which would please his father not at all."

"Why, Lady Sefton, I am not such a man-trap as that,"

Georgina assured her with a chuckle. "But it cannot signify in any case, for I do not plan to remain in town much longer. I have just about made up my mind to retire to Spalding Hall for a few months."

Lady Sefton stared, her championship of Mr. Rexton forgotten. "Are you quite mad, Georgie? Whatever for? Here all the world is making plans to come to the metropolis, and you decide to leave it! It puts me out of all patience with you. You may be sure your Aunt Elizabeth will have something to say about such a plan."

"Of course she may say what she likes, and she is free to remain here if so she wishes, but as for me, I am homesick for green fields and the hills and streams of Somerset; the metropolis begins to pall. And one of the nicest things about being a respectable widow is that I can do exactly as I please." Georgina swept a mock curtsy as Lady Sefton's mouth dropped open and then shut with a snap. "I know; it is too bad of me, is it not, ma'am?" Georgina sympathized with her. "But we shall see—there is nothing definite decided as yet."

Eventually the callers took their respective leaves, and Aunt Bess went up to rest and dress for her evening engagement with the Chandlers. Georgina instructed Geering to serve on a tray in the drawing room the very simple supper that was all she would require before she settled down happily with the third volume of Mrs. Whitebridge's latest novel. How peaceful it is, she thought as she curled her feet under her in the large wing chair, not to have to smile and smirk and laugh, or make witty conversation with people I am tired of meeting everywhere I go. Yes, I think I will go home; three months in town is quite enough for me.

The next day was so pleasant and warm it was more like late April than early March. Georgina was awake early and rang for her maid, determined on a ride in the park before it became too crowded. She drank her chocolate, dressed in one of her favorite habits, and left a message for her aunt, reassuring her that she would not fail to join her later that morning for a proposed shopping trip.

The groom who helped her into the saddle was an old Spalding retainer that Georgina had known from childhood. He knew how she chafed at the necessity of always having

a groom to attend her in town, for his services had often
been dispensed with at home.

"Mind the mare, Lady Spalding," he reminded her. "You
have not ridden her for some days, and she is fresh."

The chestnut mare with the two white forefeet was
gambolling playfully, but Georgina's touch soon brought
her under control, and although she tossed her head and
whinnied, she was obedient to the reins held so compe-
tently in the lady's gloved hands.

Lady Spalding took a deep breath. "What a lovely day,
Ives! It may not be Somerset, but I think we shall have
the park to ourselves this early. How I long for a good
gallop! And it may not be much longer before we are both
of us at home once again."

The groom touched his hat before he mounted his own
sturdy gelding. It couldn't be soon enough for him, he
thought as he followed the lady through the early-morning
streets. Lunnon! So noisy, so crowded! Even this early,
milk carts and coal sellers rumbled through the streets,
along with candlemakers and farmers' wives all crying
their wares. A pair of dirty urchins darted in front of his
horse, causing it to shy a little and Ives to curse under his
breath. Lunnon was more than a countryman could abide
for very long. He watched the black-velvet back of Lady
Spalding riding before him. She was a lovely lass, he
thought, wondering not for the first time how long it would
be before she left the Hall as the bride of some lucky lord.
If Georgina could have known his thoughts, she would
have been indignant, for then it would appear that surely
the whole world was determined to marry her off, willy-
nilly, and regardless of whether she wished for it or not.

There were a few other early-morning riders in Hyde
Park, but compared to the fashionable promenade hour
between five and six in the afternoon, it seemed almost
deserted. At that time, the park was crowded with all the
fashionables of society, come to walk and ride and chat
with their friends, both the ladies and gentlemen showing
off new toilettes and exchanging gossip.

They had not gone very far, at a gentle trot, when Ives
pulled up his horse. "Pardon, Lady Spalding!" he called,
causing Georgina to turn in the saddle and halt her mare.
The groom's horse was limping slightly, and she rode back

to where Ives had slid from its back and was expertly inspecting the injured leg.

"He's stretched a tendon is all, your ladyship," he muttered. "I thought he stumbled a while back; now what's to do?"

He looked so concerned that Georgina laughed. "You must lead him back to the stables, Ives, of course! He cannot bear your weight until the tendon heals. Go on, man, off with you!"

The groom still hesitated, so she added, "There is no need to be concerned about me, Ives. I shall finish my ride and return home safely, and since there are only unfashionable people abroad this early, who will know that Lady Georgina Spalding defied the social code by riding without an attendant? What they do not know, they cannot censure! Go on, then! The sooner you can attend to the horse, the better."

She waved her riding crop, and turning her mare, rode away. Ives stared after her for a moment before he began to lead the lame horse back to the mews. "Aye, m'lady, and much you'd care if the whole world could see you!" he muttered to himself, shaking his head, but since he knew his mistress was a horsewoman with an excellent seat seldom found in females, and that she could control her mare sidesaddle as well as astride, it was not fear of her being thrown that worried him.

Georgie cantered down Rotten Row, revelling in her freedom. In deference to convention, she nobly decided against a gallop, and promised herself only one circuit of the park before she returned to Brooks Street. Another solitary horseman was cantering towards her, and she nodded distantly as they met and passed each other. She had had a glimpse of a large man, with sharp craggy features and powerful shoulders and legs; not precisely a handsome gentleman, but one who even at a distance conveyed a strength well above most men of her acquaintance. She thought she surprised an astonished look, and smiled to herself, but then she heard hoofbeats behind her, and although she did not turn, her heart beat a little faster. Was he following her? Did he think her one of the pretty little demimondes out for an early-morning flirtation because she was unattended? If he did think that, he would be brought quickly to a realization of his mistake!

The hoofbeats drew even with her, but did not pass, and she was forced to look to her left, where she saw the stranger staring at her. She drew a deep breath and tried to pull away, but it seemed the man had no intention of allowing her to do so. For a while they galloped side by side, all Georgina's good intentions forgotten, but eventually she was forced to slow her mare when she realized the pace was distressing her. The stranger slowed as well, and Georgina felt her color rise. She refused to look at him again, and tried to keep her bearing haughty and uninterested.

"Well, here's a pretty piece of luck!" a deep voice drawled. "Never did I think to have the chance of a gallop with such as you, my lovely!"

Georgina stiffened. "You will do me the courtesy to leave me!" she commanded, turning her mare and preparing to ride away.

The stranger reached out and grasped her bridle. "Not so fast, my dear. What, let you ride away before we have a chance to begin our friendship? Oh, you are concerned that we have not been properly introduced. Allow me to do the honors; Mr. David Linwood at your service, ma'am, yes, most definitely at your service. And have you no tasks for me to perform? No dragons to be slain? No ruffians for me to run through, so I might show my homage to such beauty?"

Georgina stared into his mocking blue eyes and then at the strong hand holding her bridle. Strangely, she was not in the least afraid, even though there was no one near them she could call to for help.

"Release my mare at once, sir! I have no desire for your acquaintance, and the only ruffian I can see in the vicinity is yourself!"

The gentleman grinned down at her from his saddle, his white teeth gleaming against the mahogany tan of his face. "Well, I like that! You are a haughty little filly, aren't you?"

Georgina thought his accent very odd. He had so slow a drawl it was nothing at all like the clipped English voices she was so accustomed to. And it was not an Irish brogue, nor was he a French emigré, or a German or Italian. Before she thought, she asked in real curiosity, "Where are you from, sir? You do not speak like anyone I have ever heard before."

He laughed and removed his riding hat, causing the breeze to ruffle his dark brown hair. He was dressed in conventional style, but he did not look as if he cared very much for the set of his cravat or the height of his shirt points, and his twill riding jacket appeared to have been chosen more for comfort than for show.

"I am a Linwood from Virginia, ma'am!"

"Oh, from the colonies!" Georgina said, curling her lip. "I should have guessed from your manners, to be sure."

Mr. Linwood's blue eyes narrowed. "Much as it devastates me to contradict you, ma'am, we are no longer 'colonies,' but a free country. And neither were we defeated by Mother England in this latest war, as you will recall. A formidable opponent, the United States, wouldn't you say? Perhaps if we two were engaged in a contest, I would emerge victorious as well. Perhaps a steeplechase—I'll even give you a head start. Are you brave enough to accept my challenge? For any wager you care to name, of course. I know what forfeit *I* would choose—and well worth the winning it would be, too."

His bold eyes swept to her mouth and lingered there, and Georgina hid a tiny gasp at his audacity. "I have no interest in politics, sir, nor any at all in you and your 'challenges.' Release my bridle. Whatever customs prevail in the colo . . . in the states, here in England it is not at all the thing to be accosting ladies in the park and forcing your attentions on them. But perhaps you did not know that, living as you do among the uncouth savages."

"But you are so beautiful, how can I help it?" He drawled with another lazy smile, although Georgina had seen the quick flash of anger in his eyes at her last remark. "That chestnut hair, that gorgeous figure displayed so admirably, and especially your beautiful mouth. No, 'tis too much to ask a mere man—and one from the 'colonies' as well—to ignore. After all, as you yourself pointed out, living among the savages as I do, I have been bereft of culture and elegance for such a long time, and since Americans are so impetuous, I am sure you must excuse me if I seize the moment and steal a kiss."

He laughed and sidled his horse even closer to her, as if to make good his threat, and Georgina lost her temper. Raising her riding crop, she lashed out at the hand holding her prisoner, and he dropped the bridle. The mare, who had felt the whip as well as he had, bolted away. Georgina galloped towards the gates, wondering if he would catch her up, for she knew well he was capable of doing so. She felt exhilarated rather than frightened, and did not deign to look back. If she had, she would have seen him staring after her, his eyes narrowed and intent as he rubbed the hand she had struck. No woman, and very few men, had ever dared to raise a hand against David Linwood; the lady would be brought to see the error of her ways. He did not attempt to follow her. London society was not so large after all that he could not be sure of meeting her again, for never for a moment had he thought her anything but what she was—a fine lady, wellborn and probably very wealthy. There had been an arrogance about her that bespoke privilege and influence, not that this trait bothered him, for he would have admitted freely, if anyone should ever ask it, that he himself had more than his share of haughty pride. He was sure that she was as used to giving commands and getting instant obedience, as he was himself. Oh yes, mysterious and beautiful and unapproachable she might be, but he would meet her again. He promised himself that and the pleasure of taming her as well as he blew a kiss towards her retreating back and rode slowly after her to the gates of the park.

If Georgina thought of her encounter with the bold stranger from America in the days that followed, it was only at fleeting moments for their paths did not cross again. There were so many engagements suddenly; so many invitations to ride, drink tea, listen at a musicale, dance at a soirée, walk in the park, or attend a dinner or reception. And as her engagements increased, so did her shopping for beautiful, suitable gowns and ensembles to wear. Nothing more was said about retiring to Somerset, although Georgina thought of it one morning when, weary from standing and having her new afternoon gowns fitted, she wished she were there, wearing a comfortable old habit and riding out to inspect the early planting, and she wondered why she remained in town. And then she wondered if Mr. Linwood would think this royal-blue muslin fit her as well as her black habit, and she shook her head at her folly.

Miss Hersham did not mention her niece's future again. Georgina was glad to be spared any more lectures about the undesirability of the single state, but she would not have been so relieved if she had known that her aunt and Lady Martin had decided between them not to provoke her for the present. "For then, you know, Agnes, she will bolt for the home stable," Miss Hersham declared to her old friend, "and no amount of persuasion will get her to town again. Georgie can be very stubborn when she takes the bit between her teeth, and she has had her own way for such a long time, she does not like to be crossed. If only there was someone paying court to her besides that boring Teddy Waring!"

Her friend patted her hand. "Do what you can to keep her in town, Bess. Someone is bound to catch her eye now that all society returns for the Season. All men are not fools, after all. Besides, I have every expectation of welcoming my dear nephew Robert Holland, the Earl of Amesbury, in the very near future, so you can see how important it is that Georgie be in residence here. Now, what do you think of my surprise?"

Lady Martin sat back, her smile triumphant, as Miss Hersham's eyes grew round with wonder. It had long been the private dream of both ladies to unite Georgie and the earl. How perfect a match it would be, and how delightful to be related to each other, and since Robert had reached the age of thirty-three without succumbing to any other lady's charms, why should he not oblige them? They had spent a frustrating year, however, for when Lady Spalding was in town, Lord Holland was in the country, and no sooner had Georgie arrived in Brooks Street after Christmas than dear Robert disappeared from his own elegant town house for an extended stay in Ireland. The two ladies spent a pleasurable hour over the teacups planning their strategy and spinning their webs.

Miss Hersham complimented her niece the evening they met in the hall before Lady Sefton's ball. It was to be the first large affair of the Season, and in honor of the occasion, Georgina was wearing a new and daring gown. It was made of pale green gauze worn over a slip of emerald-green satin which was cut low over her shoulders and trimmed with tiny flowers embroidered in seed pearls. Her hair was brushed back smoothly in deep waves, and the chignon at the nape of her neck was enclosed in a net of pearls to match. At her throat and ears and on her wrists was the Spalding pearl set. Her aunt worried a bit about the neckline of her dress, for even for a married woman many years past her debut, it was very low, and she could never accustom herself to the narrow cut of the new fashions. Skimpy, she called them, used to the full skirts and crinolines of her girlhood, but even so, she had to admit that Georgie looked magnificent. She wished "dear Robert" could see her, but she knew he had not yet arrived in town, for Agnes had promised to send round a note as soon as that happy event took place. Adjusting a sarsenet stole over her own fashionable maroon silk, she strolled with her niece to their carriage, where Geering and the attendant footman tenderly helped both ladies to their seats, and Wiltshire, Georgie's dresser, handed them their reticules and gloves.

Lady Sefton's ballroom was crowded, as befitted a leader of fashion well accustomed to having her invitations clamoured over by the Ton. Georgina saw Lord Waring across the room, standing beside his sister Emmaline, who looked as if she was about to faint with nervousness. Spotting Georgina, Lord Waring made his way to her side, smiling a proprietary welcome and leaving his poor sister to scurry back to where her mother was seated among the dowagers.

"Dear Lady Spalding!" Lord Waring boomed in his hearty voice, causing several people nearby to turn and stare. It was impossible to ignore him, but then Georgina saw over his well-upholstered shoulder the sardonic grin of the stranger from America. Mr. Linwood here? Then he was no mere provincial after all, for Lady Sefton would never allow anyone not in the forefront of society at her ball. Her smile for Lord Waring turned out to be warmer than she had intended.

"How beautiful you look this evening, dear lady," Lord Waring said, his voice carrying over the hum of other conversation, as he captured her hand and raised it to his lips to kiss before he swept her a ponderous but reverent bow. "May I say that you rival all the flowers in England?"

His eyes dropped to the deep décolletage of her gown and his face reddened. Georgina hoped she would not be betrayed into laughter, for although Teddy Waring thought himself quite the dapper dog, awake on every suit, and a *nonpareil* without peer, in reality he was a very staid and conventional man. He continued by her side chatting, but never again did he allow his eyes to drop below her chin. While seeming to attend to him, Georgina noticed Mr. Linwood now in conversation with Lord Alversham and Miss Prudence Walker and her mama, and she also noticed how he managed to keep her in view.

Other guests came to greet her and to chat, and Lord Waring was forced to retreat, but not until he had put his name down for two of the country dances. Suddenly she felt a hand tug her arm, and turned to find her Aunt Bess standing behind her.

"Who is that man?" Miss Hersham demanded in a stage whisper, nodding her head towards Mr. Linwood. "I have seen him watching you, my dear, and even without knowing a thing about him, I must warn you to be on your guard! He is dangerous!"

Georgie raised her brows. "Dear Aunt Bess, how can you say so? I have not been . . . er, formally introduced, but he looks fairly commonplace to me."

"Commonplace!" her aunt repeated, drawing her a little apart from the others. "No, no, Georgie, you have the wrong of it there. He is just like one of the beasts in the Royal Enclosure. Do observe him more closely and tell me then if I am not right."

Since Mr. Linwood had turned away to meet another guest who had just joined his group, Georgie was free to stare at him unnoticed, and she had to admit her aunt was right. His evening clothes were faultless, but they did not set off his long-limbed, muscular physique to advantage. Where the clothing of other men made them look important, he wore his with complete indifference. Now that he was standing, she could see he was several inches above six feet, and there was a restless energy about him she felt was hardly controlled. It must be that harsh face, she mused, feeling a shiver at the base of her spine. It was so tanned, so powerfully carved, and the eyes so keen that above the white formality of his cravat he did seem untamed.

"Perhaps you are right, aunt. He is certainly a contrast to Sir Percival." Sir Percival Gresham was a slight youth, much afflicted with dandyism, and tonight he was a symphony of pale blue, much foaming lace, a floating handkerchief, and fobs, a diamond stickpin, and several rings adorning both his slender white hands. Next to him, Mr. Linwood

looked like a being from another world, not just a stranger
from across the sea.

Georgina turned away before he could catch her staring
and was glad to see Lady Martin bearing down on them.

"Dear Georgie, Bess!" she said as she reached their
sides. "How well you both look—I compliment you on the
emerald green, minx. 'Tis devastating with your eyes," she
told Georgie, holding up her cheek to be kissed. "And,
Bess, such wonderful news as I have. The package that I
have been waiting for arrived this afternoon; *you* know
what I mean!"

"No!" Miss Hersham said, clapping her hands. "Georgie,
you must excuse us, m'dear, there is something that I—"

"Good evenin', Lady Spaldin', your most obedient servant, ma'am," a drawling voice interrupted, and all three
ladies turned to see the man Georgie and her aunt had just
been discussing before them. Georgie was tempted to pretend she had never met him, but even though she could
hardly claim to be able to guess his reaction to such an
insult, she was sure he was capable of using it to his
advantage, and that might upset her aunt, who had already taken him in such dislike. She watched his deep bow,
and the bow he gave each of the older ladies, and was
constrained to do the pretty.

"Mr. . . . Mr. . . . ?" she asked in pretended confusion.
"I am afraid that your name has escaped me, sir. One
meets so many people during the Season that some of them
regrettably fade from memory."

His glance was appreciative. "Mr. David Linwood, ma'am.
I see I shall have to take great care to remain in the
forefront of your mind from now on, by whatever means
that takes."

Georgie ignored this remark and presented him to her
aunt and Lady Martin. After a few commonplaces, she
could see that although Aunt Bess was prepared to stay
beside her to protect her from this dangerous gentleman,
Lady Martin was big with news, and in no time at all had
excused them both and taken Miss Hersham away.

"May I beg the honor of a dance, Lady Spaldin'?" Mr.
Linwood asked, standing closer to her than she liked, although she knew if she moved away slightly, it would earn
her only a knowing grin.

"I must deny you, sir. I do not care to dance," she replied.

Deftly he flipped the small white card open and scrawled his name in two places. "Good, neither do I. I am not much in the caper merchant line, and I would so much rather sit them out so I can feast my eyes on you." His blue eyes blazed with laughter and then his glance travelled slowly from her face to her neck and bosom. "Very, very nice," he said, nodding his head after he had inspected her from head to toe. "There is a great deal to be said for culture and elegance after all. In the park, buttoned to the chin, you were lovely; tonight, er . . . unbuttoned, as it were, you are breathtakin'."

Georgie could feel the heat rising all over her body, and only by a strong-willed resolve was she able to keep from slapping him.

"How dare you?" she asked in an indignant whisper, glad he had spoken so softly, for she could not bear to think this conversation might be overheard.

"Oh, have I got it wrong again, ma'am? I thought since you were so obviously displayin' your charms, that you expected me to compliment you on them. Of course, I did see your suitor, that heavy booming-voiced man, ignorin' the beauty that was right under his nose, but I thought him overly prudish and very far off the mark as well. To liken you to English flowers—are there green flowers in England, by the way?—but perhaps he was thinkin' of boxwood, or an elm? Hardly complimentary!"

Georgie stiffened as he added, "Unless, of course, he has seen so much of you so many times that he is immune? No, it can't be that, unless the man's a eunuch."

"How dare you?" Georgie snapped again. "Oh, if I were a man, I would make you pay for these insults."

"Come, come, Lady Spaldin'! If you were a man, the occasion would hardly arrive, for although our manners in the states may be unusual, we are not as strange as that."

Before Georgie could reply, she heard Miss Kingsley calling her name, and was glad for the chance to turn away. But Clarissa Kingsley had no intention of leaving the vicinity of such an intriguing gentleman until she was introduced.

"Dear Georgie," she said, shaking her blond curls and glowing up at her, for she was a Pocket Venus of less than five feet in height, "How lovely to see you, although I declare that gown has me so jealous I can hardly speak. It is ravishing!"

"Now, that is just what I have been sayin'," David Linwood interjected, "but the lady refuses the compliment. Perhaps she will believe yours."

Miss Kingsley turned to him, her blue eyes wide as she curtsied. "Sir?" she asked, making play with her fan.

"No need to curtsy to me, m'lady, for I am plain Mr. David Linwood, and in my country, all men are equal."

"Of course I knew you were not an Englishman when you spoke." Miss Kingsley dimpled. "But where are you from, sir?"

"I am a Virginian, ma'am, from the United States."

"No!" she breathed, clasping her hands in delight. "How bad of you to hide him, Georgie, when we are all just dying to meet him. Imagine, from Virginia!"

Georgie took a deep breath. "I must rejoin my aunt, but I am sure you will excuse me, Clarissa, Mr. Linwood. I find I have no interest in our rebellious former colonies, nor in the men who inhabit them. To me, our true English gentleman is much superior in breeding, manners, and accomplishments. I apologize if I offend you, sir, but I am known to speak my mind."

To her chagrin, Mr. Linwood burst out laughing at this frigid setdown. She inclined her head and swept away, leaving a confused but delighted Miss Kingsley alone on the field and David Linwood saying earnestly, "Clarissa! What a pretty name. It suits you, little lady, so like an English flower you are. I hope I do not offend you with my compliments?"

Georgie's head was high and her green eyes were sparkling with anger as she silently vowed revenge. Lord Sefton remarked to his wife that he had never seen Lady Spalding in such looks, before he asked her what on earth was the matter with his fellows that they allowed her to remain a widow.

2

Lady Spalding had a wonderful time at the ball. She was her gayest, most flirtatious self, laughing at all the gentlemen's sallies and contributing more than a few of her own. On the dance floor, she was graceful and spirited, and when she chose to sit out, she made sure to surround herself with several of the handsomest men and the most prominent ladies, the cream of the cream, as it were. To any stranger, it was obvious that Lady Georgina Spalding was one of the brightest stars in society's firmament, sought after and universally admired.

It was not so strange, therefore, that David Linwood was not able to catch her eye even once, and when he came to claim his first dance with her, discovered that the popular Lady Spalding had disappeared and was nowhere to be found. He searched the ballroom, the hall, and even went so far as to look into the library and several salons, and although he discovered several couples enjoying the privacy to be found there, and a roomful of elderly guests at card tables in one of the drawing rooms, there was no sign of his partner.

Mr. Linwood's normal expression gave a clue to the dangerous man he was, but now a close observer would have noticed that his face settled into even harsher planes, his eyes narrowed and his mouth tightened, and he could even be seen to clench his fists before he recalled himself to his surroundings. At first he was sure she had left the ball, until he saw her aunt, Miss Hersham, deep in conversation with two elderly ladies, and when the music for the next set started, he saw Lady Spalding herself enter the ballroom and take the hand of a young man eagerly awaiting her. Mr. Linwood took a deep breath, counted to ten, and turned his back on the lady.

Georgie had spent the entire dance in the ladies' withdrawing room, the one place she was sure even a brash American would not dare to invade. She knew she had confused the two maids in attendance there by lingering to adjust her perfect gown and fussing over a hairdo from which not even one curl was out of place, but nothing was going to make her available to that odious man who had positively forced her to allow him two dances, much against her wishes. But before she began to feel uncomfortable under the maids' eyes, Emmaline Waring came in in a rush, a handkerchief to her face and her eyes full of tears. When she saw Georgina, she tried to control herself, but when Georgina asked her kindly if she could be of assistance, Emmaline burst into tears.

"Lady Spalding, I am so sorry!" she wailed after Georgina had petted and soothed her and sent one of the maids for a glass of lemonade. "But . . . but I cannot bear it!"

Georgina did not like to pry, so she did not ask what it was she could not bear, but that made no difference to Emmaline for she poured out the whole story, oblivious of the wide-eyed maids or of the possibility that others might come into the room. It seemed that she had not wanted to make her debut this Season and had begged her mother and her brother not to force her to come, but her pleading had been to no avail. And now that she was here, she hated it!

"I never know what to say or do, and if a gentleman speaks to me, I want to sink into the floor," she said between her sobs and little hiccups. "Oh, Lady Spalding, if only I could be like you! I have seen you, so assured, so easy in conversation, and I know I will never, *never* be able to be like you, no matter what Teddy says. It is all very well for him to tell me to use you for a model, but if I cannot copy you, what good does that do? And then he gets so cross with me and tells me that I am not *trying*. But I don't want to try, I hate London society! It is stupid, so there!"

She wiped her eyes and sat up a little defiantly to sip her lemonade. Georgie was a little amused and intrigued, for Miss Waring had never been so verbose before. She looked quite attractive in her indignation, with her expressive grey eyes flashing, her sandy hair escaping its severe arrangement, and her cheeks glowing in her distress.

"Besides," she continued, "it is ridiculous for me to emulate you in any way, for you are so beautiful, so slim, so . . . Just look at me!"

Georgie looked and thought it was too bad that the girl took after her brother in build, and even more unfortunate that her mother seemed to have no idea how to dress her. This evening she wore a girlish white gown much trimmed with pale blue rosettes, and nothing could have been less attractive with her pale, almost sallow complexion and sturdy, square-shouldered frame. She was very tall as well, and the muslin with all its tucks and flounces and pleats just made her look fat.

"My dear Emmaline, why should you want to copy me? I have told your brother I am much too old a model for you. Besides, you should be yourself! Remember, my dear, no one can force you to do anything you do not want to do," Georgie told her, reluctant to discuss Miss Waring's abundant figure.

Emmaline brightened for a moment, but then she shook her head. "You do not understand! Teddy has decided—and of course Mama agrees with every word he says, she always does—that it is time for me to get engaged, and . . . well . . ."

Her words died away as she looked into the mirror and saw both the attendants leaning forward, one so far forgetting herself as to let her mouth drop open in avid interest. Georgie suddenly remembered the maids as well and gave them a look that had them scurrying to the other side of the room to whisper while they rearranged some towels and scents.

"This is not the best place to tell me about it, Emmaline," she said. "If you would like to take me into your confidence, perhaps you might call on me tomorrow? I will see that we are completely private."

The girl smiled and nodded, and Georgie became aware that the music had stopped, and rose to join Mr. Rexton for the next dance. She told Miss Waring to bathe her eyes and not to reappear in the ballroom until she felt more the thing. Emmaline opened her mouth to protest, and Georgie added quickly, "If your brother should tax you with it, tell him I recommended it to you," and then she went away.

She was a little absentminded during the dance, pondering what she had just heard. Mr. Rexton was sure that he must have offended her somehow, and his labored conversation died away. Georgie was wondering what on earth Lord Waring was about, to insist on an early engagement for his sister, but when she noticed her partner's unhappy face, she put the Warings from her mind and began to tease him and laugh with him.

Mr. Rexton relinquished her to Lord Waring with regret and dislike for his successor when the dance was over, for Lord Waring had no intention of sharing Lady Spalding with this young sprig of fashion and sent him away with a few well-chosen words before he led the lady to a sofa against the wall. As Georgie seated herself and fanned her face, she asked, "Now, why did you feel you had to be so unkind to that poor boy, sir? There is no harm in him, you know."

"Of course it is to be hoped he will outgrow his pretensions," Lord Waring agreed with her, "but it is most unbecoming for him to presume on your acquaintance, silly young chub! I am surprised you encourage him, dear lady; he is much too young for you and can hardly add to your consequence. Besides, it is naughty of you to give him hope that his suit might prosper, when we know, do we not, that your future is as good as settled?"

Georgina felt her temper rising. How dare Teddy Waring criticize her, and how dare he assume she was only waiting for him to speak before she agreed to be his wife?

"One dance in a crowded ballroom can hardly be called 'leading him on,' Lord Waring," she said coldly. "Furthermore, I like Mr. Rexton; he is young, true, but he is amusing and I enjoy his company."

"We shall say no more about it, my dear," Lord Waring replied, compressing his lips. "The tone of your mind is too nice to allow you to engage in an argument, I know, but you must not mind me giving you the hint."

"Indeed?" Georgina asked, her voice even more frigid. "And what gives you that privilege, m'lord? I was not aware I had granted you any such boon. I decide what I shall do and say and how I shall behave. You forget yourself! As a widow, I am quite capable of looking after myself, and have been doing so for some time now!"

"And you are such an *elderly* widow, too!" her partner pointed out, sounding even more ponderous than ever as he attempted a playful tone. "But now I am glad I chose to sit this dance out with you, for it is plain to see that 'someone' has overtaxed herself with dancing and frivolity this evening, and is not feeling her usual gracious self as a result. I knew it would be so, for the activity you have engaged in has been astonishing. Indeed, my mama made it a point to ask me about it, this unceasing liveliness not being in your usual style. But I shall say no more on the subject, for of course 'someone' does not like instruction, even from one who has only her best interests at heart."

Georgina was so furious at this wordy lecture that she wielded her fan with even more vigor. Lord Waring began to speak of his estates, the lovely spring weather, and the various guests present at the ball, and she was not required to contribute more than an occasional nod of her head, which was just as well, for she knew that if she were to speak, she would be tempted to give Teddy Waring a setdown he would never forget.

At last the dance concluded, and she excused herself to rejoin her aunt. Lord Waring insisted on escorting her, and as he took her arm, Georgina felt as if she would like to scream. Did he think her incapable of crossing the room by herself? Suddenly the whole situation began to take on a ludicrous aspect, and she was trying to contain her chuckles as she curtsied to him before taking a seat next to her Aunt Bess.

It was not much longer before she realized that her promised sit-out with Mr. Linwood was fast approaching. She did not feel she could bear to return to the ladies' withdrawing room again, and wondered how she was going to escape this unwanted *tête-à-tête*, but then she saw Emmaline Waring standing a little apart from a group of young people, looking miserable, and she went over to her at once and drew her arm in hers.

In short order, Mr. Linwood appeared and bowed. "How fortunate I am to find you in the ballroom, Lady Spaldin'," he said, and Georgina was delighted to hear how curt his voice was with barely suppressed rage.

"Mr. Linwood," she acknowledged in her sweetest tones as she gave him her hand. "May I present a particular friend of mine, Miss Waring? We were just remarking how weary we are from all the dancing, but now we three can sit together and have a quiet coze; could anything be more charming?"

Mr. Linwood was forced to offer a crimson Emmaline his other arm before he led both ladies to some chairs placed in an alcove. The ballroom was growing oppressive from the crowds of people, the hundreds of candles burning in the glittering chandeliers, and from the fact that Lady Sefton never allowed the doors of the balcony to be opened in case some young couples might steal away for a few moments alone in the dark.

"How warm it is, don't you agree, Emmaline?" she asked. "And such a squeeze, too! This must be all very new to you, Mr. Linwood, such a civilized display of the *haut ton*, all so beautifully dressed and bejeweled." She explained to the uncomfortable Miss Waring, "Mr. Linwood is from the United States, my dear, and I am sure he has never seen anything remotely like this ball in his own new, raw country."

David Linwood looked as if he were having the greatest difficulty in keeping his hands from her throat, as she looked at him for confirmation, but he managed a polite smile. Georgina, seeing those blazing eyes, was not deceived.

"We do occasionally have dances in America," he said at last. "Not quite like this, however. I am sure American ladies would be astounded to see the gowns some English-women are . . . er . . . almost wearin'!"

Georgina stiffened. "Indeed? If they are clad in puritan grey homespun as I suspect, I am sure they would be envious of our fashions! But, Mr. Linwood, you must not apologize. I understand your dances could never be like this—how difficult to be elegant on a dirt floor in a small cabin."

"You have a remarkable conception of the United States, Lady Spaldin'," he snapped.

"I am only going by what I have read and heard about it, and of course from my observations of your own behaviour," she replied.

Emmaline had not taken her eyes from Mr. Linwood's face and she seemed to have missed the innuendos that had been exchanged.

"Do you . . . do you live in a forest, sir?" she asked.

"There is certainly forest on my property," he answered, sparing her an impatient glance. "A great deal of it has been cultivated, of course."

"Oh, you are a *farmer*, Mr. Linwood," Georgina said in

a bored voice. "How very interesting I am sure. What crops do you raise?"

Mr. Linwood leaned back in his little gilt chair and folded his arms. Suddenly he looked relaxed and pleasant, as if he were more than a little amused at her sparring.

"Most of my land is in cotton, ma'am, although we also raise vegetables, fruits, and some animals as well."

"I imagine you have trouble with the Indians? I have heard that in the colonies—I mean the states—farmers never even go out to plow without carrying a gun. How very primitive! One wonders how anyone can be found to live in such a precarious way."

Emmaline leaned forward. "Indians! Guns!" she breathed.

Suddenly Mr. Linwood abandoned any attempt to talk to Lady Spalding, and turned to the fascinated Miss Waring. Until the music ceased, he regaled her with stories of the United States, stories that owed more to invention than to truth. Georgina tried not to fume at being totally ignored, but she did not make the mistake of trying to regain his attention. She began to look about the ballroom, waving her hand and smiling whenever she managed to catch the eye of an acquaintance, for all the world as if she were competely unaware of Mr. Linwood's company and lurid tales.

By her side, Emmaline sat hardly daring to breathe, drinking in every word. Unbeknownst to either Mr. Linwood or Lady Spalding, she had tumbled into love in an instant. How handsome and strong he is, how honest and down-to-earth, she thought, her grey eyes wide with awe as he told her about a bear he had shot on his farm. How different he was from all her foppish countrymen, concerned only with their appearance, their horses, and their amusements. How she would like to stand shoulder to shoulder with Mr. Linwood, where, she thought with a little thrill, even *she* would appear tiny, reloading his gun in an Indian attack. How wonderful it would be to be married to such a brave, compelling man.

When the three were forced to part, Emmaline knew she would always cherish the memory of Mr. Linwood's smile, his masculine bow, and especially his farewell. "It has been a pleasure talkin' to you, Miss Warin'," he said in his deep drawl. "How refreshin' to find someone who is not so complacent in the ways of her world that she cannot imagine another. Lady Spaldin', your servant, ma'am."

Georgina gave him her hand and smiled, her green eyes glittering.

"May I hope you have a pleasant stay in England, sir? It is doubtful we shall meet again."

Mr. Linwood raised one eyebrow. "Do you think so, m'lady? I would not wager a ha'penny on the certainty if I were you."

As she was being driven home a short time later with her aunt, Miss Hersham, as was her wont, regaled her with all the gossip she had heard that evening. Georgina did not really attend to her, for her mind was going back over the ball; not so much Teddy Waring's proprietary manner, or Emmaline's surprising confession, but her talks with the infuriating and intriguing Mr. Linwood. She told herself she had had the best of their encounters so far, and wondered when and where he would try to renew the acquaintance, and she was running over various things she might say if he dared to try, when suddenly she heard her aunt mention his name.

"It was the *on dit* of the evening, Georgie, I am astounded you heard nothing of it! To think that Mr. Linwood, that dangerous man I warned you about, is an American and is here in England to see about some inheritance. I did not learn the name of the family, nor their location, but I did hear that there is another aspirant to the fortune. Well! I am sure after one look at Mr. Linwood whoever that may be will leave him the field without a word!" She cackled and Georgie asked, "How does he come to be known by Lady Sefton, aunt? You know what a high stickler she is about pretentious mushrooms and encroaching toadies. Whatever possessed her to invite a common farmer to her ball?"

"Now, how did you get that idea, Georgie?" her aunt asked in some bewilderment. "I have it on good authority that Mr. Linwood owns an extensive plantation in Virginia that comprises some twenty-five square miles. Not acres, mind you, miles! They say he is as wealthy as Golden Ball, that his mansion there has as many as fifty rooms filled with all manner of beautiful furnishings and paintings, and that he has hundreds of servants. The plantation is called Linderwood. Furthermore, his ancestors in England were all of the *haut ton*, and I believe he and Lady Sefton meet somewhere on their family trees. Is it not exciting?"

Georgina was spared the necessity of a reply, for just then the carriage arrived home. Pleading exhaustion, she kissed her aunt good night and went up to her room. All the time Wiltshire was helping her undress and brushing out her hair, she fumed. So, he was not a common farmer, he was a wealthy plantation owner. To think she had babbled on and on about cabins and dirt floors, Indians, and the lack of civilization. And he had left her do so, of course, because he knew how chagrined she would be when she discovered her *faux pas*. It is certainly easy to dislike the man, she thought, since he makes it a point to assist you to do so at every turn.

After she had dismissed her maid, she sat for a while in thought before the fire. She had to admit she was feeling chagrined for quite another reason as well. She had behaved badly; there was no excuse, not even Mr. Linwood's impossible behaviour, for her rudeness and bad manners. She had allowed her temper to get the best of her and she had been shrewish, ill-tempered, and definitely not a lady. Why did Mr. Linwood bring these unattractive traits to the fore?

As she climbed into her four-poster bed, she resolved that from now on, no matter what he said or did, she would remain calm, collected, and coolly self-contained.

This noble ambition lasted only until she entered the breakfast room the following morning to discover she had received three floral tributes. There was a spray of white gladioli from Lord Waring, a tiny nosegay of yellow rosebuds from Mr. Rexton, accompanying a note she knew must have taken him some time to compose, and finally, a huge bouquet two feet high and just as wide, of a dozen different blooms, all dyed a uniformly brilliant emerald green. Geering still looked astounded as he held out this offering, but Georgina had no trouble at all in identifying the sender even before she ripped open the card, and all her good resolutions disappeared in her surge of anger as she read the card: "Flowers for the victor of Round 1. I look forward to Round 2." It was signed "D.L." in bold black handwriting, and Georgina threw it at once into the fire. As she was instructing Geering to remove those particular flowers and throw them away, Miss Hersham came in.

"Dear me," she said faintly as the large vase of nodding green flowers was borne past her. "What on earth? And who sent it?"

"I have no idea, aunt," her niece lied, avoiding her eyes. "I seem to have misplaced the card, if there was one. Perhaps it was someone's idea of a joke. Come, sit down and let me pour you some coffee."

Miss Hersham took her seat at the breakfast table, her forehead creased in a frown. "But, Georgie, I cannot find it funny, nor, I am sure, do you. All those beautiful flowers, dyed such a hideous shade!"

She seemed prepared to discuss the matter for some time, but her niece changed the subject. "What are your plans for today, Aunt Bess? Would you care to come shopping with me this morning? I thought I might try to find a new bonnet for my ecru afternoon gown. You remember we were never satisfied with the *café-au-lait* straw I purchased."

Miss Hersham expressed her willingness to join her niece, since she had a book she wished to exchange at Hookam's Library and some small shopping of her own to do as well. She sipped her coffee for a moment while Georgie began to read the post, and then she said as she buttered a roll, "Do you join me this afternoon at Lady Martin's? I know she meant to speak to you about it last night; she is having a few people for tea."

She would have said more, but Lady Spalding interrupted. "No, she did not mention it to me, Aunt Bess, and I am afraid I am unable to attend in any case. I have asked Lord Waring's sister to visit me."

Miss Hersham swallowed her annoyance along with her roll at this information, for Agnes had promised to have dear Robert present so he could meet Georgie at last.

"Emmaline Waring? Whatever for, my dear?"

"She came into the ladies' withdrawing room last night crying her eyes out, and since she seemed determined to pour out her tale, and the maids were listening, I suggested she call today. She is very unhappy, Aunt Bess. It seems she hates the idea of a London Season, but her brother insisted. There is some mystery, and I admit I was intrigued."

"But how sad for her, and for you as well, Georgie! Having to become her confidante can only be tedious. And you do understand that this will make Teddy Waring sure you are going to great lengths to attach him, to show such singular consideration for his sister? I am persuaded you will be bored to death, for she is not at all in your style. Lady Martin's tea party is hardly the height of dissipation, but anything is preferable to encouraging the Warings, feeling as you do about them."

Georgie thought her aunt sounded a little tart. "Perhaps," she agreed. "But having promised to meet her, I cannot disengage. Do say everything that is proper to Lady Martin, and tell her how sorry I am that I am unable to be there. And now, I shall go and order the carriage. Do you want a footman, or will I suffice to carry your parcels? I suspect your 'small bit of shopping,' you see!"

This challenging remark threw Miss Hersham into a flurry of denials and explanations, and nothing more was said that morning about either Lady Martin or Emmaline Waring.

And so Miss Hersham went along to her friend's later that day, while Georgina waited in the smaller drawing room for her caller. Emmaline was prompt to the time they had agreed upon, but after she had removed her shawl and her gloves and taken the seat across the fireside from her hostess, she looked down at her square hands, twisting them over and over in her lap as if she did not know how to begin.

"Emmaline, do not be embarrassed, my dear," Georgie encouraged her with a smile. "Perhaps you have thought better of taking me into your confidence? If that is the case, I understand of course, and we shall say no more."

"Oh, no, it is not that!" the girl replied, raising timid grey eyes to Georgina's face. "It is just that I have had time to think and come to realize that perhaps the Season will not be such an unpleasant experience as I had feared."

Georgina raised her eyebrows. She was not to know that it had been hours before Miss Waring had been able to sleep the night before, for she had been remembering the handsome, strong, and intriguing American she had met. For a while she daydreamed that he would come to feel for her as she did for him, but this rosy-colored vision was too impossible to sustain for someone as practical and honest as she was. No, he was more apt to prefer someone like

Lady Spalding, she told herself sadly, so beautiful and spirited and assured. But never, never would his eyes alight with any degree of pleasure on a plain, stout girl with no wit and little conversation. She had cried a little at that, but then she told herself that if she were just allowed to stay in his vicinity, she would be happy. Just to be able to watch him smile and talk and dance would be wonderful, and perhaps he would even remember that they had met and smile and bow to her! She brought her mind back to Lady Spalding's drawing room with difficulty.

"You see, Lady Spalding, I told you that Teddy—my brother, that is—wanted me to come to town this year so I could become betrothed to some eligible gentleman. But I did not mention that his main reason for that is because he wishes to have my affairs settled before he contracts an alliance himself. I am sure I do not have to tell *you* anything about that, for you must know it anyway!" She blushed and continued, "Teddy, you see, does not feel that Mama is capable of handling an affair of this nature by herself. In fact, he has gone so far as to tell us both that if it is left up to the pair of us, we will probably insist on bringing some completely ineligible fortune hunter into the Waring family, for you must know I am odiously wealthy. But I have resolved to *try* to do as he wishes, for the family's sake."

Georgina tried to follow this involved paragraph without any emotion showing on her face, but she did not dare to comment on it and only nodded her head as if she understood.

"And although I think it is too bad that Teddy feels he is the only one who should decide whom I should marry— for after all, how could he know if I will like the gentleman he chooses?—he is very determined. And as Mama has always said, when Teddy makes up his mind to do something, nothing on this earth will make him change it."

She sighed, for she knew there was not even the remotest possibility that Teddy would choose Mr. David Linwood from America. She had already met two young men Teddy considered suitable, and both of them had been remarkably like him: respectable, stuffy, and dull. Emmaline was no wit, no intellectual, but she had a sense of fun that had been left out of her brother's makeup.

"Besides," she added, "Teddy is determined I shall become engaged within two months. He says he has other

things to do this spring than parade suitable husbands
before me, and that I shall have to make up my mind
quickly." She must have noticed Georgina's horrified expression, for she added, "Of course, he did say that if I
showed a particular partiality and the man was acceptable,
he would take that into consideration."

"But . . . but," an astonished Georgina broke in, "how
can this be? He cannot make a gentleman propose!"

"Yes, he can!" Emmaline said with a little sniff. "All he
has to do is mention my dowry. Thousands and thousands,
and two estates as well. He has told me there is to be no
question of 'love.' In fact, he has forbidden me to think of
it, for he says that is something that people of our station
should not be concerned with. Teddy says kindness and
consideration are all I should hope for, and indeed, dear
Lady Spalding, I know he is right. I am not beautiful—
why, I daresay some people would consider me an antidote."

Georgina got up in a whirl of primrose skirts and came to
put her arms around her guest, she felt so upset at this
unflattering assessment. She wished she might have had a
few words with "Teddy" about everything he "said."

"You are no such thing, dear Emmaline! Do you— forgive me for asking—do you have a dress allowance?"

"Yes, Teddy has put what seems to me to be a great deal
of money at my disposal," the girl answered. "But Mama
hates to shop, and she said I could do it perfectly well by
myself with that expensive French maid Teddy found me.
Only . . . I have not liked to ask her, for I don't think she
approves of me."

"It is not her place to approve of you—the very idea!"
Georgina said, rising to walk quickly up and down the
room. "If you would like me to, Emmaline, I would be glad
to help you with your shopping. Your ensembles should be
chosen with a great deal of care. You must forgive me for
saying so, but you are tall and sturdy, and the gown you
wore to the ball last evening did not do you justice."

"*You* would help me?" Emmaline asked, her eyes wide.
"Oh, how famous! I knew the gown was all wrong, but
Mama says a *jeune fille* must always wear white or pink or
the palest of blues, and no jewelry except pearls. I know I
look terrible as a *jeune fille*."

Her voice was so matter-of-fact that Georgina had to
chuckle. "Perhaps we can make you a little less green, my

dear. I shall call on you tomorrow morning. Kindly inform your maid that we will be going shopping and that I will have a great many instructions for her to follow, about your hair and toilettes. You shall, I fear, find me a very managing female."

"Lady Spalding, you are too good," Miss Waring said in a gruff little voice, as tears came to her eyes.

"Pooh!" the lady replied, waving her hand. "I shall enjoy it. Come, now, Emmaline, no crying, that is my first instruction. It makes your eyes red, and what is worse, the tip of your nose as well. My second order is that you shall call me 'Georgie.' I am not that much older than you, and since we are bound to see a lot of each other, it will be more comfortable." While Emmaline nodded her head, she added, "Now, what time can you be ready in the morning? I have an early riding engagement, but perhaps by ten?"

Miss Waring promised to be waiting on her doorstep at that precise moment, and went away much happier than she had been in a long time. If Lady—no, Georgie— was indeed going to help her, perhaps all was not lost. All the way home she dreamed of entering a drawing room looking absolutely stunning, and seeing before her an astonished Mr. Linwood, his eyes glowing with admiration and desire as he hastened to her side.

Miss Hersham made no mention of her tea party that evening at dinner, but she seemed in the happiest of spirits until, over the veal fritters, removed with a salmon mousse, some chicken in Madeira sauce, and buttered tiny peas, Georgina told her about Emmaline Waring's remarkable confession and what she had promised to do to help the girl. At that, she frowned.

"But, Georgie, do consider. There can be nothing more misleading to Lord Waring than your taking his sister under your wing. He will be sure you are only intent on aiding her to hasten the day when the two of you can announce your own engagement, unhampered by m'lord's younger sister. I warn you, Georgie, he is sure to take this as a sign of your interest in his suit."

Georgina chuckled. "Then I will be quick to disabuse him of his illusions, for Lord Waring is in great need of a stunning setdown. He considers himself my future husband, and he was terribly possessive at the Sefton ball, for he is so sure that all he has to do is come up to the mark, and I will be transported with delight, almost unable to murmur my overjoyed acceptance. What conceit! He has never attempted to question my feelings, for if he had, he would have seen there is no chance for him. When I told you I did not wish to marry again, I certainly meant it, but if ever I should be tempted, it will not be by the likes of Teddy Waring."

Miss Hersham nodded. "It does not bear thinking about, of course." Especially *now*, she added to herself. "But do have a care, Georgie. Your kindness to Miss Waring is sure to be remarked."

Her niece laughed as she picked up her fruit knife and began to peel an apple. "If I were as green as Emmaline Waring, you would do well to be concerned, but at my age I am sure I can handle the gentleman."

Miss Hersham shook her head as she ate her cream cake, but she said no more, for her mind was still on what had transpired in Lady Martin's drawing room that afternoon, and the very eligible Earl of Amesbury. She had been pleased to see that her friend had not overstated her nephew's attractions. Lord Holland was over medium height, with an aristocratic face made up of distinguished features. It was plain to see that he was dressed by the finest tailors, but such was his presence that you were not even aware of his fine clothes. He was a slim man, more wiry than powerful, and Miss Hersham had especially liked his straight bearing and long slender hands. Beneath a pair of slashing black eyebrows, his grey eyes twinkled engagingly as he bowed to his aunt's old friend and told her how delighted he was to make her acquaintance at last. Miss Hersham succumbed at once, for m'lord's voice was deep in timbre and warm in tone, and she did not know how any woman could resist it, or the smile that accompanied it and caused the dimple in his chin to deepen.

Miss Hersham had watched him as carefully as she could without being obvious. She noted that he took the time to speak to all the guests, but there was no special attention paid to the two younger ladies that her hostess had invited to draw him off the scent. "For, Bess, if Georgie is the only lady present who is under the age of forty-five, dear Robert is sure to suspect what we are about. 'Ware hurry! You know how silly men can be when they feel they are being pursued."

Miss Hersham was suddenly glad that Georgie was not present, for now when Lord Holland did meet her it would seem more natural and unplanned. Still, she could not help but feel a pang when she saw Clarissa Kingsley flirting and smiling, or Miss Tewkesbury deep in conversation with this paragon of masculinity.

By the end of the week, however, both ladies were about to scream with frustration. If Georgie went driving in the park, Lord Holland was at his club; if she attended a reception, that was the evening he was engaged for dinner in quite another part of town, and the afternoon of Lady Ward's riding expedition to Richmond, dear Robert had to refuse the invitation, for he was in the City attending to business with his lawyers.

"I declare I could shake them both!" Lady Martin exclaimed when she called on Miss Hersham on Friday afternoon. "It is almost as if they are thwarting us deliberately, although of course that cannot be. But whatever are we to do, Bess? It is impossible for Robert to fall in love if he never gets to meet the gel."

Miss Hersham suggested a theatre party, or perhaps an evening at the opera, but Lady Martin shook her head. "No, no, that will never do. Even though we are such old friends, Robert is sure to be on guard. He knows how much I want him to marry—I have been introducing eligible girls to him for years, and he treats it as a game. No, we must think of something better than that."

But unbeknownst to both ladies, Georgie was at that very moment making Lord Holland's intimate acquaintance, and in a way that neither could have planned in a million years. She had, quite literally, fallen into the gentleman's arms.

She had gone shopping with Emmaline Waring that afternoon, and in stepping down from her carriage in Bond Street, she had tripped over a loosened sandal string. Lord Holland, who was passing the carriage at the time, and who had paused to stare at this beautiful unknown lady with the delightful throaty chuckle and glorious chestnut hair, saw her throw out her hands to save herself, and he pushed past the footman holding the door of the carriage open and caught her neatly in his arms. His face was bemused as he stared down into those surprised green eyes and at her sensuous mouth, half-opened in amazement, and for a moment his arms tightened as if he did not mean to let her go.

To both of them, it seemed as if the world faded away for a moment, but then the street noises came back, the clinking of the horses' harness, the rumble of another carriage passing by, Emmaline Waring's voice exclaiming at the near-accident, and the footman's stifled cough.

Lord Holland gently set the lady on the flagway, and, still holding her hand in his, made her his most elegant bow.

3

"I beg your pardon, sir!" Georgina said as the gentleman released her hand. "I cannot think how I came to be so clumsy."

He looked down at her, his grey eyes a little cynical. "I refuse to believe it an accident, ma'am, for I am sure you are in general a most graceful creature."

His deep voice was as warm and intimate as his words were insulting, and Georgina stiffened. Behind her, Miss Waring spoke up, "Oh, Georgie, are you all right? Look there, your sandal!"

Before she could move, the gentleman knelt before her to tie her sandal ribbon again, murmuring, "You must allow me the privilege!" Georgina exchanged a startled glance with Emmaline over his dark head. She knew the whole episode was improper, for although she was of course grateful that he had saved her from a bad fall, she could not like having her shoe tied in public by a complete stranger. She could feel his warm hands on her ankle and calf and she forced herself to stand still although she drew herself up even straighter and her expression changed from bewildered gratitude to a haughty stillness. She was not used to being treated without respect; why, it was almost as if he thought she was not a lady at all, but she knew that to create a scene would only make the situation worse.

When he rose to his feet again and dusted off his knee, she nodded coldly. "Thank you, although it was unnecessary for you to bother, sir. I am sure I could have managed the few steps into Mme. Barbette's. I thank you for saving me from a tumble, and I am so sorry to have inconvenienced you. Now, you must excuse me. Come along, Emmaline."

She inclined her head in dismissal, and Lord Holland was

forced to step aside and allow her to enter the shop. He stood staring after the two girls for a moment, and then he shrugged his shoulders and continued on his way. His first impression, that she was an expensive bit o' muslin who had contrived to throw herself deliberately into his arms in order to gain an introduction, had to be discarded in the light of her subsequent behaviour. If she had been interested in attracting his attention, she would have remained to talk to him, smiling and flirting until he asked her name and her direction. As he strolled along in the bright spring sunshine, swinging his malacca cane, he wondered who she was. The younger, plainer girl had called her Georgie, which was entirely in keeping with his first impression. Lord, the Mimis, Fifis, Margies, and Nancys he had known! And he had been misled by her ripe mouth and the aware expression in her green eyes into thinking her a high flier. She was no simpering, blushing virgin, of that he was positive. But although she was one of the most sensuous-looking women he had ever encountered, it was now obvious that she was a lady as well. It was an interesting combination, and one he had seldom met.

Robert Holland, the Earl of Amesbury, was very well acquainted with all the ways a woman had of getting his attention, for he had been pursued by matchmaking mamas for years for his title and his wealth, and by their eager daughters for his good looks and deep, caressing voice. It was no wonder he was a little cynical. He had once confided to his good friend Freddie Wilson that there was nothing the ladies had not tried with him, from dropped fans and handkerchiefs (rank beginners in their first season) to sprained ankles and errant bonnets bowled along to his feet by the March winds (intermediates in the art of dalliance), to runaway horses and once even a young lady who wandered into his bedroom late one night at a house party and claimed she walked in her sleep (the more advanced practitioners). Lord Wilson laughed. "I know you have the devil's own luck with the ladies, Robert, but you cannot be so conceited as to think they are *all* after you. Perhaps the horse did bolt, and the bonnet escape m'lady's head." He shook his head. "I do mistrust the lovely sleep-walker, though. And how did you handle that, I wonder?"

An unholy smile crept over m'lord's face. "You are right to be suspicious; lord, if you had seen the nightgown she was wearing! Perhaps someday I will tell you, but believe me, Freddie, at my age I have seen all the tricks," Lord Holland replied, his lip curling. "Sometimes, as you are well aware, I have even pretended to be taken in by them for a while, but when the time comes that I decide to wed, it will be my own decision, and not the result of a clever trick."

Now he smiled to himself, for it appeared that Freddie had been right, and not every lady was as intent on snaring him as he had thought. This Georgie had not lingered, there had been nary a trace of a smile, never mind an inviting one, and she had given him no idea where she might be found again. Although it might be a clever ploy to gain his interest, to pretend indifference at first until he began to pursue her, somehow he did not think so.

Perhaps she had not cared for him? Somehow he found this thought lowering, and he told himself he would be on the lookout for the lady in the future, although he knew if their paths never crossed it would not overset him. True, she was beautiful, but London was full of beautiful ladies. He raised his hat and bowed to Lady Amsterdam and her two daughters, who were passing in an open landau, and was pleased to see the eager smiles and waves he received.

As it turned out, he saw the mysterious Georgie just two nights later at the theatre. Lady Martin had discovered that morning that he was engaged with some of his cronies to attend Kean's new play before going on to supper at Grillon's, and she dashed off a note to Miss Hersham. Both ladies had taken up a daily correspondence, to the annoyance of their footmen, who felt they were wearing a path between Brooks Street and Portman Square. As soon as Lady Martin found out what her nephew's plans were, she would inform her conspirator, who would then reply with her niece's agenda for the same time period. Now it appeared that all was at last in tune, for Georgie and her aunt had been invited to join Lord and Lady Jersey in their box that very same evening, in company with General Bates and Lord Waring, and it was not impossible that Miss Hersham might catch the Earl's eye and be able to perform the long-awaited introduction at one of the intervals.

Lord Holland, who was in the pit, spent the time before the first act in surveying the house through his quizzing glass, and so he saw Georgie's party enter and take their seats. Tonight she was dressed in a floating white half-gown of spangled net, worn over a silk slip, and her hair was arranged high on her head, with only a few curls allowed to fall and touch her bare shoulders. He noticed the heavyset figure of Teddy Waring leaning towards her and realized that his lady of the loosened sandal had impeccable birth and credentials indeed, for Teddy Waring would never recognize anyone unworthy of his rank. Lord Holland resolved to visit Sally Jersey's box at the first interval.

David Linwood was also at the theatre that evening, in company with the Seftons, and as their box was almost directly across from Lady Spalding and her party, he did not miss the lady's entrance either, and was delighted at this opportunity to further his acquaintance with the haughty Englishwoman who was in such need of a setdown. It was just as well for Georgina's peace of mind that she was innocent of both their presence and their intentions, or she might not have been able to keep her mind on the performance unfolding before her.

When the first-act curtain came down, Lord Waring turned to ask her how she was enjoying the play. Georgina knew Mr. Kean was one of London's foremost actors, forever being lionized by society, but she thought his performance in this particular vehicle overdone. Before she could do more than begin to explain her reasons, Lord Waring very kindly undertook to tell her exactly what she must think of it, as if he thought her incapable of forming an opinion without his advice. He failed to see the militant sparkle his instruction brought to her eyes, but before she was completely out of patience, Lord Waring's discourse was interrupted by visitors.

Lord Holland was the first to knock, but only because Mr. Linwood found himself delayed by Lord Sefton, who was anxious to solicit his opinion of the London theatre.

When Georgina saw the gentleman who had saved her from falling that day in Bond Street, she was puzzled by her aunt's reaction to the guest. Miss Hersham started, and her eyes grew wide as she exclaimed to herself, "My word!" Then she almost elbowed Teddy Waring from his seat, declaring that she must sit beside her niece for a moment, and ordered him to go away and fetch some punch or visit with others of his friends. As the bewildered Lord Waring left the box, Miss Hersham smiled and beck-

oned to the Earl, who was shaking hands with General
Bates.

"Lord Holland, how delightful to see you again. And are
you enjoying the play?"

The gentleman bowed and smiled. "Very much, Miss
Hersham. And yourself and Miss . . . Miss . . .?"

Georgina thought her aunt quite flustered and wondered
at it even as the older lady beamed and said, "Of course
you do not know my niece; I forgot she was not with me at
Lady Martin's tea. May I present Lady Spalding? Georgie,
my dear, this is Agnes' nephew, Robert Holland, the Earl
of Amesbury."

The Earl bowed, and Georgina inclined her head with a
slight smile. She was still feeling a little miffed at the
gentleman for treating her in such a cavalier way, but she
had to admit he was everything an English gentleman
should be from the top of his well-groomed dark head to his
polished evening pumps. He was handsome, elegant, old
enough to be both debonair and devastating, and at the
moment, his grey eyes sported a knowing twinkle, as if the
two of them were in some conspiracy over a deep dark
secret. When he spoke, she remembered his other attribute—
that warm, deep voice she was sure had sent many a
shiver up many a feminine backbone before tonight.

"Perhaps I should confess, Miss Hersham, if it would not
put your niece to the blush, that although we have never
been formally introduced before tonight, Lady Spalding
and I have met before."

He paused as Miss Hersham turned to stare at Georgina.
"You have? Where could that have happened, for you never
mentioned it to me, Georgie."

Her niece unfolded her fan and waved it gently before
her face, taking her time in answering. She decided to play
the game with him until she saw where he was leading. "It
was very unusual, Aunt Bess, but I am not surprised it
slipped my mind; one runs into so many people during the
Season, don't you agree, sir?"

"Definitely! A crush wherever you go. But it is not
every day that such a lovely lady as yourself falls right into
my arms. That made it impossible for me to forget, and I
certainly enjoyed it more than if you had merely 'run into'
me."

" 'Pon my soul!" Miss Hersham exclaimed. "Fell into your arms? Georgie?"

Lord Holland patted her hand and laughed. "There was a slight matter of an untied sandal string, you see, and Lady Spalding tripped getting down from her carriage. I was so fortunate as to be there to . . . er . . . catch her."

"So fortunate, how kind, just imagine!" Miss Hersham breathed.

Georgina chuckled and served the ball back into m'lord's court. "You certainly saved me from an ignominious spill and possible injury, and yet I had the feeling that you were not best pleased at the time to be playing the *galant*, sir. Perhaps I was delaying you from an appointment? I apologize for my clumsiness again."

"I found those few seconds to be more than just enjoyable, Lady Spalding. May I also apologize for *my* clumsiness?" His grey eyes were intent on her face, and when he saw the recognition of his meaning in her eyes, he added, "Just so. It was badly done of me. I should have known better."

To the confusion of her aunt, who, although she was pleased at the rapport that was growing between Georgie and Lord Holland, did not understand a word of what they were saying, Georgina chuckled again. "How could you know, m'lord? Parliament has yet to decree that those who are entitled to be so addressed must wear a badge proclaiming them a 'lady.' Perhaps you should bring it up on the floor? It would save so much confusion in the future!"

Lord Holland put back his head and laughed out loud. "*Touché*, Lady Spalding. My compliments!"

He would have said more, but just then there was a stifled cough, and he turned to see Lord Waring behind him, and an attendant with a tray of drinks.

"Good to see you again, Waring," m'lord said, taking two of the glasses and presenting them to Miss Hersham and Georgina. Lord Waring reddened a little as the ladies thanked him. After all, he was the one who had had to push through the crowd, buttonhole a waiter, and escort him to the box, and yet here was Robert Holland getting all the plaudits. It was too bad!

Talk grew general for a few moments, and then another knock sounded at the door. Lady Jersey laughed and patted her hair. "What a crowd we are attracting this evening, my love," she whispered to her husband. "I shall try very hard to pretend it is all on my account, but somehow I suspect Georgie Spalding is the honey that is luring so many bees!"

But the gentleman who had entered the box came directly to her side and bowed. "Dare I hope you remember me, Lady Jersey?" David Linwood asked. "We met at Lady Sefton's ball."

The lady gave him her hand. "Of course I remember you, sir. As if anyone could forget you, as you are very well aware. Besides the novelty of being American and thereby automatically intriguing, you have a way with you that sets you apart."

Georgina had to agree. The box seemed to have shrunk in size now that the tall, powerful figure of Mr. Linwood had invaded it. Her glance went from Lord Holland to the American. Although they were both tall and dark, any comparison ended there, for while Mr. Linwood exuded masculinity and strength, the earl seemed contained and casual. His grey eyes were cool and controlled, Mr. Linwood's blue eyes blazed fire, and m'lord's face and slender hands seemed almost pallid and too finely drawn next to the other's dark tan and rough-cut features. The gentleman . . . and the commoner, she thought, and she inexplicably shivered a little. She was recalled from her reverie by Sally Jersey asking, "Are you acquainted with the others, Mr. Linwood? I know you have met Miss Hersham and Lady Spalding; may I present Robert Holland, the Earl of Amesbury, and General Gates, and Lord Waring?"

Georgina thought Lord Holland stiffened a little as Mr. Linwood turned towards them and bowed.

"Ladies, a distinct pleasure to see you again," he said in his harsh, drawling voice. "And a pleasure to meet you, m'lords, General."

He bowed to the other men and then he stared straight at the Earl and his expression seemed almost menacing. "How very strange it is that we should discover each other this way, m'lord. I was sure that when we two met it would be in some lawyer's dusty rooms, not in such elegant company. But then, there was no doubt that we were fated to meet, and one place is as good as another, I suppose."

Lord Holland inclined his head, and when he spoke his deep voice had lost most of its warmth. "As you say, Mr. Linwood, it is surprising, but as Lady Spalding was just remarking, there is no way of keeping track of the people you run into in town at this time of year. Some meetings are delightful, others most unpleasant. I am sure at least that our *last* meeting will be in some lawyer's dusty rooms. Would you care to wager on it?"

Georgina, who was looking from one to the other, sensed the tension between them, and wondered at it. She saw Mr. Linwood clench his fists at m'lord's cold statement, but before he could answer, the Earl added, "You would be most unwise to bet on the certainty. Till then, sir. Your servant, ladies, for I must excuse myself to return to my friends."

Bows were exchanged, and smiles, but Georgina thought the earl looked displeased, as if he wished he had not had to speak to Mr. Linwood. And what did their remarks about lawyers mean? There was something between the two of them, that was sure.

David Linwood came to take the seat beside her and grinned down at her, all the blackness gone from his expression. "How delightful it is that we keep seeing each other, Lady Spaldin', but I did tell you the other night that it would be so, did I not?"

"I am surprised to find you still in England, sir," she replied in an even tone, determined not to be drawn into argument. "I rather thought you would be making haste to return to your own country. Surely you are needed there on such a vast plantation as you own."

The others were all deep in conversation for the moment, so he bent nearer to her and whispered. "That rankled, when you found out, did it not, *ma belle*? How disappointin' to learn I am not only wealthy but as well-born as your lovely self!"

Still Georgina controlled herself. "I was ashamed of my bad manners, certainly, sir. But before I was quite overcome with remorse, I remembered your own provocative behaviour."

"Oh, we have no need for mincin' ways and foppery in Virginia, my dear; we speak our minds! And to tell the truth, I enjoyed sparrin' with you. I have the feelin' I will always enjoy a good set-to with you—of whatever nature it may be."

His eyes travelled over her face, lingering on her mouth in what was becoming a familiar gesture, and then calmly admiring her slim neck and white shoulders. Georgina sat very still, her chin raised.

"Quite finished with your inspection, sir?" she asked as his eyes returned to her face. "I hope you approve?"

"You are everythin' a man could desire, and you know it," he snorted. "But I came to ask you if I might call on you, perhaps join you some mornin' for a ride in the park? I notice you have not returned there alone; can it be you were afraid of meetin' me?"

Georgina tilted her head and appeared to give serious consideration to his provocative question. "I would be a liar if I said I was not afraid of you, for I find you a very frightening man, Mr. Linwood. And for that reason, although I am sorry to be rude to a guest in my country, I would rather you did not call. As for riding, I find myself too occupied with all my old friends to have the time for any more early-morning gallops. I am sorry."

She thought his face grew harsher as she spoke, but he was still able to smile at her. "There is no reason for you to fear me, *ma belle*, for I would never hurt you, and you would be sure to find our time together pleasurable . . . in every way. My promise on it!"

She looked astounded. "I fear we are talking at cross-purposes, sir. We were discussing a ride in the park, were we not? No, I think I must forgo the treat."

He bowed his head in mocking disappointment. "Ah well, you may deny me, my dear, but I will keep turnin' up, you know."

"Like the proverbial bad penny, you mean?" Georgina asked.

He did not seem offended, but before he could reply, Lord Waring was there to point out that he was blocking his seat, and since the candles were being dimmed, perhaps it was time for the gentleman to return to his own party? Mr. Linwood took his leave and Georgina noticed as the curtain went up that Lord Waring was in a pet. She realized that he had planned on an intimate chat, and the appearance of not one, but two other men who had man-

aged to monopolize her attention had not pleased him at
all.

No one came during the next interval, but since Lord
Waring was quick to suggest that Georgina might enjoy a
stroll outside the box before the final act, she was not to
know of it. Taking her hand and placing it in his arm, Lord
Waring began to tell her how grateful he was she had
taken his sister under her tutelage. Georgina tried to make
light of it. "It is such a little thing, m'lord!" she said. "I
understand your mother does not care for shopping? It is
no trouble at all for my aunt and me to take Emmaline up
with us. You must not refine too much on it."

"How like you, noble creature!" he breathed, patting her
captured hand. "But I know, although of course I will
spare your blushes and not mention it, that there is another reason for your goodness. That reason makes me so
happy I cannot tell you."

"I pray you will not, sir," Georgina put in quickly. "There
is no need for your joy. I would do the same for any one of
my friends, believe me."

"Not every one, dear, *dear* Lady Spalding!" he insisted.
"But I will say no more at this time. We understand each
other very well, I am sure. How could it be otherwise?"

Georgina was aware that Lord Waring understood her
not at all, and was preoccupied the rest of the evening
wondering how she was to tell him that what he was taking
so for granted was far from the truth, and that she had no
intention of marrying anyone, least of all himself, when he
refused to hear anything that did not coincide with his own
views.

By the time the carriage had left her and Miss Hersham
in Brooks Street, Georgina had a headache from pondering
this problem and fending off Lord Waring's unsubtle hints
about their future together, and much to her aunt's regret,
decided to retire at once.

As Miss Hersham went up the stairs behind her, to fetch
a bottle of lavender water for her brow, and some pastilles
to burn, she told herself that even if it was disappointing
not to be able to discover at once what Georgina thought of
Lord Holland, there was plenty of time, and in the same
way that Lady Martin tried to disarm her nephew, so she
realized she must be very careful as well. Georgina had

declared her aversion to marriage, and she would suspect at once if her aunt made Lord Holland a topic of conversation too often.

Miss Hersham looked forward to meeting her friend tomorrow for a comfortable coze and the making of further plans. All was going well; she must not be impatient. Accordingly, she kissed her niece good night and tripped off to bed, and Georgina was left to a few moments of quiet reflection. How disappointed Miss Hersham would have been if she had known that her niece promptly put the elegant earl in the back of her mind and thought only of Lord Waring and the dangerous Mr. Linwood before she fell asleep.

The following morning, Georgina had an appointment to go shopping again with Emmaline Waring. She wished she might cancel it, and all future meetings as well, but she told herself it was unfair to punish the girl because her brother was imperceptive and insistent. Emmaline was so much happier now. Her French maid had risen to the challenge, as Georgina had been sure she would, and had applied a golden rinse to her mistress's sandy hair that made it much less mousy. After trying several different hairstyles, they had decided that since Miss Waring's hair refused to curl, it looked best brushed smooth in a classical but soft chignon.

Georgina had also convinced her young friend that pleats, flounces, and knots of ribbons and lace, especially all on one ensemble, did nothing at all for her heavy frame, and they had ordered several severely cut gowns and afternoon dresses in gold and bronze colors with a few delicate pastel silks for evening wear. None of these were pink or white, since these shades tended to make her skin look even more sallow than it was. Miss Waring, in consequence of their shopping, began to appear to greater advantage, although she would never be a beauty.

This morning she was to have the final fitting on her costume for a masquerade ball to be given in a few days by Lord and Lady Stern. Georgina was aware that the wish of Emmaline's heart was to appear as Marie Antoinette in court dress, or perhaps as a shepherdess, and had had to take a firm hand with her.

"Some other period of history, my dear!" she admonished the girl, who stood staring in rapture at an elaborate gown of white satin draped over enormous hoops, completed by a towering head of nodding plumes. "You cannot wear such a thing, and as for the shepherdess costume with its little apron and tiny laced-in waist, it is not to be thought of! Only Clarrisa Kingsley can wear it, and if I know her, she probably will!"

Emmaline sighed and allowed herself to be convinced that a flowing gown of golden draperies with a loose hip girdle of gold thread would be much more becoming. Georgina also chose a one-shouldered Grecian costume in leaf green for herself.

"But what are we supposed to be, Georgie?" Emmaline asked after the important matter of slippers, wigs, and masks had been decided and they were driving home.

"Whatever we choose! That is the advantage of the classical Greek robe, not that either yours or mine really is, of course. You may be Aphrodite or Diana or just a nameless nymph. Perhaps you might choose to be the goddess of love; just think how that would enliven the conversation." She thought for a moment and added, "Perhaps not. I do not think Lord Waring would approve."

Emmaline giggled, and thanked Lady Spalding once again for all her help. Then, carefully not looking at her new friend, she said in a gruff little voice, "You will never know how I wish you might be my sister, but even though Teddy is determined on it, somehow I cannot believe it will ever come to pass."

Georgina stifled an impatient exclamation and said, "No, I will never be your sister, Emmaline, but we can still be friends. You must not be misled by your brother's pursuit of my hand, for he is far off the mark there. I shall never marry again."

She thought to give the girl the hint, in hopes she might tell Lord Waring. Emmaline's eyes grew wide as she asked in disbelief, "Not marry again? You? Oh, I understand. It must have been wonderful to be married to a man you loved so much that you cannot contemplate replacing him with *another*. But perhaps in time . . ."

"Never," Georgina said firmly as they reached the Waring town house. She changed the subject by saying she looked forward to seeing Emmaline at the masquerade, and warned her she was not to ruin her costume with any elaborate jewelry, when only a simple wreath of flowers was appropriate.

Lord Stern's estate near Hampton Court had the advantage of being but a short drive from London, and early on the evening of the ball, Georgina and her aunt joined a stream of carriages to be driven to the party. It was warm for April, and it promised to be an entrancing affair, for it seemed from the crush of the traffic that all the *haut ton* had been invited.

Miss Hersham wore an evening gown she had owned as a girl, proud she was still able to lace it almost as tightly as she had done thirty years ago. Her wide skirts took up so much room they threatened to crush Georgina's green draperies.

"I do beg your pardon, my dear," she said, trying to sweep her hoops to one side. "I do not remember hoops being such unwieldy things, but perhaps I have become reconciled to the fashions of the new century at last."

Georgina laughed. "It is difficult to imagine how you managed to dance and ride and even alight from a carriage, Aunt Bess. I am glad I never had to learn to control them."

"Ah, but what a stately curtsy you could make in them, my dear. I shall be delighted to show you, when the occasion arises. I wonder if Lady Martin will be in costume? I know Agnes considers herself too old for such folly, but I tried to get her to join the rest of us. And her nephew— such a handsome man, don't you think? —will he come as Bonny Prince Charlie or perhaps Sir Walter Raleigh? I swear he would make a more devastating Antony, for example, than the original. Don't you agree with me?"

She looked sideways at her niece, who was staring out at the turnpike they were travelling, thinking she struck just the right note by not mentioning Lord Holland every other thing, but just often enough to remind Georgie of his existence. She failed to see the tiny smile her niece repressed so quickly. Aunt Bess, with her heavy hints, left no doubt what goal she had set as her heart's desire, but Georgina would not spoil her fun for anything. Idly she wondered if her aunt was in league with Lady Martin, and if Lord Holland was being pressured too. And then she wondered if he minded very much before she told herself that that was a matter of no concern to her.

When at last they came up the winding drive to Stern Hall, it was to discover that it had been recently renovated. Neither Lord nor Lady Stern was an admirer of the classical architecture that had suited their ancestors, and so instead of a formal front, rigid with symmetry, there was now an attractive freestanding house in the Gothic style that fit comfortably into the surrounding landscape. The front door was reached by only a pair of wide steps, and to the right of the front hall a tower rose three stories and was adjoined by a glassed-in conservatory with views to the park through floor-length windows.

From the hall, the guests proceeded through a circular gallery crowned with a rotunda, much gilded and carved, and from there to the drawing room. Georgina looked about her with interest and decided she liked the new informality of the house. Her hostess was delighted by her compliments, and begged her to explore sometime during the evening, before she turned to greet her next guests and Georgina and her aunt passed into the ballroom.

Lady Martin had not dressed for the masquerade, and it was easy to spot Lord Holland standing beside her, even though he wore a scarlet domino over his evening dress, and a black half-mask. She noticed there was another gentleman present in a scarlet domino, and she was sure it was David Linwood, from his height and broad shoulders and the impatient way he moved. She let this gentleman sign her dance card, told Lord Holland she would be pleased to waltz with him, tried to pretend she did not recognize Mr. Rexton as Romeo, and resigned herself to a country dance with Lord Waring. He was resplendent in a crushed-velvet doublet and hose and knee breeches of slashed satin. Over all, he wore an enormous ruff and on his head a cavalier's cap of matching velvet, with several drooping feathers. Georgina thought his sister looked much better than he did, as she watched the young lady positively beaming at the larger scarlet domino and agreeing to a dance. Georgina was quick to move away from Lord Waring, by excusing herself in a cold voice, to greet others of her friends. She was determined this evening to show her indifference to him in such a way that his vanity would be hurt and he would give up his relentless pursuit of her hand.

The ball commenced as Lord and Lady Stern led off the first set, and Georgina prepared to enjoy herself. Her first partner was the brawnier scarlet domino, and she was more sure than ever that it was David Linwood. He held her much too tightly, much too close, but although he kept the beat and minded his step, he did not seem at ease on the floor. Georgina decided to tease him, and when they came together, she whispered, "You have the look of a man who would rather be elsewhere, sir!"

His blue eyes blazed at her through the slits of his mask. "How ungallant of me, ma'am, if it were so! Although, to be truthful, I would rather we were somewhere else. You notice I include you in my exile? Perhaps in a quiet, deserted alcove? On a dark garden path? Ah, that would fulfill all my desires."

"How very rash of you," Georgina said as she danced under his upheld arm. "You cannot be sure, after all, who I am, and if you were to find yourself alone with me, what a surprise if I am not whom you suspect."

"My dear Lady Spaldin', think you to mislead such a man as I? I assure you, I knew you in an instant. The mask cannot fool me, nor the blond wig. And although I have not held you in my arms before, I have inspected your figure often enough to recognize it at a glance." His arm tightened on her waist as they went down the set, and Georgina's lips tightened as well.

"Shall we desert the ballroom so I might prove I am right?" he asked next, bending over her. "And then I can prove as well that you have nothin' to fear from me!"

"I think not, Mr. Linwood," she snapped, and he laughed out loud.

"So, you have been watchin' me closely as well, have you, and my domino and mask are no disguise."

Georgina was not to be drawn into further argument. "There is an air about you that is not English, sir. I cannot describe it . . . not without being rude, and I have decided I will not be rude again. When do you leave for your home?" she asked, abruptly changing the subject.

"There is a matter of business I must attend to here in England, Lady Spaldin', before I am able to take ship.

And, I might add, an additional matter I have every intention of resolvin' before I leave."

"Indeed? I wish you good fortune, sir!"

"You wouldn't, *ma belle*, if you knew what it was!" he drawled, but Georgina ignored the statement and spent the remainder of the dance commenting on Lady Stern's new interiors. Mr. Linwood allowed her the diversion.

When the first waltz struck up, Georgina found the other scarlet domino bending over her hand.

"Fair nymph, you behold me in attendance!" he said, striking a dramatic pose. Georgina curtsied.

He took her in his arms, and she was struck again with the difference between the two men. Whereas Mr. Linwood grasped her tightly, the earl held her with calm assurance, and he needed only a gentle pressure of his hands to let her know how he wished her to follow his lead. "How well you dance, m'lord!" she could not help remarking.

"I am considered fairly adept," he agreed. "But tonight, with such loveliness in my arms, how could I help but be inspired?"

The deep voice was intimate again, and Georgina leaned back a little against his arm to look up at as much of his face as the mask did not cover. She thought his grey eyes cynical and his smile a little twisted as if he mocked her, himself, and all society. Did he think she knew of her aunt's machinations and approved of them? Had he determined in that case to hold her at arm's length by indulging her in a light flirtation?

She shrugged, pretending indifference herself, even as she saw her aunt tap Lady Martin with her fan and incline her head in their direction. She hoped Lord Holland did not see their smiles and nods of approval.

"Are you complimenting me, m'lord?" she asked in what she hoped was an amused tone. "I must tell you I do not fear you will turn my head, for I have been on the town forever, you know, and I am more than two-and-ten."

"You have not been on the town forever, m'lady," he contradicted her, turning expertly with the music. "You married while you were still very young. Since then you have been in almost constant mourning and not much in society until this year, and so, in spite of your widowhood, you are still almost a green girl."

"Well, I see I need not fear to be overcome with your flowery compliments!" Georgina retorted, her color rising at his cool words. "A green girl? I am twenty-five, and old enough to take care of myself!"

Lord Holland tightened his hands just a trifle. "It is to be hoped so, especially where Mr. Linwood is concerned. Allow me the liberty of warning you not to trust him, my dear Lady Spalding. He is a dangerous man, and I can see that he is attracted to you. Your inexperience, even your widowhood, will not deter him from taking advantage if he can."

Georgina was becoming annoyed at the earl's calm assumption that she needed his worldly advice, and she said sharply, "You will please allow me some expertise in matters of this kind, m'lord. I repeat, I am well able to take care of Mr. Linwood's attentions."

Lord Holland sighed. "Well, you have been warned. But permit me to say one more thing, do not ever be alone with him if you can help it, for I have seen how he looks at you."

"And how is that, m'lord?" she asked in innocence, although her eyes glittered behind her mask.

"As if he would like to swallow you whole, m'dear," he said wryly. "He is more than capable of doing so if you allow him any break in your defenses."

"How do you know him so well?" Georgina asked in real curiosity. "I thought you met for the first time at the theatre, yet you both appeared to bear the other some animosity. Now, why should that be? You cannot consider him England's enemy still?"

Lord Holland did not answer for a moment as the waltz came to a close. As he drew Georgina up from her curtsy, he said, "He may not be England's enemy, no, but I know him for *my* enemy, and with good reason. I believe he will serve you a bad turn as well, if he is allowed to do so."

Georgina looked at him in dubious wonder as he took her arm to lead her from the floor. "Well, I will not pry any further, and I thank you for your good advice, sir!" she said. And then she added, "At least I suppose in courtesy I should do so, even if I do consider it unnecessary interference!"

He smiled at her in approval, his grey eyes warm, and remained beside her after they reached the sofa where

Lady Martin and Miss Hersham were seated together.
Georgina thought both ladies a little distracted, as if they
had had some startling news, but she was delighted that
whatever it was had drawn them off the scent, for neither
one of them made any mention of the delightful picture she
had made dancing with the earl.

In the meantime, Emmaline Waring had had the exquisite happiness of dancing with Mr. Linwood. Although
they exchanged very few words, the lack of conversation
did not cause her cup of enchantment to empty. She did
not feel she could converse in any case, it was so intoxicat-
ing to be so close to him. To be in his arms, to feel his
strength and masculinity, to be near enough to smell the
lotion he used, to admire those keen blue eyes and his
powerful features—it was as close to heaven as she had
ever been. And at the end of the dance, she thought for
one moment that instead of curtsying to him, she would
have to throw her arms around his neck and beg him to
kiss her, since she could not help herself. This made her
blush. She would have been thrilled if she had known Mr.
Linwood thought her much improved from their first meeting, but suddenly her brother was beside them, bowing
and drawing her away. She did not even hear his whispered
censure of her partner, nor his orders that she was never
to dance with the man again, and she did not pay much
attention when he took her over to Lord Handford and
bade her entertain him well. "Thirty thousand, no fortune
hunter, good title and family, comes from our county, and
thinks just as he ought. See to it, Emma—you know what
I mean!"

Emmaline went so far as to smile in a dreamy way at the
young man, her thoughts far away, and her brother bustled over to Lady Spalding to claim his dance. Throughout
it, Georgina replied to his best *bon mots* and heavy compliments with distant looks and icy comments, and when
Lord Waring bowed at the conclusion, she was sure she
had let him know in no uncertain terms what she thought
of him and his suit. She was wrong. Lord Waring was
delighted with her coldness, for he was sure dear Georgie
had no idea who her cavalier had been, and he could only
applaud her demeanour with a stranger. It was just as it
should be, he thought, for of course her admiration and
growing love for him would make her very stiff with other

men. He went away determined to do all he could to force his sister and Lord Handford to the altar in short order so he could devote himself wholeheartedly to his own engagement with Georgina Spalding.

All unsuspecting, Georgina danced with Mr. Rexton and with Lord Holland again, and several other gentlemen of her acquaintance. Sometime after supper, she found herself beside her hostess, who said she would be delighted to show her around the Hall and tell her just what improvements she had made—and how very expensive and time-consuming it had all been!

Several people noted Lady Spalding's departure from the ballroom. The Earl, and Lord Waring as well, saw Lady Stern by her side and relaxed, while Mr. Linwood decided to follow them. The ladies had entered the conservatory, and he lingered in the hall outside, pretending an interest in many portraits of the Sterns' ancestors which hung there, when Lady Stern's butler came to find her with a note on his silver salver. She excused herself to Georgina.

"Some silly problem in the kitchen. French chefs are all very well, Georgie, and the supper was delicious as always, but François has a temper that is positively frightening. Do feel free to look around while I am gone, my dear."

Georgina thanked her for the tour, and took a few turns about the conservatory. She could not see the vistas of the park through the long windows this late at night, of course, but the room was pleasantly cool and decorated with several lovely flowering plants, as well as some bamboo sofas and chairs. She was about to sink into one of them and enjoy her solitude for a few moments more, when she became aware she was no longer alone.

She whirled to discover a scarlet domino, hands on hips and legs spread wide, staring at her with relish, and she knew it was not Lord Holland who raked her body with those blazing eyes and whose mouth widened in a smile of complete satisfaction.

"And now I have you alone, as I have wanted for so long!" he said, striding toward her while she tried hard not to retreat. Somehow her feet moved of their own volition and she did not stop until she found herself backed against a wall, David Linwood followed her step for step, like a panther hunting prey, she thought wildly. Before she could speak, he reached out and removed her mask.

"We do not need this anymore, *belle*, and I want to see your face," he drawled, his hand caressing her neck and bare shoulder as he took the mask away.

"How dare you—" she began, but he put a large hand over her mouth.

"None of that conventional indignation, *belle*, if you please! You know very well how I dare; I told you over and over I would, did I not? Americans go after what they want . . . and get it!"

Georgina felt her breath coming fast in her throat as he put one strong arm around her and pulled her tight against his chest. His other hand came up to hold her chin fast, and she realized that she had never been so vulnerable in her entire life. Short of screaming, there was no way she could stop him from doing whatever he wanted to, and she was not at all sure he would not throttle her if she tried. Helplessly she watched those intent blue eyes drop to her breasts and then travel up to her eyes, before they went again to her mouth. He was in no hurry, and it seemed she had been standing his prisoner for hours before he bent his head and kissed her. At first there was just a gentle pressure of his lips, as if he were investigating uncharted waters, but all too soon he began to move his mouth with more insistence over hers, becoming more and more demanding, as if to tease her with his control over their embrace. He put both his arms around her and pulled her even closer to his broad chest before he parted her lips with his tongue and began to explore her mouth. Georgina could not move, could not even try to twist her head away, and when she tried to close her lips, he refused to allow it. All the time he was kissing her, she had not taken a breath, and just when she thought she must faint, he raised his head and frowned down at her, his hands moving to grasp her arms in a cruel grip, until she was sure she must cry out with the pain.

"But what is this? I understood you were a widow, *belle*. What a cold marriage you must have had! Why, any fifteen-year-old maid receives a man with more passion than you have just displayed."

He dropped his hands and stepped away from her as if

he were amused and somehow, she thought, disappointed. Her mind was whirling with questions. What did he mean? Of course John had never, *would* never have dared to kiss her like that. She had not realized a kiss could be so deep and consuming, with two mouths joined as one, demanding and unrelenting, and it had frightened her, although she could not deny the faint quiver of response that she had begun to feel take hold of her just as he raised his head. Now she tried to steady her breathing as she replied, "Perhaps it is because I dislike having to kiss you, Mr. Linwood. I am not in the habit of being *forced* to accept an embrace."

He laughed at her then, and she clenched her fists. Strolling back to her, he took her chin in his hand again. "I would say you were not in the habit of acceptin' embraces at all. You have not the least idea how to go on, do you, Lady Spaldin'? What a dull dog your husband must have been. Or was it a marriage of convenience and perhaps never consummated at all? Who would have thought that such a voluptuous and seductive woman as you appear to be would turn out to be so inexperienced and virginal? What cruel jokes the gods play on mortal men!"

His laugh was openly mocking, and Georgina wished she had the courage to strike him.

"Never mind, *belle*," he consoled her, tracing her swollen lips with one strong finger. "I am feeling magnanimous, so I will show you how to go about it. What would you care to wager that in only a few lessons you will live up to your looks with a vengeance? And how gratifyin' it is that in a way I will be your *first* lover. I am a very good teacher, you know, and I will try to restrain my impatience to reach the final lesson. You may consider tonight an introduction to love's delights, and think yourself fortunate. You see, I would not bother if I thought you truly cold, for I have no time to waste on such women, but I am sure that you will be a delight to instruct, and an apt pupil."

He bent his head again, but this time he just brushed her lips lightly, his hand moving possessively over her bare shoulder as he did so, and then he let her go and turned his back on her to light a cigarillo. Georgina took advantage of his distraction and picked up her skirts to run from the room. She heard his jeering laughter as she gained the tower room and came face to face with the Earl of Amesbury. She knew he heard as well, for one of his black eyebrows rose, and his grey eyes turned cold.

"Burned, Georgie? So much of my good advice, and your *supposed* expertise in handling men." He sounded nonchalant, as if it mattered little to him what happened to her, but then he added more formally, "Allow me to escort you back to your aunt, Lady Spalding. Like you, everyone has unmasked, and the ball is . . . er . . . over."

4

When Georgina came downstairs late the following morning, it was to discover that her aunt had already left the house.

"I believe she has gone to visit Lady Martin, m'lady," Geering informed her, pouring her a cup of coffee after she had refused all the various dishes awaiting her pleasure on the sideboard of the breakfast room. "She said she did not know when she would return, and begged you to excuse her." Geering coughed. "If I may be so bold, ma'am, I take it Lady Martin is in a spot of bother, and Miss Hersham has gone to bear her company."

Georgina shrugged. She was glad Aunt Bess was out, for she had no wish to discuss the masquerade now, and she did not feel she could bear to listen to her aunt enthuse about the marvelous Earl of Amesbury without screaming in frustration. Georgina had not slept very well.

"Thank you, Geering, that will be all," she said, and the butler bowed and left the room. She was not to enjoy her solitude for long, however, for a few moments later he returned, carrying a long white box.

"This has just been delivered, m'lady," he said as he presented it to her.

Georgina untied the satin bow with unsteady fingers and opened the tissue paper inside. She was aware the butler had lingered to adjust the burners on the sideboard, but as she lifted out the flowers she found enclosed, she forgot his presence.

"How very beautiful!" she exclaimed. "I wonder what they are?"

In her hands she held a spray containing dozens of tiny flowers with white throats and petals of a very pale green.

She bent her head, but there was no scent from the exotic blooms.

Geering, an old family retainer, was bold enough to cough again. "Excuse me, m'lady. I believe they are orchids from the tropics, although I have never seen any quite like that. Mr. Ryden-Jones across Brooks Street raises them in his conservatory, and his butler, a particular friend of mine, showed them to me one day. His specimens cannot compare to these, however, being much larger and purple in color."

Georgina laid the flowers down carefully beside her cup and searched the box for a card. They had to be from either Mr. Linwood or Lord Holland, for Teddy Waring would never send such a strange offering and Mr. Rexton probably could not afford them. She was not too surprised to see her name on the envelope in that familiar bold black handwriting, for she was sure the Earl was disgusted with her after the fiasco at the ball.

"Thank you, Geering," she said, turning the envelope over in her hands. "Take them away and put them in water, if you please, and perhaps you can ask your friend how I should care for them as well?"

The butler bowed again, his face expressionless, although his mind was busy going over m'lady Georgie's beaux, and discarding one name after the other. It was obvious to him a new contender had entered the lists, and he wondered who it could be.

Georgina waited until the double doors had closed behind him before she tore the heavy vellum envelope open.

Dear Belle:
    There *are* green flowers in the Americas, as you can see, and more lovely than the English flowers I sent you last. And you, like these, are already less "green" than you were before last evening. Do not disappoint me by leaving London before our next lesson.
                                D.L.
I look forward to the morning I send you a spray of *scarlet* orchids. Let it be soon!

Georgina did not know whether to burst into tears or throw her coffee cup at the wall. Two men, in less than the space of a single day, had accused her of being green. And she, who had begun to pride herself on her sophistication, had to admit, in all honesty, that there was a great deal of truth in their assessment.

The flowers surprised her. They were so delicate and fragile and so very unlike the overpowering Mr. Linwood. Somehow the gesture seemed unlike him as well, for he was not at all the type to shower a lady with bouquets and trinkets and love letters. Not, she told herself as she returned his note to its envelope, that this could be considered a "love letter"! Not at all! It was more a challenge, and she wondered if she had the courage to pick up the gauntlet he had thrown down. Or should she, as she had decided to do just before she dropped off to sleep in the grey of an English dawn, leave town and return to Somerset? She would be safe there, she knew. The question was, did she really want to be safe?

She could still remember how his mouth had felt on hers, and his caressing hand on her bare skin, and although she had been shocked and frightened, something that she had never been aware of in her had responded to his passion. Her marriage had not been one of convenience and it had certainly been consummated, but now she realized that in matters between the sexes, she knew almost as little as Emmaline Waring! John Spalding had been a rough-and-ready soldier and his kisses had been hearty smacks accompanied by bearlike hugs. When he came to her bed, it was always at night when she was half-asleep, and after a vigorous few moments he would roll off her and immediately fall asleep, leaving her to stare at the ceiling, her hands clenched and her eyes wide as she listened to his snores. If he should still be there in the morning, he would slap her bottom and call her a good gel before he climbed out of bed and, talking all the while about his hounds or his favourite horse, hastily don his dressing gown and leave her alone.

And she had imagined that that was what marriage and lovemaking were all about. She writhed a little at her naiveté. No wonder the Earl and David Linwood had called her green. But did she really want to find out any more? Part of her was still a little afraid of what she might discover if she stayed near David Linwood, yet another part wanted to go on and on until she knew all there was to know about this strangely exciting and thrilling pastime.

And perhaps then she would be able to bring men like David Linwood and Robert Holland to their knees. It was a heady thought, and she smiled as she picked up her neglected coffee cup.

At the same time, in Portman Square, Miss Hersham was putting down her coffee cup with a snap and saying "Good God!"

"Well you may say so, Bess!" Lady Martin agreed, throwing down the letter she had been reading aloud to her friend. "Was there ever anything more vexatious than a *man?* And Cousin Bertie is the worst of the lot. To write to me, not only demanding my attendance but also commanding me to 'get up a party' of as many as I care to invite, to come to Upper Littledean for a long stay—and in the height of the Season, mind you—it is too bad. And all because he has decided to make out his will—one more time—and wishes to compare dear Robert, who has been his heir forever, with some mysterious distant relative no one has ever heard of before, so he can decide which one he will leave his fortune to. Make his will indeed! He has made any number of wills; I think it is an obsession with him, having all the lawyers scurrying back and forth from town and in constant attendance, to make him feel important." She tapped the letter before her and added, "And whom, I ask you, can I persuade to leave town at this time, especially to stay at Carew Court, for a more boring location I have yet to see. Tch!"

She shook her head, and Miss Hersham went right to the heart of the matter. "If dear Robert goes out of town, you know that will put paid to any alliance he might contract with Georgie. Drat the man, although I should not say so of your cousin, Agnes."

"You may say so with my blessing, for I have called him much worse, time out of number," her friend said graciously.

"But who *is* Cousin Bertie?" Miss Hersham asked next.

"He is Bertram James St. Denis Holland, Marquess of Carew, and he considers himself the patriarch of the family. You are not to think he is about to stick his spoon in the wall, however, Bess, for he is only sixty-and-two and in excellent health, although he likes to pretend his days are numbered. I really do not know why they are not, after the life he has lived, the old roué. He never married—indeed, he has always been so eccentric, no one would have him in spite of his fortune. That is not to say he does not have an eye for the ladies." Lady Martin snorted. "My, yes! In his day, he held the title of England's Premier Rake. The stories I could tell you about the man would make you stare. One *inamorata* after another for years and years and years. The entire family breathed a collective sigh of relief when he retired to the Court at Upper Littledean and took up brass rubbings from old tombstones instead."

Miss Hersham did not comment on this unusual hobby. "I take it he has enough money to make it imperative for Lord Holland to attend him at this time?" she asked, secure in her position of a bosom bow who was entitled to ask any impertinent questions that came to her mind.

"Unfortunately, yes. Besides a fortune in Funds and his various estates, there are also the Holland Emeralds, and they, let me tell you, are worth a trip to the end of the earth to secure."

"I do not believe I have ever heard of them," Miss Hersham replied, looking puzzled.

"Only because they are so hideous, no one has ever worn them to our knowledge. They are worth a king's ransom, but I ask you, Bess, who would ever contemplate being burdened by a stomacher weighing several pounds, these days? And the most revolting medieval crown to match."

"A stomacher and crown?"

"And they are such historic and valuable antiques, they can never be broken up and reset. They are of no use to anyone, and a great deal of trouble besides for whoever possesses them, for they must be kept in a special vault, and I know Cousin Bertie hires a man from Bow Street to guard them as well."

"My! How very unusual!"

Lady Martin picked up the letter again. "But a party, Bess. I cannot think who—"

"Why, aunt, you have the beginnings of your party sitting beside you right now," Lord Holland said, coming in to give his aunt a kiss and Miss Hersham a bow. "I see you have received great-uncle's summons too. Surely you can persuade Miss Hersham to accompany us, aunt, for she is your best friend, is she not? And then, of course, we must invited Lady Spalding as well."

He turned aside to get himself some breakfast, and Lady Martin kicked her friend under cover of the table and beamed, while Miss Hersham clasped her hands together over her head like a victorious prizefighter. Both ladies were a study in normality when the Earl came back to the table.

"What an excellent idea, Robert," Lady Martin agreed, and then she added in a glum voice, "But I am sure neither Bess nor Georgie would care for it, especially since I have just been telling Bess the truth about Cousin Bertie and Upper Littledean."

She sounded so innocent, her nephew chuckled. "That was not well done of you, aunt. You should have painted a rosy picture of pleasant walks and drives, scenic views and salubrious air, and then thrown in any number of interesting castles and churches to visit, to make them all eagerness to see such treasures for themselves. But come, ma'am, how can you desert your friend in her hour of greatest need?"

His grey eyes were sparkling with fun as he smiled at her, and Miss Hersham found it difficult to imagine any woman able to deny him anything he asked for, including herself.

"I should certainly be pleased to bear dear Agnes company, m'lord," she said. "But Georgie . . . and in the height of the Season, too . . . I do not think she would care for it."

Her voice sounded so mournful, the Earl was forced to cover his mouth with his napkin for a moment. He knew well what these two old tabbies were up to, but he, like Georgie, had no intention of spoiling their treat.

"Then we must bend all our efforts to convince her that town life is growing flat, that she looks pale and in need of country air, and that there will be several interesting people there to amuse her."

"*What* interestin' people?" his aunt inquired in her blunt way.

The Earl considered. "I can ask Freddie Wilson and his sister, Constance. She is a pleasant girl who loves the country and is most agreeable as well. I am sure I can convince them to join us."

"Well, that is only you and I, Bess and Georgie—if we can get her to come, mind!—and Lord and Lady Wilson. Not much of a party!" his aunt snorted.

"You are forgetting Cousin Bertie—Lord Holland, I

mean," Miss Hersham reminded her. "From what you have told me of him, Agnes, I am sure he will be most . . . er . . . unusual and entertaining."

"And I have forgotten the mysterious lost heir as well. Have you any idea who he might be, Robert?" Lady Martin asked.

The Earl was well aware who his rival was and had known for weeks, for Cousin Bertie had notified him of the man's identity as soon as his lawyers had discovered the family connection. Life had been a little flat at Carew Court through the winter months, and Cousin Bertie was not adverse to stirring the pot for his own amusement. But the Earl had no intention of making the man's identity public as yet. He had his own reasons for wanting Lady Spalding at the Court, along with Mr. David Linwood, his very distant second cousin.

He acknowledged to himself that his reaction when he found Lady Spalding alone with the American last evening had been surprising. The look on her face as she rushed from the conservatory made him angry enough to want to challenge the man, and for a moment the dangerous temper that he kept hidden so carefully from the world almost got the best of him. Then he shrugged mentally as he assessed the situation.

Georgina Spalding was nothing to him, and the fact that she had been so rash as to disregard his warnings told him she was no better than she should be. She had joked with him about her title, and "Lady" Spalding she might be in name, but it was obvious she was no better than the lowest bit o' muslin who strolled the fashionable streets, or the opera dancers who flirted with the wealthy gentlemen in the boxes, all in search of a protector. Perhaps she was not even as good, for they at least were honest about their occupation. He could see why she might find her widowhood frustrating, and if she was so inclined, who was he to say her nay? Besides, if she were to stay at Carew Court with Linwood and himself, there was every chance he might be able to cut the gentleman out of yet another conquest. Lady Georgie was beautiful; he would not mind in the slightest indulging her in an affair.

Besides, he was determined the man would have no part of the Holland fortune, even if he had to kill him to make sure of it. He had never considered himself overly patriotic, but the thought of all that English wealth going to an American, whose country was nothing but a rat's nest of colonial rebels who had turned their back on the mother country, made his blood boil. No, if he had anything to say about it, Mr. David Linwood would return to Virginia empty-handed of both the Holland fortune and the lady's favours as well. He had started certain investigations of his own to make sure of it.

Now he smiled at his aunt and lied to her without a qualm. "I have no idea, Aunt Agnes, but his attendance must add spice to our adventure, don't you think?"

He excused himself then and went away, leaving the ladies to put their heads together, much cheered, to begin their campaign to get Georgie to agree to a trip to Upper Littledean.

But this turned out to be a formidable task. Presented with the perfect solution to her vexing problem of avoiding Mr. Linwood. Georgina found herself most unwilling to take advantage of it. She told herself it would be cowardly to run away, for she was feeling much braver with every minute that passed that she was not in his company. Surely she had made too much of his lovemaking! She would know better next time how to go on, and since she had no intention of ever being alone with him again, she did not see how he was to continue his lessons, unless he kidnapped her. She did not think even *he* would go so far, although it was a delicious thought to speculate about.

She thanked him for his spray of orchids when they met at Mrs. Manning's reception, her voice even and controlled and polite, and she looked him right in the eye as she did so. She was able to sweep away from him with her head held high, sure she was in command of the situation, but it was just as well she did not see the delighted smile of genuine amusement that passed over Mr. Linwood's craggy features as he watched her stiff back as she left him.

In vain Miss Hersham reminded her how much she enjoyed the country and how delightful it would be to inspect a part of it she had never visited. Lady Martin's entreaties were useless as well, even up to and including her pointing out that by removing herself from town, Georgie would be free of Lord Waring and his tiresome suit at last. The ladies were at their wits' end when Lord Holland took a hand.

Informed by his aunt that dear Georgie was being difficult, he sent her a note asking her to join him for a ride in
the park that very afternoon, to try out his new team of
chestnuts. He mentioned he would be driving his high-
perch phaeton, so if she was at all nervous, he would
understand her refusal completely.

Thus challenged, Georgina dashed off a note declaring
she would be delighted to join the Earl at three, for she
found high-perch phaetons an exhilarating way to travel,
and went upstairs to choose her most devastating afternoon
gown, a new one of sea-green silk.

It was going to be a little awkward climbing up into the
phaeton with any degree of modesty, she thought, eyeing
her narrow skirts, as the Earl got down and came around
to assist her. He waved her footmen away, while his tiger
stood to the horses' heads, and somehow Georgina found
herself deposited high above the cobblestones by a pair of
wiry arms she would not have believed to have had such
strength, for she knew she was no feather. She grasped
the seat tightly as the Earl sprang up beside her and took
up the reins, but when he raised his brows in inquiry, she
was quick to unfold her parasol and tilt it at a becoming
angle over her shoulder.

"It is quite safe, m'lady," he assured her with his warm
smile. "I should think myself most remiss to overturn such
a beauty as yourself! What a lovely dress! But then, you
are always turned out in the first stare of fashion. I do
think you should refrain from wearing that particular shade
of green, however—with your eyes it is almost more than a
mortal man can stand!"

Georgina thanked him for his compliment, and then conversation languished, for the Earl had his hands full. The
team was fresh and the streets were crowded. Georgina
watched those long slim hands controlling the restless team
with such ease and admired his skill. At last they reached
the park, and after leaving the crowded entrance behind,
the Earl settled his team into a steady trot and turned to
her again.

"How well you control them, m'lord!" she enthused. "I
am sure it is not an easy task, yet you make it appear so
simple."

He smiled that intimate smile of his and said in his deep,
warm voice, "Perhaps it is because I find horses like women,

m'lady? A firm hand on the reins is all that is required in both cases, for they both like to know who is master. Don't you agree?"

Georgie tried not to frown. "I am not entirely sure I approve of the comparison, sir!"

"But do consider, dear lady. On the dance floor, it is the man who leads. Granted, no reins are necessary, but don't you yourself prefer a man who takes control, who lets you know what he wishes you to do?"

"On the dance floor, certainly, m'lord," she replied, wondering what on earth the Earl was about. He had never been so suggestive since the first afternoon they had met, when he mistook her for a little demimonde. To her relief, he changed the subject.

"I am sorry to hear that you do not feel able to join our country party at Upper Littledean, ma'am. I am sure I can promise you any amount of . . . mm . . . entertainment, if that will change your mind!"

Georgina ignored these provocative words. "It is kind of you to invite me, m'lord, but I cannot like leaving town at the height of the Season."

"Perhaps if I tell you that Mr. Linwood is to be among our number?" he asked casually, nodding to Lady Jersey and her party.

Georgina stiffened. "Mr. Linwood! Whatever will he be there for?"

"Mr. Linwood, as it turns out, is a very distant second cousin of mine, and as such, the missing heir."

"So that is why you do not like him," Georgina said, her eyes narrowed in thought.

"Perhaps . . . and there is something about the man as well—a certain crudeness—I cannot say. He acts the gentleman, he dresses the gentleman, and if my uncle's lawyers are to be believed, he is in truth a gentleman, but for all that, I find it hard to accept him as one."

Georgina was thinking hard, but before she could frame a reply, the Earl asked, "Afraid, Georgie?"

"Of what should I be afraid, m'lord?" she asked in her haughtiest voice, ignoring his use of her nickname.

"Who knows? Of me? Of Mr. Linwood? Or perhaps you are afraid of yourself? I did not think you a coward, but if you do not have the courage, we will say no more. What a pity."

"It is not a question of courage, sir!" she snapped, grasping the handle of her parasol so tightly she was sure it must break. "It is a question of whether I would find the stay amusing—"

"Come, come, dear lady. What could be more amusing? To watch Mr. Linwood trying to maneuver himself to my cousin's good graces, to be on hand to observe how I attempt to foil him, to have the chance to choose between us in a lonely rustic setting . . . what can there be here in London to compare to it, and to give you so much . . . pleasure?"

Georgina was not sure she had heard him correctly. Choose between them? She must have misunderstood him. "I shall promise only to reconsider, m'lord," she said.

"Let your answer be 'yes,' if you please, m'lady. Your presence is the only thing that will make this entire affair at all agreeable."

He pulled up his team by the lake for a moment and turned to lean nearer to her and to look down into her eyes. "Say, 'yes,' Georgie, say 'yes,' " he whispered. Georgina felt breathless and confused. Robert Holland was much too handsome, much too assured, and much too persuasive, and there was something about the man that made her want to agree with everything he asked. She felt a sudden yearning to lean towards him in turn and receive his kiss. She gasped and straightened, pressing back against the seat and wondering what on earth was the matter with her, as he added, "Do not cry coward, m'lady. I *dare* you."

"Then I accept your challenge, sir, and I will be delighted to accept your aunt's kind invitation as well, but if I am not accorded amusement of the most unique kind, I shall be very disappointed."

She tried to sound casual and worldly, and the Earl turned away for a moment so she would not see his laughter.

"Trust me, Georgie, I shall see to it," he said, giving his horses the office to start again. In a softer voice he added, "It shall be my first consideration in order of importance, my dear. I promise I shall not fail you."

Georgina had the sudden thought that she was not any more in control of this situation than she had been in David Linwood's arms at the masquerade, and in point of fact had been manipulated for the Earl's own purposes, but stung, she said in a rush, "I am sure it will be most enjoyable, and to tell the truth, I have been longing to get back to the country. Is Upper Littledean good hunting country? Tell me about it and the Court, if you please."

The remainder of the drive was spent with the Earl describing the estate and the surrounding countryside, and telling her as many stories about Cousin Bertie as he felt fit for a lady's ears. When he himself insisted on lifting her down from the perch when they regained Brooks Street, he held her for a moment in his arms before he let her slip gently to the walkway. As he did so, there was a look on his face that seemed almost a twin to the blue fire in David Linwood's eyes, but it was gone so quickly, and the Earl was so formal and polite as she thanked him and said good-bye, that Georgina was sure she must have been mistaken.

It was not to be supposed that Lord Waring would fail to hear about the proposed party at Carew Court, and he did everything in his power to be included, even though he knew it was unfortunate to have to leave town just when Emma seemed to be attracting such an eligible *parti* as Lord Handford. But what else could he do? There were the handsome Earl of Amesbury and Mr. David Linwood to consider, and just the thought that his Georgina would be forced into the close proximity that a country house party entailed, with two men he could not approve of, made him break out into a cold sweat. And so he bent every effort to be charming to Lady Martin, dropping ponderous hints about his availability and interest, and was rewarded by the lady's densest stare of incomprehension.

"Surely it would not appeal to you, Teddy," she said. "So boring, these family affairs. No, no, I will not ask it of you. Besides, it is your sister's first Season—you should be in town, just in case."

No amount of cajoling could change her mind, and Lord Waring went off in despair to seek his mother's advice. This retiring woman, so out of the world, had often been helpful to him before. She was a tiny little thing who had been overwhelmed first by her bluff, stout husband and then, after his death, by her only son, as like his father as two peas in a pod. Over the years she had become resigned to having her opinions neglected and ignored, and the beauty and personality she had possessed had faded away. People were often unaware she was even in the same room with them, and if asked to describe her, were hard put to remember a single feature of her pale, quiet face. But Teddy often sought her counsel; not, to be sure, in hopes of hearing anything helpful from her. It was just that sometimes enumerating his problems and laying before her the various ways he might go in resolving them brought the solution to his mind. Now he paced up and down her drawing room while she sat over her sewing and watched him with her wide blue eyes.

"You see, Mama, it is of the first importance that I be here to accept Lord Handford if he does come up to scratch! I must tell you, I am most pleased with Emma. Somehow she seems to have attached William, although I could not tell you how she went about it."

He frowned as he considered this, unaware that his sister's dreamy state of love for Mr. Linwood had brought a softer expression to her face, and her casual way of treating the younger peer had piqued his interest. He set himself the task of making her notice him, but although she was always glad to dance with him, or sit and talk, he knew her attention was elsewhere, and this spurred him on to greater and greater efforts to succeed with her.

"And I cannot like Lady Spalding going to Upper Littledean without me," Lord Waring continued. "You know how flighty women are, even the best of them, Mamma, and there is Mr. Linwood, whom I cannot like, and the Earl of Amesbury. Especially the Earl; you know his reputation!"

His mother made a small sound of distress, and he went on as if she had agreed with him, "But then, when I did everything but beg Lady Martin to let me join the party, she denied me! But Emma notwithstanding, I must be there!"

Lady Waring cleared her throat, and he turned, astonished to see her hand raised and her face a delicate pink.

"Dear Teddy," she said shyly. "might we not . . .? No, that would not do, for he might not wish to come, and perhaps it would be too pointed to single him out that way, but really I do not see what else you can do, and even if I do not quite like it, I suppose I must do what I can to help. . . . Oh dear!"

"Whatever are you babbling about, Mama?" his lordship asked in some amazement, for he had not heard so many words, even as disjointed as they were, from his mother in years.

Lady Waring turned a deeper shade of pink and said, "Only that you must contrive to get Emma and Lord Handford invited as well as yourself, and I do think, even if I cannot like it, that I had better come too."

"Mama, you are all about in your head!" her devoted son snapped. "Haven't you heard a word I have been saying? If I cannot get Lady Martin to invite *me*, how the devil—I beg your pardon, Mama, but I am at my wits' end—how can I get her to include a number of other guests?"

"But you don't have to ask her," Lady Waring replied, overturning her sewing basket at her daring. Her son saw she was almost scarlet now, and wondered if he should summon her maid, since his mother was clearly unwell. "You see," she whispered, "I shall write and ask Bertie—I mean the Marquess—myself! I am sure he will be glad to invite us all, for Carew Court is huge and Bertie lives in great state. Ten or a hundred more guests can make no difference."

"*You* will write? To *Bertie*?"

Lady Waring got down on her hands and knees to pick up her threads and needles, and with her head averted, was able to say, "I . . . I knew him once, very well, a long time ago!"

"Well, 'pon my soul! *Mama!*" her son exclaimed. "I cannot believe it of you. When was that, and where, and how did it come about?"

As Lady Waring regained her seat and lowered her eyes, he added hastily, "No, no, never mind! I don't need to know, don't even want to! Well, well! The perfect solution to the problem! Write the old gentleman a letter, Mama, and be sure to ask him to include Lord Handford in his invitation. I am sure it must be correct for such *elderly* old friends not to stand on ceremony!"

He looked in dubious wonder at his blushing mother as he prepared to take a hasty leave before she could feel the need to tell him all about her former relationship with Bertie Holland, who not so many years ago had been such a great rake. Cautioning her that he wished to surprise Lady Spalding, and so would appreciate it if the whole affair could be kept very quiet, he hurried from the room, shaking his head in stunned amazement.

Lady Waring felt a stab of resentment at being called "elderly" by her son, for she was only fifty-two, but since she had not contradicted him since he reached the age of five, she did not dare to do so now. Besides, in confessing she knew Bertie Holland, she had used up her slender stock of courage. She folded her sewing and went obediently to her escritoire to write her letter.

Miss Hersham was delighted when Georgina returned from her drive with Robert Holland and announced almost defiantly that she had decided to go to Carew Court with the others. Miss Hersham had admired the spray of orchids, for Georgina had had them placed in the drawing room, but when she asked who had honoured her niece with such a beautiful tribute, she had been shocked to discover they had been sent by Mr. Linwood. They must have cost the man a fortune, and it was such a distinguished attention, she could not help but feel a qualm of fear. But with Georgie making plans to go to Upper Littledean, she was relieved, for this would remove her from the gentleman's orbit forever. Miss Hersham had not reached the age she was without being able to recognize the power that a man of Mr. Linwood's persuasion could exert over even the most sophisticated woman, and she did not want to see Georgie caught in his web. Especially when dear Robert was becoming so very attentive. When Georgie let slip some days later that the American was the missing heir and would certainly be a member of the party, her spirits plummeted again, and she put on her bonnet and stole and ordered the carriage to take her to Lady Martin's so she might seek her advice.

"It is so very worrying, Agnes," she said, after pouring out her tale. "Mr. Linwood! At Carew Court! With Georgie!"

Her friend patted her hand. "But Robert will be there as well, my dear. Be calm! I do not like it myself, for in observing the man, I swear he almost crackles with masculinity, and so we must be very clever and foil any of his attempts to attach Georgie before Robert has a chance to fix his interest with her. Much as I dislike playing *duenna*, I suggest that both of us take turns watching over her. She must never be left alone where he can get at her. We must be very attentive, not only to Georgie, but to Mr. Linwood as well!"

As Miss Hersham raised an inquiring brow, Lady Martin

explained, "If he is engaged in conversation with us, he can hardly be chasing your niece! Oh dear, I am afraid we are going to hear more about America and the customs prevailing there than we have ever cared to know. For Georgie's sake, and for Robert's as well, we must avail ourselves of every opportunity to hang on his sleeve." She shook her head. "I fear Carew Court will be even more tedious than usual this visit."

Now it was Miss Hersham's turn to pat her friend's hand. "At least, Agnes, that tiresome Teddy Waring will not be there to plague us and complicate things. *That* is something to be thankful about at all accounts."

The house party bound for Carew Court near Upper Littledean did not take coach for some ten days more. The ladies had shopping to do, for what was worn in town would not do for a rustic setting. Then too, there was the closing of their London establishments, orders to be given to the servants, and invitations to be refused. Freddie Wilson was engaged for a race meeting he did not care to miss, and David Linwood had written to Georgina that he hoped she would be able to curb her impatience, for he was so involved with lawyers that much to his regret they must postpone their next lesson until they were both installed at Carew Court. Georgina threw this missive in the fire and shrugged in disdain.

Robert Holland was delighted it was all taking such a long time, for he was expecting a letter to arrive from overseas, and he was anxious to hear the report of a certain underling who was haunting the docks for him as well.

5

Carew Court had been built in 1665 in the Palladian style by Rogert Pratt. Its red-brick exterior was symmetrical, a single handsome block much adorned with pediments and columns and several chimney stacks, and topped with an octagonal cupola. The servants' wing extended behind, so that the whole mansion formed a large T. The north front, which was the main entrance, was reached by travelling up a long winding drive through a beechwood forest. About half a mile from the Court, the vista opened up to reveal several acres of sweeping lawns and gardens containing marble statues and a large fountain. There were wide gravel walks throughout, one of which wandered through a small grove of birch trees before ending at a marble bathhouse near a lake.

A set of shallow curving steps led up to the front door, and the visitor entered the most impressive part of the house, the Great Hall. This massive room ascended for two stories, and a pair of matching stairways rose along its sides to meet in a gallery that ran along the back and provided entrance to the Great Dining Chamber. At the rear of the Hall itself was the Great Parlour, another high-storied room hung with dark oil paintings of landscapes and portraits of former Hollands.

The Court was decorated with all manner of furnishings belonging to these ancestors, as well as such new acquisitions as had caught Cousin Bertie's eyes. Thus a much-carved high-backed chair of the early 1600's might sit next to a lacquered table of Chinese design, the mate of which Bertie had admired in Brighton Pavilion. The Marquess was a great admirer of the Prince Regent.

The State Bedroom, however, had been kept intact,

exactly as the Lord Holland who built the Court had had it prepared for Charles II. It was not known whether His Majesty had ever honoured it with his presence, but Cousin Bertie was much taken with it. He liked to go there every now and then and stretch out on the Royal Bed to stare up at the tester complete with ostrich plumes so far above him. Like all the rooms of the Court, it had a high ceiling, and the walls were hung with crimson-and-gold tapestries depicting gods and goddesses at play. Every post and moulding, every carved garland, was heavily gilded, and the four-poster bed itself was an enormous affair, draped with crimson and gold velvet and separated from the rest of the room in its raised recess by a carved balustrade.

The Marquess was not aware how ridiculous he appeared in his mansion, for he was barely five and a half feet tall, with tiny hands and feet and a rotund, portly figure. His little round face sported a pair of twinkling brown eyes, a button nose, and rosy cheeks, not, alas, from good health and the effects of fresh air, but from his propensity for wine and old brandy. He was not bald, but what remained of his hair circled his head like a monk's tonsure. It was pure white and he wore it long, while above it his bald pate gleamed in a perfect circle. It gave him a deceptively saintly air, and it was the only saintly thing about him, for he was not at all monkish in either his behaviour or his speech. He tended to bounce when he walked, perhaps in an effort to make himself appear taller, and he could also be seen to bounce up and down in his chair as well, if he became excited. Amid his huge formal rooms and massive furniture, he looked very much like a naughty child escaped from his nanny.

He had been delighted to hear from Lady Waring, and happy to include her, her children, and Lord Handford in his party. Dear Lavinia, it has been such a long time since we met, he thought. I wonder if she was happy with Stuffy Waring? But she was a widow now; how old would she be? He counted back on his fingers and nodded. Perhaps she would not be averse to a *liaison de coeur*? She was only fifty-two, and he had a mere ten more years in his dish, and they were not ready to cock up their toes to the ceiling yet! He fell in readily with the lady's suggestion that they surprise the others, and did not mention these additional guests in any of his communications with Lady Martin.

Lord, it would be amusin' to see Aggie's expression when
he produced the Warings! He rubbed his little hands together and laughed out loud, a high-pitched chortle, as he
decided he could hardly wait for the fun to begin!

The various coaches left London the first week of May
and made their way north to Lincoln before they left the
main roads and drove through the countryside for another
day's journey until they reached Upper Littledean. Georgina and her aunt had accepted Lady Martin's invitation to
ride in her coach, and there was another coach following
them that contained their maids and all the luggage, and
several grooms and outriders to escort them on their journey. Georgina's man, Ives, trailed her chestnut mare.

Now Lady Martin stared out of the coach window and
sighed. Her sighs had become progressively more in evidence the nearer they came to Carew Court, and in an
effort to distract her, Miss Hersham asked her again, for
what Georgina was sure was the fiftieth time, if she thought
dear Robert was before them.

"He left London the same day we did, but driving his
curricle, with his valet and baggage going ahead, he has
surely made better time. I daresay he will be there to
welcome us, along with Cousin Bertie." She sighed again.

Georgina had been amused, on the three days they had
been travelling, to piece together such snippets of information as her two companions let drop while talking about the
current Marquess, and she had to confess she was anxious
to meet the gentleman, he sounded so unique and had led
such a varied life. Lady Martin did not approve of him,
that was plain to see, but Georgina found it hard to believe
such an elderly man could be half as bad as she painted
him. However, the first person she saw at Carew Court
was not her host, but Mr. Linwood. He had been coming
down the stairs when they were admitted by a very tall
and stately butler, and he paused to smile at her as she
inspected the Great Hall.

Lightly running down the remaining steps, he came and
bowed to them. "Ladies, how pleasant to see you again,"
he drawled, his blue eyes sliding around to Georgina as if
to add: "especially *you*, dear Lady Spalding." "I trust you
have had a good journey?"

Lady Martin gave him her hand and a warm smile. "As

good as it could be, under the circumstances, thank you, Mr. Linwood. And when did you arrive?"

"I have been here some two days. I sent my man ahead with my baggage and rode north. I wished to see as much of the countryside as I could, you see, and it is impossible to do so in a swaying coach."

"How adventuresome of you, sir," Miss Hersham said, trying to make her tone admiring. "Had you no groom, no companion?"

"No, ma'am, I did not, but I shall not make that mistake again. I had the bad fortune to run into a highwayman—at least I think robbery is what he had in mind. He fired at me so quickly, however, that perhaps he meant murder instead."

Both older ladies gasped, and he smiled and reassured them that he had taken no hurt and had been able to frighten his assailant away. Georgina concentrated on removing her bonnet and gloves and giving them to Wiltshire to hold.

"Lady Spaldin'," he said, forcing her to turn and face him. "Even though I have discovered that you have highwaymen in England, I will not tell you they are unknown in my country."

"Indeed?" she murmured, as if uninterested in his adventure. "And where is the Marquess? I would like to meet him and thank him for including me in his invitation."

Mr. Linwood grinned again. "He has gone to bathe. Would you care to come into the Little Parlour to await his return?"

"Thank you, Mr. Linwood, so kind," Aunt Bess said, bustling up and taking Georgina's arm. "My niece and I would prefer to retire and rest, if someone will show us to our rooms."

"Of course, Jenks, call the housekeeper at once!"

The butler bowed as all three ladies thought that Mr. Linwood appeared to be taking possession of Carew Court already, and resented it. Lady Martin considered him pushy and encroaching, but still she smiled and thanked him for his courtesy.

"I shall have tea sent to your rooms as well, ladies," he added.

"It is unnecessary of you to disturb yourself, sir," Lady

Martin was forced to say. "I have been giving orders in this house for years!"

"Of course," he murmured. "Forgive me, but I forgot you are a member of the family too."

Lady Martin gasped as he smiled at the others. "I cannot tell you how glad I am you have finally arrived, for the Court has been very quiet with only myself and the two Lord Hollands in residence, and we badly need new faces to leaven this family party."

"Ah, my nephew has come before us, has he?" Lady Martin asked, recovering her aplomb. "That is good news!" she added, nodding her head to Miss Hersham.

"He is bathing with the Marquess. I must say that that is one refinement I shall take back to Linderwood when I go. The plunge pool in the bathhouse can easily hold half a dozen people and is most refreshin'. You must try it, Lady Spaldin'!"

Again those blue eyes blazed at her, as if he were picturing her swimming in it, naked and alluring.

Before Georgina could reply, a very tall middle-aged woman neatly dressed in black bombazine with a bunch of keys at her waist arrived in the hall and curtsied. Lady Martin introduced the others to Mrs. Farrow, the housekeeper, and in not many more minutes they were on their way upstairs, followed by their maids and any number of footmen who were unloading the coaches.

In the confusion, Mr. Linwood caught Georgina's eyes again. "Until later, *belle*," he drawled, and winked at her.

Georgina turned away without a word, and climbed the marble stairs, her back very straight and stiff.

After Lady Martin was settled in her customary chamber, with Miss Hersham installed next door, the housekeeper led Georgina down a long hall and opened the door to an attractive bedchamber, complete with dressing room. "If there is anything at all you need, m'lady," she said, "please do not hesitate to call on me."

"Thank you, Mrs. Farrow, it looks wonderful," Georgina said, looking about her with interest. "There is one thing however. Does this room have a key?"

The housekeeper stared hard at her before she recalled herself. "Of course, m'lady." She half-closed the door and showed Georgina the key in the lock, and pointed out a matching key on the ring at her belt.

Since she still looked a little surprised, Georgina said in a casual voice, "I have a great dislike for sleeping in an unlocked room. I have felt this way since I was a child. Thank you, Mrs. Farrow, now I am sure I will be comfortable."

The housekeeper curtsied and excused herself, saying that she would see that some tea was brought shortly, and Georgina wandered over to one of the windows to inspect the view. Behind her she heard Wiltshire come in and instruct the footmen where to place the trunks.

Georgina's room was on the north side of the Court and overlooked the lake. The gardens were attractive and looked well-cared-for, but beyond the park, the wild hills and moors of Upper Littledean stretched before her in the warm spring sunlight, as empty and untamed as they had been centuries before. She opened the window and took a deep breath, feeling better already, for instead of the persistent odours of town, here there was only the scent of the earth, and green new growth. It was not Somerset, but it was attractive in its own way.

She lingered there at the window, remembering her reaction to the sight of David Linwood again. Even in the hall, with him doing the pretty for the old ladies, she had been aware of his strength and determination, and she wondered if perhaps she had not been very foolish to let the Earl goad her into coming. She had very few weapons at her disposal and they seemed weak and puny things. True, she could lock her bedroom door, but David Linwood would not be deterred by that, and she could not always be in the company of others, for that would drive her mad. Nor did she think that her plan to be cold and distant would keep him away. Helplessly she leaned her forehead against the glass, biting her thumb in thought. What was she to do? And then there was the Earl as well, and his flirtatious, suggestive words. Was he also to become a danger?

As if her thoughts had conjured him up, the Earl appeared on the path from the birch grove in company with another man, and Georgina forgot her problems with a hearty chuckle. Next to his tall relative, the Marquess, for so it had to be, seemed almost a dwarf, and he had to skip now and then to keep the pace the Earl set. Robert Holland was not talking, she noticed, but the Marquess

was busy waving his hands and conducting a nonstop monologue. Suddenly the Earl looked up at the Court, and
Georgina stepped back a little so he would not think she
had been staring at him and spying.

The two men passed beneath her window and entered
the house by a door she could not see, and Georgina turned
back to the room and began to settle in for her stay.

When the first dressing bell rang, Wiltshire came back
with the evening gown Georgina had chosen, freshly pressed,
over her arm. As Georgina washed and dressed and sat
down at the dressing table to have her hair arranged, she
questioned her maid about her accomodations.

"Coo, it *is* a big place, ma'am!" the girl exclaimed. "But
my room is adequate, and all the maids share a large
sewing room near the service door, so I will be handy if
you need me."

Georgina smiled at her in the mirror and then turned her
attention to her appearance. She was wearing a gown of
amber silk that had been much admired in town, so she
hoped it would not be too sophisticated for the Court. It
was cut with a high collar and little sleeves, and she knew
it flattered her figure, with its severe lines and absence of
trimming. With it she had chosen her amber beads, and
after picking up a light stole in case the Court should be
drafty, she wandered down the hall, wondering if she should
stop and inquire if her Aunt Bess was ready to accompany
her. She decided not to, since she was anxious to meet her
host, and went down the marble stairs to the Great Hall.
The butler bowed and led her to the Parlour, opening the
door for her and unbending far enough to smile at her as
she entered.

There was only one occupant in that vast chamber. A
large fire burned on the hearth, and there were enough
candles so that she had no trouble at all identifying Mr.
Linwood lounging at his ease before the blaze. He straightened up and came towards her, and Georgina wished she
had waited for her aunt, even as she put up her chin and
extended her hand.

"Mr. Linwood, I see we are the first," she said, trying in
vain to release her hand from his warm grasp.

"An unexpected treat, *belle*," he said, staring down at
her before he led her in the direction of the fire. "I have
missed you, and the continuance of your lessons as well."

Georgina chose a chair that was somewhat apart from the rest. "Will you not join me on the sofa, my dear? I am sure you will be more comfortable," he said, releasing her hand at last, and going to sit across from her.

"Thank you, no. Mr. Linwood, I am glad we are alone for a few moments, for I wish to speak to you. I must ask you to cease to annoy me. Believe me when I say I have no desire for your instruction, and since we will be together here for some time, it can only be uncomfortable if you persist."

He raised his brow and then crossed one neatly breeched leg over the other. "But why did you come, then, dear Georgie? I was sure you had made every effort to be invited here because you missed my touch, for if you did not want me to continue my pursuit of you, it was very rash of you to follow me. I think the lady doth protest too much."

"I did not follow you. How dare you?" she exclaimed, leaning forward a little in her distress that he should put such an interpretation on her actions.

"There is no need to be shy about it, *belle*. You and I do not need to conduct ourselves as society's conventions dictate. I am delighted to find that you, like I, are unafraid of going after what you want. I definitely approve, for now I can conclude both pieces of business at once. The inheritance . . . and your lovely self!"

Georgina was horrified at his assumptions, and would have denied them vehemently, but just then the double doors were thrown open and the Marquess of Carew bustled in to join them. Both Mr. Linwood and Georgina came to their feet at his approach.

"Well, Davey, you sly dog!" he said, bending back his head to stare up at his tall relative. "I see you have already captured this lovely lady, and are enjoying a *tête-à-tête*, and wishing me at the devil, no doubt, for interrupting you. You must be a Holland if that is so— we were ever notorious womanizers. My dear, you must be Lady Georgina Spalding, You are exquisite. That chestnut hair, those lovely eyes, your beautiful form. I kiss your hand in admiration."

Suiting his action to his words, he did so, and Georgina looked over his bald pate at Mr. Linwood's laughing face,

somewhat stunned to have her attributes so glowingly
catalogued at first meeting.

The Marquess relinquished her with reluctance. "A glass
of sherry, my dear? Davey, if you please, do the honours."

As Mr. Linwood moved to a large table where a tray of
decanters and glasses had been set out, the Marquess took
her arm and led her to the sofa beside the fire. She noticed
he kept running his hand up and down the soft inner skin
of her arm, and could well believe he had been a great
rake.

"It is too bad of you, Lady Georgie," he said next, his
brown eyes crinkled shut in his amusement, "to remind me
of what I am missing at my advanced age. Alas! To be
forced to step aside for younger men. Only my man, many
memories of conquests in the years past permit me to do so
with any degree of composure." He nodded his head at
David Linwood, who was offering them their sherry on a
silver salver. "However, you must admit, he is a fine
figure of a man. I do so like height and presence." He
bobbed up and down on the sofa for a moment before he
took a sip of wine and added, "I am proud of him, and
Robby too. Worthy descendants of the Holland line, and
sure to lead all the ladies a merry chase as well."

"I strive to . . . er . . . do my humble best, cousin," Mr.
Linwood drawled, sipping his sherry in turn and winking
at Georgina. Before this extraordinary conversation could
continue, Lady Martin and Miss Hersham came in, es-
corted by the Earl. Georgina did not know whether to be
glad or sorry. Surely she had never met anyone remotely
like the Marquess of Carew before!

After the introductions were performed, and the Marquess had welcomed her aunt, Georgina noticed that Lady
Martin went to sit beside Mr. Linwood. This was surprising, for she knew she did not care for him, and resented his
appearance and the possibility that he might do her dear
Robert out of his inheritance. Until Jenks announced dinner, Lady Martin kept Mr. Linwood in conversation, leaving Georgina and her aunt to converse with the others.

"So it begins—*en garde*, my lady!" Robert Holland said,
his deep voice so soft only Georgina could hear.

"None of that whispering sweet nothings in Lady Georgie's
ears, mind you, Robby," the marquess commanded, interrupting Miss Hersham in mid-sentence. "Your pardon,

ma'am, have to keep an eye on these young men, you know. Lady Georgie is much too sweet a honey pot."

Miss Hersham agreed fervently, thinking of the neatly trapped Mr. Linwood as he continued, "But let us have no ceremony, for this is in the way of a family party—all good friends here, eh?" Georgina saw him glance quickly at the Earl, and then at David Linwood, and his smile broadened. "Let us be Bertie and Bess, Davey and Robby, Georgie and Agnes, and when the others appear, we will include them in our game too." He chuckled to himself. "No stiff 'milords' or 'miladies,' here, if you please. Besides, since both Robby and I are Lord Holland, it will be too confusin'. I shall be Cousin Bertie to you all."

Georgina could not help smiling and stole a look at the Earl, wondering how he liked his pet name.

"I shall call you 'Robert,' never fear, m'lord," she confided as he offered his arm to lead her to dinner.

"*You* may call me anything you like," he whispered close to her ear as they followed the Marquess and Miss Hersham, and were followed in turn by Mr. Linwood and Lady Martin, still deep in conversation. They all went back through the Great Hall and climbed the stairs to the Dining Chamber. Georgina could not help but be impressed with this room, so massive you might seat a hundred guests, and stiffly formal as well. She was glad the table had been shortened by several leaves, as she prepared to take the seat the Earl was holding out for her. The Marquess saw her and beckoned.

"We will not stand on ceremony here either, dear Georgie. Come and sit beside me, dear lady, and I shall place your aunt on my right hand to play gooseberry."

"Bertie!" Lady Martin exclaimed. "For heaven's sake!"

He chortled and bent over Miss Hersham. "No need to feel neglected, ma'am, I am only funnin'. Agnes, stop looking so sour and sort out the boys."

Georgina looked up at the "boy" holding the chair the Marquess had indicated, but the Earl did not display any indignation at his cousin as he seated her and took the place beside her. He was obviously used to the Marquess' eccentric ways. Mr. Linwood found himself between Miss Hersham and Lady Martin, and directly across from his rival. Somehow Georgina was glad the table was so wide. Tall footmen came to stand behind every chair, as others entered the room carrying laden trays, and Jenks stood at the sideboard attending to the wine.

"What very large servants you have, m'lo . . . Cousin Bertie," she could not help remarking.

"It is a trifling idiosyncrasy of mine, my dear. I do not like to have little dabs of people about me, scurrying around and twittering. They make me nervous. Some height and stateliness are necessary in those who serve me, if I am to be comfortable."

Georgina must have shown her surprise, for she had seen the thick cushion on his chair and the way the footman adjusted his stool since his feet did not reach the ground. Seeing her expression, he added, "You are too nice to point out that I myself am only of *medium* stature, are you not? But I *feel* tall inside, as tall as Jenks there, and that is what is important." He waved his wineglass at her and continued, "Never forget that, my dear. It is how you feel inside yourself that counts, not what the world thinks. Do try some of the partridge and the new peas. Jenks, the wine."

The dinner was excellent, consisting of several courses and removes. Since they were such a small party, talk was general, and seemed almost too informal for such a dignified room. The footmen were removing the fish course when Miss Hersham remarked, "I trust you find our English dishes palatable, Mr. Linwood . . . er, David? What did you think of the fare at the inns you stayed at on your way from town?"

"Not to compare in any way to the cuisine here, ma'am. That turbot in the wine sauce, for example— delicious. It makes me glad I reached the Court safely after all."

"Safely? Why ever should you not?" Cousin Bertie demanded, his little brown eyes intent.

"I was shot at, cousin, only a few miles from town."

"Shot at? You never mentioned it. But I thought the highwayman problem was under control at last."

"If the man was indeed a highwayman," Mr. Linwood remarked, nodding his head at the baron of beef the footman was holding. He stared across the table at the Earl and continued, "The man fired on me without even askin' for my purse, and when my horse stumbled and he missed, he took to his heels at once. I sent a bullet after him, you may be sure, and I took good care to be on my guard after that."

"Did you fear he might return, sir?" Miss Hersham asked nervously as the others all watched the two men whose eyes were locked together.

"Who knows? If he was only after my money, I would expect him to search out easier prey, but if he meant to do me an injury, there was every possibility he might have at me again."

"Since you are here among us, *cousin*, we can safely assume he did not," the Earl said gently. "Thank you, Jenks, the claret I think."

Mr. Linwood looked away from the Earl's face at last. "No," he drawled, "I did not see him again."

The Marquess took a sip of wine. "I am sorry, my boy. Not a very warm welcome to England as you have had."

Mr. Linwood grinned at him. "There are welcomes and welcomes, cousin. It would take more than that to overset my nerves. But I do believe I will remain on my guard until my ship has cleared the Channel and is beatin' for Virginia."

In spite of his grin, his tone was almost menacing, and there was a long moment of silence before Lady Martin remarked, "So interesting, America. I am most anxious to learn all about it."

"Oh yes, and I as well!" Miss Hersham agreed. "We are most fortunate to be able to hear about it firsthand."

Georgina looked at the two of them, wondering what they were up to now, but then the Marquess began to question her about her home and her late husband, and she thought no more about it.

She spent the evening playing whist with the Earl, her aunt, and Lady Martin, for the Marquess took David Linwood away to play at billiards, and they were not seen again until the tea tray came in.

Bouncing up and down in his chair, the Marquess leered at Georgina and shook his head. "What a shame I did not think to put you in the State Bedroom, Georgie! *You* would do it justice, I know, although I have seldom installed anyone there in late years." He giggled a little at his memories and added, "But I promise to take you on a personal tour tomorrow, just the two of us, you know!"

He winked at her, and Miss Hersham wondered if she

and Agnes would have to add Cousin Bertie to their list of men that must be kept away from her niece.

Georgina smiled and thanked him, aware he had made great inroads on a bottle of brandy since dinner, and glad she was past the age of blushing. She assured him her room was very comfortable and that she did not think that a Royal Bed would be at all conducive to peaceful slumber.

Cousin Bertie opened his mouth, but before he could say whatever outrageous thing he had in his mind, the Earl interrupted to ask her if she would care to ride with him in the morning. Georgina was glad to turn to him and agree, but the Marquess was not done with mischief-making yet. "And you must take Davey as well," he said. "That way both Miss Hersham and I can be comfortable, knowing you are chaperoning each other. Georgie is much too ripe a plum to be left alone with either of you."

The Earl let no sign of annoyance cross his handsome face. "I would be delighted, of course, if *Cousin* David would care for it."

A time was agreed on, and the party broke up to go to bed, but not before Lady Martin told the Marquess, in an angry whispered aside, that he was behaving very badly.

"Know it, don't care. And don't you try to ruin things, Aggie. Most entertainment I have had in years . . . and more to come. You'll see!" He chortled, and Lady Martin rolled her eyes heavenward.

After Georgina dismissed Wiltshire and told her not to disturb her in the morning until she should ring, she waited until the maid's footsteps faded away down the corridor before she climbed out of bed and went and locked the door, feeling a little foolish as she did so. But just as she was dropping off to sleep, she thought she heard a sound at the door, and sat up to peer through the darkness, her eyes wide and her ears straining. She could not see if the handle was being turned, but she was sure she heard the clink of metal, and froze, clutching the bedcovers to her breast. There was a moment of thick silence, and then, quite clearly, she heard a low masculine chuckle, and to her relief, footsteps going away.

She lay down again, her heart pounding, but it was a long time before she slept.

The following morning dawned bright and sunny, and after she drank her chocolate and had been dressed in her new forest-green habit, and had pulled on her shiny black boots, she took up her gloves, crop, and riding hat and went down to breakfast. Lady Martin was there alone, eating heartily, and she greeted her with a fond smile.

"The food is the only thing that makes Carew Court at all bearable," she said as Georgina remarked on the huge strawberries and clotted cream. "I do apologize, my dear, for Bertie. I think he is worse than he was the last time I visited, so impossible and silly. The very idea of flirting with you at his age."

She shook her head, and Georgina was quick to say, "There is no need for your concern, ma'am, for I think he is a dear. A little unusual, to be sure, and yes, I agree he enjoys setting us all about every which way, but I am sure he is harmless."

Lady Martin snorted as she buttered her scone and reached for the marmalade. "He will never be harmless until he is buried in the family vault, and I wouldn't be at all surprised if he managed to return to haunt the Court even then. It is just the silly sort of thing he'd enjoy, moaning through the corridors and frightening the maids. Just look at the way he is stirring up trouble by pitting Robert and the American against each other. The expressions on their faces last night made me shiver."

Remembering, Georgina had to agree with her as she ate her breakfast, her face sober.

At that moment, the two men they were discussing were walking down the front steps to wait for her to join them for their ride. They had managed to avoid each other most of the time since they had arrived at the Court, by meeting only at dinner, but now that there were other guests, with more to come, they knew they would be thrown into each other's company more often. It was not a particularly enchanting thought for either of them.

This morning Mr. Linwood glowered; the Earl looked grimly amused.

"Good morning, *cousin*," he said, nodding his head. "A good day for a ride, wouldn't you say? Perhaps I can show you some parts of the estate you have not seen? The moors, for example?"

"Whatever you like, m'lord," Mr. Linwood snarled, the scowl still on his face. "I will certainly endeavour to follow wherever *you* lead!"

The Earl gestured at the grooms who were bringing up the horses. "Cry peace, man," he said in an undertone. "We are forced to be here together; let us not add to Cousin Bertie's enjoyment of the situation by being at each other's throats so obviously. Besides, it can only distress the other guests."

"Especially Lady Spaldin', eh?" Mr. Linwood sneered. "And you of course would not want anything to upset her, now, would you? I saw you looking at her last evening, and I have to inform you, m'lord, I have the prior claim."

The Earl's eyebrows rose, and a close observer would have seen his face pale a little and his hands in their tight pigskin gloves curl into fists. "You must excuse me, *cousin*, if I wait to hear that from the lady's own lips. The customs that prevail in the States may be different from ours, but I have heard no announcement that the lady has chosen you."

"Nor will you. Did you think I meant marriage?" Mr. Linwood looked incredulous. "No, no, I travel alone. But that lady very badly needs a lesson in behaviour."

The Earl smoothed his riding gloves, his grey eyes lowered. "And you, of course, are prepared to administer this lesson?"

Mr. Linwood grinned and swung his riding crop so vigorously that it cut through the air with a loud swish. "I look forward to it, m'lord. Oh, how I look forward to it."

The Earl stared for a moment, his face very still before he said in a casual voice, "One hopes you would not feel the need to use your crop."

Mr. Linwood stared at his black whip, and taking it between his hands, he bent it as if testing its resiliency. "I would lie if I told you I had never used a whip on a woman before, for I have when it was necessary, many times. Let us hope it will not come to that where Lady Spaldin' is concerned."

He seemed on the point of saying something more, but then he shrugged his shoulders, and with a visible effort relaxed his harsh features into a smile again. "I must admit there are two things the English excel at, sir," he remarked, pointing to a black gelding a groom was holding. "Their horses . . . and their women. While I am here, I intend to enjoy both, to the fullest."

He stared at the Earl as if to challenge him, but for a

moment Robert did not reply, but only smiled back, a glinting smile that did not reach his eyes, and when he spoke, his voice was quiet yet imperative.

"It is always dangerous to underestimate your opponent. I beg you do not make that mistake. Ah, there you are, Bodkins," he added in a louder voice, strolling down the remaining stairs to greet the head groom, who had known him since his childhood.

Above them, Georgina paused for a moment on the top step, her hand clutching the railing. She had not been able to hear what Mr. Linwood and the Earl had been discussing, but the sight of those two straight figures facing each other, and the looks on their faces, as well as the way the American swung his crop, told her it was no pleasant conversation.

She took a deep breath and called, "Good morning! Have I delayed you, m'lo . . . I mean Robert? David?"

Both men turned and watched her come down the steps, the white chiffon veil on her severe black riding hat floating behind her. The Earl murmured something to the head groom, and before Mr. Linwood could step forward, Bodkins was there bowing and offering to toss the lady into her saddle. Georgina patted her mare's chestnut neck and assessed the mounts her escorts were riding.

"I hope you will remember, sirs, that this little lady is no match for those two horses you are riding."

The Earl mounted his large roan and smiled at her, although Georgina thought he seemed a little abstracted. "No point-to-points today, m'lady, and no neck or nothing either, I promise. Ready, *cousin?*"

Mr. Linwood nodded, his expression bleak, and Georgina found herself riding between the two men as they trotted down the wide drive. The Earl led them through the park, and then onto a narrow forest path, where of necessity they had to ride in single file, and at a walk.

"How lovely it is, with the sunlight coming through the beech leaves," Georgina remarked, determined to act as if there was nothing out of the ordinary in this ride.

The Earl glanced over his shoulder. "I promised Mr. Linwood a closer look at our moors, m'lady. We shall soon be out of the woods."

Behind them, Mr. Linwood's soft drawl came clearly. "There is one other thing that England can boast over the

States, m'lord. Here you can ride like this through dense forest and not have to worry about Indians attackin' you. But perhaps there are things, even here in your civilized country, to be afraid of; things that still make people lock their doors at night in order to be safe."

His voice held a hint of scornful laughter, and Georgina concentrated on holding her back very still.

"You are referring to robbers, Mr. Linwood?" she asked, only turning her head a little. "But there are all kinds of robbers, after all, are there not? Some of them are interested in other booty besides gold and precious gems."

There was a short pause until David barked a loud laugh, causing Georgina's mare to shy a little. As she controlled the prancing horse, he said, "And some of them want all the booty they can gather! To a determined man, the locks were never made that could delay the inevitable . . . forever!"

Georgina was delighted to see the heath opening up before them as they reached the outskirts of the wood. She wondered what the Earl was making of this remarkable conversation, glad they were now in the open where their pace could be quickened and there would be no further opportunity to converse.

For the next two hours, the threesome rode the open heath, occasionally climbing a gentle hill for a better vantage point. The Earl pointed out the various landmarks, and named them. There were a few scattered farms, and some grazing sheep, but no villages in sight, and the heath looked almost empty under the May sky, unsoftened even by the wildflowers that grew there. Georgina asked their names, and was pleased that the Earl could identify them. Eventually they turned back towards the Court, which looked impressive even at this distance, since it was the only large building as far as the eye could see.

As they approached the front gates, they noticed a carriage coming towards them, and pulled up to wait for it. The Earl shaded his forehead with his hand and squinted a little before he smiled.

"Just as I thought, it's Freddie and his sister, Constance. And in time for luncheon, trust Freddie for that!"

He waved his crop, and hands could be seen waving back as the smart carriage slowed for the turn into the drive. The coachman and grooms touched their caps as the riders prepared to escort it up the drive. There was a flurry of activity as the riders dismounted and the occupants of the carriage climbed down, and Georgina and Mr. Linwood were presented to the newcomers. Georgina liked them both immediately. You would know them for brother and sister anywhere, for they were both tall and slender, with butter-blond hair and a rather prominent family nose, and they both had identical warm, open smiles.

As they were chatting with David Linwood, Georgina could not help smiling, and looked up to see the Earl with a questioning look in his eyes. "How fortunate it is that Miss Wilson is so tall," she explained. "She will win over the Marquess in a moment."

He laughed and offered her his arm. Georgina saw the sudden black look on David's face and accepted with alacrity, sweeping her riding skirt to one side as she prepared to climb the steps.

"We shall see if you are correct, Georgie," he remarked. "And yet I feel m'lord will still prefer you, even if you are not quite so tall. Connie is a wonderful girl, but I doubt she has ever flirted in her life. Freddie says it is becasue she is the only daughter midst seven sons, and was brought up as one of them. Cousin Bertie is a great admirer of femininity, of course, in case you hadn't noticed."

"Thank you for your explanation, m'lord," she said in a demure voice. "That characteristic of his had escaped my notice! And here are Lady Martin and my aunt!"

She dropped his arm as they stepped through the front door, and went to kiss the older ladies. For a while there was a great chatter and confusion as the others were introduced, and the housekeeper came to show them to their rooms. Everyone agreed to change quickly and meet again for luncheon in half an hour.

True to Georgina's surmises, the Marquess was struck by Miss Wilson's height, and paid her many a pointed compliment. Georgina waited to see how she would react, for she was past her first girlhood by a couple of Seasons and showed great elegance rather than conventional beauty. Now, although she nodded and thanked the older man, she did not seem to be attending to his attentions. Freddie Wilson, who was seated beside Georgina, whispered, "Good old Connie! Told her, y'know, about the Marquess, for Robert had warned me he is a trifle eccentric. But Connie never attends to what she does not want to hear. You'll see she can be completely oblivious."

Georgina was able to judge this for herself, for when the Earl mentioned that he was sure the lady had long, beautiful legs, she continued to eat quietly. There was a moment of stunned silence among the others at the Marquess' boldness, and she looked up to find everyone's eyes on her.

"I beg your pardon, did you say something, sir? I am so sorry, I was not attending. This soufflé is delicious; might I beg permission to visit your chef for the recipe? Mama would be so pleased!"

Cousin Bertie was forced to retreat, having learned that drawing a bow at this particular prey would produce no blushes, stammers, or lowered eyelashes, and Georgina silently applauded, looking forward to getting to know Miss Wilson better.

As they were all leaving the dining chamber, there was a knock on the front door, and Georgina, who happened to be glancing at the Marquess, saw how his face lit up with deviltry.

"Now, who can this be?" Lady Martin asked. "Our party is complete, is it not?"

"You'll see, Aggie, you'll see!" The Marquess crowed as he bobbed down the stairs. Jenks was opening the front door, and Georgina leaned over the gallery railing in time to see Lord Waring escorting his mother and Emmaline Waring into the Great Hall, followed by young Lord Handford.

"Oh no, it can't be!" she cried, much shocked.

"Good God, it needed only this!" Lady Martin exclaimed as Miss Hersham moaned behind her.

The Earl raised his eyebrows, Freddie looked to his friend for an explanation, and David Linwood never took his eyes from Georgina's face. Only Miss Wilson seemed unconcerned, for she had gone to inspect a family portrait that hung at the back of the gallery.

"Lavvy! My lovely Lavvy!" the Marquess exclaimed as he reached the last step and hurried forward to greet these new guests. He put his arms around Lady Waring and lifted her clear off the floor, whirling her around so exuberantly that her skirts belled out, showing half her legs. Lord Waring's mouth dropped open as his mother was firmly and thoroughly kissed, still held tight in the Marquess' arms. Emmaline was not attending, for she had spotted the tall figure of David Linwood on the stairs above her, and she could not restrain a happy sigh. When she had learned that they were all to be part of a house party at Carew Court that contained Mr. Linwood, she thought she must die of happiness. The fact that Lord Handford was also to join them did not bother her at all. So deep in her dreams during the journey had she been that she had not even noticed his presence, or her mother's blushes, the closer they came to Upper Littledean. Now she was forced to drag her thoughts from the American as she heard her brother's outraged voice. "Here, I say! Mother, stop that at once! Whatever can you be thinking of?"

The Marquess put the lady down, but not before giving her one final kiss and a crushing hug. "I hope she is thinking just what I am, of course. You must be Teddy, glad to see you, my boy. Your mama and I are very old, and very . . . um . . . intimate friends. And this is Emmie, of course. Fine, fine figure of a girl. And Lord Handford? What's your first name, son?"

Lord Handford bowed and managed to get out that his first name was William, his brown eyes popping and his face red.

"Good! Now, Willie, Teddy, and you too, Emmie, dear girl; you must all call me Bertie. We have decided on an informal party—my darling Lavvy. So many years. As soon as you have unpacked and rested, we must have a long *private* talk."

The Marquess bounced up and down and winked as he seized the lady's hand, and Georgina had to stifle a laugh as she saw the expression of horror on Lord Waring's face. She was still angry that he had followed her here, for not for a moment did she think Lady Martin would serve her such a trick. She followed the others down to the Great Hall, determined that Teddy would pay for this.

Robert Holland whispered in her ear, "My, my, Georgie. Now you will have three gentleman to choose from—or have you arranged for more to come as well? I hope I do not get lost in the crowd."

Georgina's eyes flashed at him until she saw he was

laughing at her. "It may be funny to you, sir," she whispered back, "but I could kill Teddy."

"I'll be glad to help you," he said in a complete agreement. "And yet, I don't think it will come to that."

At her look of incomprehension, he added, "It appears he will not have time to pursue you, m'lady, for he will be so busy chaperoning his mother."

6

After everyone had been introduced to the newest guests, the Marquess personally insisted on escorting Lady Waring to her rooms, and he was closely followed up the stairs by her son, and trailed by Emmaline and Lord Handford in the care of Mrs. Farrow, the housekeeper. Georgina told herself that her stiffness and lack of a smiling welcome had been lost on Teddy, for he seemed so stunned by this new development involving his mother and the Marquess that his own greeting to her had been a little abstracted. Perhaps the Earl was right? Lady Martin took Miss Hersham off with her in high dudgeon, both ladies whispering and shaking their heads, and the gentlemen of the party excused themselves to inspect the stables. Georgina smiled at Miss Wilson and asked her if she would care to stroll through the gardens with her. "Unless, that is, you are too tired from travelling, Miss Wilson," she amended.

"Of course not! I am never tired. But come, Georgie, you must call me Connie, by royal decree, remember? Let us fetch our shawls so we might spend more time outdoors; I noticed as we came up the drive that the gardens are very fine."

A short time later, both girls were wandering down one of the gravel paths, admiring the formal beds.

Georgina tilted her sunshade over her shoulder to protect her face from the bright sunlight, and Connie remarked, "It seems a strange pastime for the Marquess—gardening, I mean. I would not have thought he could be interested in such mundane things, he is such an unusual man. Have you known him for long, Georgie?"

Georgina admitted she had met him for the first time only the day before, and her companion nodded. "Then I can speak freely, as I could not have done if you were a distant relative of his. Let us hope he does not get up to his tricks with Miss Waring, for she is so shy and so young. But perhaps his pursuit of her mother will forestall that. In any case, I can see it will be our duty to protect the girl if necessary from his outrageous 'slings and arrows.' "

She smiled a little as Georgina chuckled at her wit. "I must tell you, Connie, the arrival of the Warings and Lord Handford was completely unexpected by everyone, including Lady Martin, who was asked to get up the party in the first place."

"Another of Cousin Bertie's tricks?"

"Yes, instigated by Lord Waring," Georgina said bitterly, her green eyes darkening in anger.

Miss Wilson observed her carefully. "Ah, lies the wind in that quarter, my dear?"

Georgina looked at her as she added, "Forgive me for presuming on such short acquaintance, but did Lord Waring follow *you* here?"

Georgina nodded glumly, and now it was Connie's turn to laugh.

"And you, of course, are not interested in that worthy young man. How could you be?"

By this time they had reached the fountain in the center of the gardens, and as old friends who do not even need to confer, they sat down on one of the marble benches that was placed around the gravel circle so they might admire the play of the water and the statuary.

Miss Wilson continued, "I think this may well turn out to be the most singular house party I have ever attended. Already the currents are developing. First there is the noble Teddy, torn between his desire to be with you and his duty protecting his mother. Then there is Miss Waring, and that tongue-tied young lord who has presumably been dragged along so he might fix his interest with her. What a shame that she, like you, does not care for his suit! Oh no, Miss Waring's heart has been given elsewhere!"

Georgina turned from her contemplation of the dancing sprays of water and stared at her companion. "It is? How could you possibly be sure on such short meeting?"

Connie laughed and adjusted her slipping shawl. "It is a little hobby of mine, my dear. While seeming not to pay much attention to the doings of others, I must confess that

I like nothing better than watching and drawing my own conclusions. Real life can be more fascinating than the best play, you know. I hope you will be my confidante—indeed, it is only the thought that the two of us may occasionally compare notes on this ill-assorted group that will make my stay enjoyable, for what is the use of ferreting out intrigues if there is no one to confide in? Say you agree."

Georgina was happy to do so, for she began to think Connie Wilson a sensible woman, and one whom it would be a pleasure to know better and call friend. Then she recalled the lady's last statement.

"But Emmaline! You do not know it, but I have been in a way an older sister to her while we were all in town, for her mother did not know how to dress her, and she was so miserable and shy. I like to think she has come on very well, but I can think of no one she could be in love with, unless it is Lord Handford."

"No, she is barely aware of him, although he seems to find this intriguing. When I first saw her she was staring at Mr. Linwood with her heart in her eyes, and she never looked at anyone else until she was forced to."

"David Linwood? Poor Emmie! He would eat her alive if he knew."

"If he could be bothered to take the time, but of course, as you are well aware, Georgie, Mr. Linwood has quite another object for his gallantry in mind . . . you. Oh, this is such fun."

Georgina spoke a little sharply. "It may be amusing to sit back as an observer, Connie, but it is not at all pleasant for me."

"You do not care for him, my dear?" Miss Wilson asked.

"I . . . I don't know. Sometimes he fascinates me, and yet there is something about him . . ." Her voice died away, and her companion did not press her for a more lucid explanation.

"There is certainly something about him," she agreed cordially instead. "And the Earl too, although I think his attractions more refined, more gentlemanly. Of course, I admit to bias; Freddie and I have known Robert forever, and I must tell you that my fiancé, Captain Sir Albert Adams, is his very good friend as well."

When Georgina congratulated her on her engagement, she said, "It is not announced as yet, and you will please not mention it. My father is being positively gothic, for he says that until Albert returns from his diplomatic mission in Vienna and proves he is still of the same mind, he will not hear of our betrothal. Albert, you see, has a wonderful sense of humour, and my father thinks him fickle and frivolous. He will find out." She nodded her head in calm assurance and added, "In the meantime, I sit and wait for him, but while I do, I amuse myself by observing the tangles in other people's lives. See there, Miss Waring is coming to join us, so our speculations must be at an end for now. Let me just say, Georgie dear, if you want to talk to me at any time, or seek my poor advice, I would be most happy to oblige, and not from a spirit of mischief-making, mind, but only to help you if I can."

Georgina thanked her and pressed her hand as Emmaline came up the path, her pale face flushed with her hurry. Now the three of them began to walk down to the lake, and conversation became more general. Georgina tried not to be stiff with Emmie, for she knew it was not her fault that Teddy had brought them all hot-foot after her. Careful questioning of the girl by Constance Wilson brought out the facts of their invitation, but Emmaline did not seem much interested in her mother's old beau, her brother's machinations, or Lord Handford's suit. The only thing she volunteered was how pleased she was to see Mr. Linwood at Carew Court, and then she blushed. Georgina's heart sank. Connie had been right, and Miss Waring was indeed enamoured of the dangerous American. She noticed that the girl kept looking about her, as if to catch a glimpse of him, and had all she could do to bite her tongue and not give the silly creature a setdown for her folly.

They were all interested in inspecting the bathhouse and the marble plunge pool, which to Emmie's eyes looked very deep.

"See there," Connie pointed out, "you may stay near the steps if you cannot swim. We must try it some hot afternoon—what do you say?"

"Only if we can be assured complete privacy," Georgina murmured, and Emma agreed, albeit reluctantly, that she would be happy to make one of the party.

A short while later, Lord Handford appeared and asked if he might join them, even as he took up a position by Miss Waring's right elbow. It was plain to see that there was no way he would allow himself to be dislodged. As Georgina and Connie followed along behind, Connie whispered, "Poor young man! Not that it will do him a bit of harm to realize he is not the be-all and end-all of every maiden's dreams. Men can be so arrogant, even the best of them. They need to be put in their place every once in a while, for that is the only thing that makes them at all bearable." Georgina laughed and agreed, thinking of the setdowns she had in mind to give in the immediate future.

As the foursome regained the main gardens again, they saw the Earl and Freddie Wilson in the distance, but of Mr. Linwood there was no sign. Emma drooped, and Lord Handford insisted on taking her back to the Court to rest.

It was unfortunate that Miss Waring had allowed herself to be removed, for a short time later David Linwood came around the corner of the East Front and hurried to their sides, bowing with exaggerated elegance and taking an arm of each lady to escort them.

"How fortunate that I left the others," he said, staring down at the bit of profile that was all Georgina would allow him to see under her rose-colored parasol. "Now I have captured the prettiest guests for myself. Not even inspecting the horses in the Marquess' fine stables can compare to the pleasure of your company, ladies, and the opportunity to converse with you.".

"I do not think we should allow ourselves to be overwhelmed by the compliment, Georgie," Miss Wilson said absently, pausing for a moment to observe a bed of dark purple iris grouped around a life-size statue of Cupid. "For, of course, horses cannot speak and I cannot imagine Mr. Linwood making such a cake of himself as to stand about trying to hold a conversation with a horse."

The gentleman gave up trying to get Georgina to look at him, and turned his head sharply to observe Miss Wilson, who gave him a sweet, absentminded smile.

"Of course I have known men to speak to their mounts," she continued. "Quite silly, some of them are, petting and chatting them up. Georgie and I are delighted that you are not amongst their number, and prefer even our poor feminine company. Georgie, do not fail to notice the tulips by the boxwood hedge. What a lovely display."

By the time the threesome had regained the main entrance, David Linwood was wearing a very puzzled frown.

Miss Wilson had taken over the conversation exclusively, and carried on a gentle monologue, only occasionally asking her companions their opinions, which she did not bother to wait to hear before she started on yet another tack. All the innuendos that he had planned to startle Lady Spalding with went unsaid, for he was never allowed to get a word in edgewise. Georgina was having a great deal of trouble keeping her expression indifferent as Connie bid him good-bye.

"So pleasant to have had this chat, sir. I have been longing to hear all your descriptions of America, your opinions of the future course of your country, and your philosophy of life. Most refreshing. Come, Georgie, my dear. You know we promised to attend Lady Martin, and I fear we are very late. Mr. Linwood."

She nodded her head in dismissal, and as the two women went up the steps, David Linwood heard her continuing her chatter, and the frown deepened on his dark face. Lady Spalding had not said one word to him, nor he to her. By God, he would make sure they were alone the next time they met.

When Georgina went to her room to summon Wiltshire to help her to dress for dinner, she found that a note had been delivered from the Marquess:

> My dear Georgie:
> I have planned a special surprise this evening, so I beg you to wear your prettiest gown. Perhaps a green one? I shall say no more, for it is a secret, puss. *A bientôt!*
>
> Bertie

She had to smile. The Marquess was certainly enjoying his house party, even if no one else was! She wondered how Lord Waring had spent the afternoon, and chuckled to herself as she washed, hoping he had been very busy chasing after his mother and the Marquess, perhaps even going with them to inspect the State Bedchamber.

She was not to know how close to reality her imaginings were. Teddy had indeed trailed his mother and the Marquess, in spite of Cousin Bertie's broad hints that he take himself off and leave them alone. When the first dressing bell rang, Bertie bent over Lady Waring and whispered,

"We must contrive to meet privately, Lavvy. Sorry to say so about your son, but it's intolerable the fellow can't take the hint. Is he by any chance slow-witted?"

Lady Martin and Miss Hersham had spent the afternoon in the Little Parlour, devising ways they would like to use to dispose of Bertie, and after agreeing that hanging was too good for him, shooting him too quick, and chaining him to a dungeon wall too painless, had decided that the most satisfying thing they could do, given the chance, was to tie him and Teddy Waring together and drop them into the lake, each with a large stone to his feet. Then they reviewed their plans to keep David Linwood away from Georgina and how best to promote the suit of dear Robert at the same time.

Georgina did not make the same mistake as she had the evening before, and so she was one of the last guests to appear in the Great Parlour. She wore a gown of pale green velvet trimmed with a deep flounce of creamy lace that accented the low round neckline and fell over her arms in graceful folds.

The Marquess hurried to welcome her. "Perfect, my dear Georgie, perfect, and just what I hoped to set off my surprise!" he said, patting her hand and guiding her towards where the others were grouped around the fireplace, holding sherry glasses and making desultory conversation. Only the Earl was not present. Connie Wilson, stunning in pale blue silk, sent her a warm smile and continued to talk to Emmaline Waring, as tall and sturdy as ever in a gown of gold, thus forcing her to remove her longing eyes from David Linwood's face. The American stood before the fire, and on either side of him, looking together like a small but determined guardian escort, were Lady Martin and Miss Hersham. He raised his glass in a toast to Georgina, and both ladies burst into speech, causing him to turn to them with a strained smile. It is doubtful that even Mr. Linwood had ever found himself so popular with dowagers before, and he was looking a little confused.

Freddie Wilson was having hard going trying to make conversation with milords Handford and Waring, and had just decided that, friend or no friend, he was going to tell Robert exactly what he thought of this ill-assorted group, and soon. The Marquess led Georgina to where Lady Waring was sitting on a sofa, and proceeded to take the place between them, bouncing up and down as he held both their hands.

"Now, this is very nice and just what I like, to be so close to dear Georgie and my very dear Lavvy."

Georgina thought Lady Waring much improved, and could tell she had overcome her distaste for shopping in order to purchase a new and becoming lavender gown.

The Earl appeared just as Jenks announced dinner, and apologized for his tardiness by saying he had had an express from London, and in reading it had forgotten the time. "What you were waiting for, Robert?" Freddie Wilson asked quietly, and Georgina, who was smoothing her gown where Bertie had bounced on it and creased it, could not help overhearing.

"No, that has not arrived as yet, but this was promising, Freddie, most promising. Tell you later."

The Marquess sorted everyone out to his own satisfaction again in the Dining Chamber, and another delicious dinner commenced. When the final course had been removed, and the ladies were preparing to leave the gentlemen to their port, he jumped to his feet and said, "We will not be long, my dears, for I have a special treat for you all this evening!" He giggled and nodded to Georgina, who thought him strangely excited, and Lady Martin sniffed.

As she shepherded the other women from the room, she said, "I wish to speak to you, Bertie, as soon as it may be contrived—and alone. Your behaviour has been such that I must and will see you."

"Go on, Aggie!" he crowed. "This is my party and I shall do just as I wish. Not that I am not happy to attend you, only not tonight. Tonight we must have our surprise." He bounced back into his chair and blew her a kiss, which fortunately she did not see, for she had turned her back on him and was leaving the room in a huff.

The ladies returned to the Great Parlour. Miss Hersham took up the fringe she had been knotting, and sat down beside her niece. Georgina thought she seemed tired, and reminded herself to ask her aunt later if she was feeling quite the thing. Whenever Mr. Linwood was around, Aunt Bess positively bloomed with conversation and questions, but in his absence, she had little to say. Emmaline Waring was talking shyly to Lady Martin, who put aside her anger at her cousin to try to put the girl at her ease. Her mother stared into the fire, a dreamy little smile playing over her lips, while Miss Wilson proceeded to inspect the Parlour, only occasionally glancing back at the others.

Cousin Bertie was true to his word, and in a short time the gentlemen appeared.

"Come, ladies, now for the event of the evening! You must all follow me, for it is not here, oh no, not here at all." He came and offered his arm to Miss Hersham. "Feel I've neglected you, ma'am. Would not offend you for the world. You, there—Teddy, is it?—take your mother, and the rest of you come along!"

He led the little parade down the Great Parlour and unlocked a small door at the end of it before taking up a large branch of candles. Before them a narrow flight of stone stairs wound upward. It was chilly and somewhat airless, Georgina thought, as Freddie Wilson climbed beside her, his hand cupping her elbow in support.

"What on earth are you doing, Bertie?" Lady Martin asked, and the Marquess turned to peer over the railing at her.

"Come along, Aggie, and don't spoil the fun."

At the top of two flights of stairs, there was another locked door. The Marquess knocked on it, and from her position somewhat below him on the stairs, Georgina could see a small peephole open, so whoever was inside could inspect the group.

"Oh, it's you, guv," a cockney voice exclaimed, and everyone could hear very plainly bolts being drawn back, the door unlocked, and a heavy chain withdrawn.

The Marquess waited impatiently, bouncing up and down. "Hurry it up, Fickles, hurry it up!"

They could not hear the man's reply, but when the door was thrown open, he said plainly, "And you 'old your 'orses, sir! This 'ere door takes time!"

The Marquess skipped inside, holding his candles high and dragging a bewildered Miss Hersham with him. They were closely followed by the others.

They found themselves in a medium-sized room made of stone, with no windows and very little furniture. Georgina heard her aunt gasp and looked at the man who had opened the door, and her own eyes widened. He was very tall, taller even than David Linwood, and a good deal heavier, with a huge chest and powerful arms, but what really surprised her was his brilliant red hair, and the fact that he held a leveled pistol on the guests, and had a heavy truncheon tucked into his wide leather belt as well.

"Very impressive, Fickles, but put that down. I told you I was bringing my guests up tonight." The Marquess turned and beckoned to the others. "Come in, all of you, no need to be afraid. Sometimes Fickles can't forget his Bow Street Runner background. And now you are going to be among the few in the world today who have ever seen the Holland Treasure. I shall open the safe, Fickles, stand aside."

"Beggin' your pardon, guv," the man replied, not moving from his position before a dark green curtain, "not until the gentry morts and the coves wot's with 'em turn their backs. You knows the rools."

The Marquess giggled. "Excellent man, Fickles. In my excitement I forgot. Friends, you must all turn around and face the other way. Isn't this the most amusin' thing?"

Lady Martin sniffed, but she did as she was bid, and the others followed suit. Georgina happened to catch sight of David Linwood's face, and she was surprised to see that he seemed to have gone a little pale under his tan, and his expression looked strained. Her eyes swept past him to see the Earl observing him carefully. His glance caught Georgina's for a moment, but he gave no sign he had noticed her watching them both.

She could hear the curtain being pulled to one side, and then a series of soft clicks. At last the Marquess told them to turn around again, and there before them, behind the heavy door to a large vault, were displayed an ancient medieval stomacher and crown resting on a bed of black satin.

"My word!" Miss Hersham said faintly. Teddy Waring coughed, Miss Wilson gave the objects about the same inspection she had the purple iris that afternoon, and the others stood in a shocked and quiet circle.

"Now, isn't that something like?" Cousin Bertie asked proudly. "The ancestral treasure of the Hollands. What do you think of that, Davey? There can be nothing like it in America, I am sure!"

Mr. Linwood moved forward, and Fickles seemed to stiffen as he eyed the American. David did not appear to notice, for his eyes were busy assessing the gold and what seemed to be hundreds of emeralds of all sizes and shapes.

After the others had inspected it as well, the Marquess beckoned to Georgina.

"Come here, my dear." He reached into the vault and withdrew the crown, and handed it rather quickly to his guard. "If you would be so good, Fickles, as to put it on the lady's lovely head . . ."

Mr. Fickles did so with reluctance, and when he took his hands away, Georgina thought her neck was going to break, the crown was so heavy. She stared at the others as the Marquess burst into speech.

"See what a match the emeralds are to Georgie's eyes. I remarked it the moment I first set eyes on her, and in thinking it over, I decided that the Holland Treasure should go to whoever wins her hand, for it would not be just for another lady to display these jewels. So, Georgie, my dear, I hereby abdicate my power to name my heir and give you the choice. Which one shall it be? Robby or Davey?"

There was a stunned silence, and Georgina stood frozen, for surely this went beyond mere eccentricity.

"Here, sir, I *say!*" Lord Waring exclaimed, breaking the spell they were all under. "Your remarks are in bad taste, for the lady is as good as promised to *another!*"

The Marquess peered at his red face. "Well, it's nothing to me if you want to enter the lists too, Teddy, but I beg you to reconsider. You'll only make a fool of yourself. Look at my nephies—*you* can't hold a candle to 'em. Besides, you can't inherit, ain't a Holland. I don't know why you're buttin' in." Then in a loud aside to Lady Waring, he added, "Pitty the boy takes after old Stuffy, my dear, instead of your side of the family, and appears to have less than moderate understanding as well, Too bad, too bad."

"*Bertie!*" Lady Martin said in an awful voice.

Georgina looked for a second at the Earl and saw his grey eyes twinkling and his lips quivering in amusement at her predicament, but when she transferred her gaze to David Linwood, it was to find his blue eyes blazing at her and his lips compressed into a tight line—of what, she did not know. Disgust? Determination? She reached up to remove the crown, and Fickles hurried to assist her.

"This is ridiculous," she said, trying in vain to keep her voice light. "I do not choose anyone, m'lord, for I do not intend to marry ever again."

The little Marquess whirled and stared at her in disappointment, looking just like a baby whose candy has been taken away from him. Then he giggled and shook a playful finger at her.

"Now, Georgie, of course you do. It is just that it was such a surprise. But you are sure to pick either the Earl or Davey, for I know you can't want to marry *him*."

He waved his hand in a dismissive gesture at Teddy Waring, who was turning an alarming shade of purple, as his mouth opened and closed like a fish's.

"And since it appears you have no decided preference as yet," the Marquess continued, "why, then, let the wooing begin. Gentlemen, you have been challenged, for I am quite determined the Holland Emeralds will never adorn another lady."

"And they will never adorn this one," Georgina snapped, turning her back on the vault and preparing to leave the room. "You cannot order people to marry to suit yourself—how gothic." She ruined this indignant speech by adding as she massaged her neck, "Besides, that crown is so heavy, I think it would break my neck, or . . . or anyone else's. And as for that stomacher, sir . . . well!"

The Marquess hurried to her side. "Talk to you later," he hissed, as everyone strove to listen. "Must be private, for after all, not all are members of the family. There's that Willie—he's too quiet to be trusted, to my mind, and the Waring chappie as well—not much in his brain box, can't know what he'll get up to."

He turned back to the others. "Let us all go back to the Great Parlour while Fickles secures the vault. It is cold here, and we cannot take the chance that the future Marchioness might catch a chill."

He shooed them all before him down the stairs. From her position in the lead, Georgina could hear the whisperings of the others behind her, and then the crash of the heavy door, and the chain, bolts, and locks being put back in place. She marched towards the fire, absolutely furious at the Marquess, the Earl, David Linwood, and Teddy Waring. *Men!*

Constance Wilson came to stand beside her and whispered, "Calm yourself, Georgie. I know the man's impossible, but your only course is to pretend indifference, as if the whole thing is so bizarre it is beneath your notice. A little indignation is reasonable, certainly, but the sparks you are giving off now look very, very suspicious."

Georgina took a deep breath and nodded her head, glad Connie was there with her sensible advice. She moved to help her aunt to a chair by the fire, and stood beside her to ask how she did. The Earl, entering the room, saw what she was doing and nodded his head in approval.

The others wandered in and took their seats. The atmosphere in the room was more than a little strained, as if no one knew quite what to say or how to behave after the scene just witnessed. The Marquess seemed to sense their unease, for he rang for Jenks and ordered him to bring brandy and some wine for the ladies, and then he took up a position in front of the fire, tucking his hands under his coat tails, as he proceeded to rock back and forth on his heels and beam at his successful ploy.

"Come now, you must admit that for unusual entertainment, you will have to go far to top that of Carew Court," he said, smiling at them all. "But tell me, if you please, what did you think of the Holland Emeralds?"

Miss Hersham was determined to draw attention away from her niece, and was quick to reply. "They must certainly be very rare, Bertie. How old do you suppose they are? And how did they come into the possession of the family?"

"No one knows," he admitted. "It seems they have always been here, passed down from father to son as part of the estate. For myself, I suspect it was a Crusader who brought them back from one of the Holy Wars." He shook his head sadly. "Those knights, you know, not at all what they should have been, in spite of trying to make good Christians of the infidels. Wouldn't put it past some pious old Holland to have killed a royal prince for those jewels."

He managed to look chagrined at such unchristian behaviour, and the Earl strolled forward to lean against the back of the wing chair where his aunt was sitting.

"At least it appears that we do not have to worry that they will be stolen again, cousin. I have seldom seen such stringent precautions taken, except perhaps for the Royal Treasures."

Cousin Bertie's eyes lit up, and for several minutes he regaled them all with stories of how he had had the vault specially built, as well as the room that contained it, and how he did not begrudge paying Fickles a large salary to watch the emeralds as well.

He concluded by saying that although he supposed an army with a careful plan of assault might be able to make away with them, he did not see how anyone working alone could ever do so.

At this David Linwood spoke up for the first time since they had all gone up into the tower. "Let us hope you are correct, Bertie," he drawled. "But after all, locks were made to be broken, guards disarmed, and treasure stolen."

He looked at Georgina as he spoke, but she refused to return his glance, although she could feel his eyes on her face like hot probes.

Jenks returned with two footmen and began to circulate among the guests, asking what they would care to drink, and under cover of the general conversation, Lord Waring came over to Georgina and said, "My dear, I am sorry that you were exposed to such a distasteful experience. Of my own feelings in the matter, I shall say nothing, since I know you enter into all my sentiments so completely. Surely the man is mad. I think it would be best if we made our preparations to leave the Court as soon as it can be arranged. I shall speak to Miss Hersham, and we will not talk of this again."

He nodded his head at his wisdom, compressing his lips, and Georgina felt her temper rise. Although she was still very angry at the Marquess, it had never occurred to her to cry coward and quit the field, yet here was Teddy Waring, without even so much as a by-your-leave, calmly assuming he had the right to control her affairs, and expecting her to obey him without question.

"You take too much on yourself, m'lord," she said as coldly as she dared. "I have no intention of leaving, although you, of course, must do as you think best. As for your speaking to Aunt Bess, I beg you will not, for if you should manage to convince her to go with you, I would lose the comfort of her companionship. Somehow I do not think she will consider it. The Marquess is a strange man, but he is not mad, and he cannot force me to do his will. I fail to see why you presume to tell me what I must do, and as for your judgment of Bertie, that can only be the result of his assessment of your character. It is obvious that he has offended you."

Lord Waring drew in a startled breath, and it was some seconds before he even attempted to reply to this stunning setdown.

"I fear that 'someone' has had her head turned by all the attention she is receiving; ah, frailty, thy name is woman," he said finally, with a return to his heavy playfulness. "But I also know that 'someone' is too nice in her requirements, too refined in her manners, to care for the ravings of an old rake, and as for flirting with the Earl of Amesbury or that crude American, it is not to be thought of by one whose ladylike demeanour must always inspire admiration. I shall wait, dear Lady Spalding, for you to come to your senses, and for now, since I see that 'someone' is not her sensible, good-natured self, I shall say no more. We both know your future . . . this is mere flourishing."

He bowed and left her side, and Georgina did not know whether to dissolve into hysterics or empty her wineglass over his pompous head.

She saw Emmaline Waring giving her a pitying stare, and remembered that the girl had told her that when Teddy set his mind on something, nothing could change it, and she realized that it would not be as easy to discourage him as she had thought.

Mentally putting this problem aside, she went to make the further acquaintance of Lord Handford, who was chatting with Lady Martin.

Nothing more was said about the Marquess' remarkable proposal, and certainly neither the Earl nor David Linwood made any push to gain her side or monopolize her attention.

For Georgina, it was a very long evening.

7

It was also a very long night. After she had dismissed Wiltshire and carefully locked her door, even going so far as to push a heavy table against it, Georgina threw another log on the fire, and wrapping a blanket around herself, settled down in the chair by the hearth to think.

Surprisingly, it was neither Robert Holland nor David Linwood who came first to her mind, but rather her indignant reaction to Teddy Waring's ultimatum that she leave the Court immediately. Now, why did that put me in such a tearing temper? she wondered. It was certainly the sensible thing to do, and no one would consider it at all strange, after the way the Marquess had embarrassed her, if she took her departure as soon as her coach could be summoned from town. It was what any gentlewoman would do, she told herself, for certainly no lady would want to continue to reside here when everyone would be watching her every move, talking about her constantly, and wondering which man she would choose in the end. And if she did not leave, what interpretation might not the others put on that? That she was willing to go along with the Marquess' ridiculous proposition? That she wanted to be the consort of either Lord Holland or Mr. Linwood?

And yet, just the thought of going made her determined to remain. Am I deceiving myself? she wondered, getting up and dropping the blanket to pace the floor in agitation. Am I becoming so attracted to David and Robert that all my protestations about wanting to remain single must sound empty and untrue to the others? They certainly were beginning to sound hollow to her own ears! She put her hands over her hot cheeks and moaned. She did not know why, she only knew that nothing could drag her away from

Carew Court right now. But perhaps Teddy was right, and her head had been turned by all the attention she was receiving? Even if Cousin Bertie had been indecorous in what he proposed, it was certainly flattering to be chosen as the only lady ever to wear the emeralds in her generation.

She dropped into the wing chair again, wrapping the blanket securely around her, and drew her feet up under her to keep them warm.

She wished she knew what Robert thought about all this. Was he disgusted . . . revolted, even? And would he consider marrying just to gain control of Cousin Bertie's title and vast wealth? How lowering it would be to discover later that that was the reason he asked her—if ever he should do so, she added hastily to herself.

And then, of course, there was David Linwood to consider. Was she really as afraid of him as she told herself she was? Or was she honest enough to admit that when he had kissed her that night at the masquerade, she had not been quite as indignant as she pretended to be, and that in fact she had enjoyed the strange new feelings of warmth and abandonment she had begun to feel as his hands and lips caressed her. There was something about being held in his strong arms and forced to do his bidding that had drawn a response from her she had never known. At least he seemed to want her, so perhaps if she chose him and he became the heir, she would not have to pretend his attraction for her was real. Georgina sighed. She was not so green that she supposed that every man, even when he was drawn to a woman physically, wanted to marry her, and she had to admit she had seldom seen a man less ready for domesticity than David Linwood. No hearth and home and the patter of little feet for him! Just picturing him in such a setting made her lips curl in amusement.

At last she dozed in her chair as the fire died down to glowing coals. She woke sometime later to find herself in the dark, for her candle had gone out, and the room was growing cold. Shivering and stiff, she climbed into bed, where she lay and stared up at the ceiling until dawn.

It was very early when she decided that she would not sleep at all this night. She splashed some cold water on her face before she put on a simple muslin morning gown and pulled a brush through her tangled hair, fastening it back with a matching ribbon. Taking up a large shawl, as well as the book she was currently reading, she made her way quietly through the sleeping house and let herself out the French doors of the Little Parlour. She felt she had to be alone, and although she knew it would be dangerous to wander about alone at any other time of day, now only the servants were beginning to stir, and she would be safe.

The early morning smelled fresh and full of promise, and she drew a deep breath. Everything always looked better in the daylight; surely if she could be by herself for a while to think, she would be able to decide what her course of action must be. She slipped down the gravel path leading to the lake, not caring that the early-morning dew was wetting her kid slippers or that the mist rising from the cold ground was causing her hair to curl wildly around its ribbon.

When she reached the lake, she did not pause, but continued around the shore, determined to find a secluded place where there was no chance of being spotted from the house.

Georgina had been like this even as a small child, often stealing away when she had a problem or when she felt hemmed in by the company of others. Solitude was a very necessary and precious thing to her, and this morning she could not bear to think of talking to the other guests, not even Connie Wilson or her dear Aunt Bess.

Robert Holland had not slept well either, and like Georgina, had sat for a long time before the fire in his room in a brown study. He was more than a little surprised to discover how much he had sympathized with Lady Spalding last evening. What Cousin Bertie had done was more than too bad, it was unconscionable, and would have sent many another lady into hysterics or a dead faint. Georgina had handled it with as much dignity as anyone could muster, and he had been astounded to find that he was proud of her. It cannot be that I am falling in love with the chit, he told himself sternly. Not after thirty-three years of avoiding matrimony! No, no, it was simply admiration for her courage and presence and dignity.

But even if he were not in love, he was now more determined than ever that David Linwood would not win either the Holland title and fortune or Georgina's hand. He had not missed the American's reference to locked doors. Could it be possible that he had wronged the lady, and that she was not wanton after all? It sounded very much to his carefully listening ears as if Georgina had locked her door against the American. He smiled to himself, hoping it was true. As for David Linwood's announcement that he had the prior claim to her, he disregarded it. It was just the kind of brash boasting you would expect from a foreigner.

He rose at last and stretched and made his way to bed. He would talk to Freddie and Connie in the morning; perhaps among the three of them they could discover a way he would make sure that Linwood was thoroughly routed, and that in the process of doing so, he himself would not be forced to take that short but final journey down the aisle of Westminster Abbey.

Just before he dropped off to sleep, he had the sudden thought that even if he were in love with Georgina Spalding, there was no way he could court her now, for to her eyes and the eyes of the others, it would appear that he was interested only in the inheritance and the emeralds, since he had made no real push to fix her interest before now. Now, why do I find that so depressing? he asked himself as he punched his pillows in frustration.

David Linwood slept better than either of them. He had gone outside after the others retired to bed, to stroll up and down the drive in front of the Court, enjoying a last cigarillo and the evening air. He was finding his stay at Carew Court a trying experience, for he was used to a great deal of physical activity, and these gentle, and to him useless, little activities that made up a gentleman's day were wearing, not only to his spirits, but to his health as well. He promised himself a hard, taxing gallop the following day.

But of course, no matter how his prolonged stay in England wearied him, it must be endured, and surely it could not be much longer before the Holland inheritance would be his. Forget the title—he neither needed nor wanted it—and he certainly had no intention of abandoning the country of his birth, which was so rich in opportunity for a man of great wealth, not even for such an estate as this. Yes, he decided, he would accept Georgina's hand in marriage, for he supposed he was forced to do that, and at least she was beautiful and spirited, and would bring him the emeralds as well, and when they were safely in his possession, he would make a grand gesture and refuse the title and the estates, throwing them back into these superior English faces as worthless things he could not be bothered to possess.

He wondered how Georgie would like America, not that he cared whether she did or not. She would grow accustomed . . . to a lot of things! He grinned there in the dark before he ground out the stub of his cigarillo and took himself off to bed.

Used to rising early, he was the only one up besides the servants when Georgie found a little cove on the far end of the lake where two small brooks joined together and ran into the main waters. There was a stretch of grass there, already being warmed by the sun, and behind it some graceful birches for shade if she should need it. She looked back at the Court, but all she could see of it were the roof and the massive chimney stacks, and feeling herself free of company at last, she spread out her shawl and sat down on it, resting her arms and her chin on her drawn-up knees while she stared out over the lake. As the sun climbed higher, it grew warmer, and soon that warmth, and the gentle buzzing of the dragonflies swooping down over the quiet water, forced her to lie back and close her eyes. In only a few moments, she was fast asleep.

The Earl had been so fortunate as to find Freddie and his sister in the breakfast room, along with Lady Martin, who was apologizing profusely for her cousin's behaviour. He signalled to Freddie over her head that he wanted to see him later, and nodded his head in Connie's direction as well. Freddie winked and applied himself to his ham and biscuits, while Robert went to get himself some coffee.

When Lady Waring and Emmaline came in, Freddie was quick to rise and go help his sister from her chair. Connie looked at the scone she had just buttered, and sighed as she picked up her skirts and rose to excuse herself. In the hall, her brother told her that Robert wanted to talk to them, and the two of them strolled up and down the Great Hall until the Earl was able to escape the early-morning civilities in the breakfast room.

"You're a Trojan, Freddie, always thought so," Robert said as he led them both to the front door, where a footman was waiting to open it for them.

"And what am I?" Connie demanded in mock reproof. "I

am the one who was dragged away from the table before I was ready, and who had to pretend that I always butter scones I have no intention of eating!"

The earl kissed her cheek. "You, my darling Connie, are the Trojan's more Trojan sister! Let us go outside, for I have to talk to you both, and I do not want to run the risk of anyone overhearing us. You won't be too cold, will you, Connie? Do you need a wrap?"

Miss Wilson smiled up at his face, knowing that the anxiety he expressed was not for her comfort, but that she would delay matters by insisting on going to her room to change her clothes.

"I am fine, Robert, for it is a lovely morning!" she said, taking an arm of each man as they started for the gardens. "I wonder where Georgina is? I do hope she is not skulking in her room after last night's fiasco, but somehow I do not think it of her. She seems a woman of courage, don't you think?"

She peeped at the Earl and smiled when she discovered him nodding his head in agreement.

"Yes, I think so too, and that is what I want to talk to you about. Cousin Bertie has really put a spoke in the wheel now. Whatever am I to do?"

Freddie laughed. "Seems to me, dear boy, that all you have to do is treat the lady to some of your famous address, and then order the ring and plan the honeymoon. Can't see her preferring that Linwood chap—why, he's not even an Englishman."

"I would not be too sure of that," Connie broke in. "He is a completely fascinating and compelling man."

"Hold fast, you two. I have no intention of marrying anyone, not even for the title, but I am determined that that damn American shall not stand master here, nor shall he enjoy the lady's favours either. But what can I do to prevent it?"

Freddie opened his mouth to speak, and caught his sister's quelling frown. He closed his mouth and shrugged as Connie took a seat on a bench near the lake and said, "Of course, if you cannot like her, Robert, there must be no thought of marriage. Perhaps if you tell her frankly that you know how difficult all this is for her, and that you have the greatest respect for her own wish to remain a widow,

and will do everything you can to help her retain that
state, it might serve the purpose. But with David Linwood
forever in her eye, I do not see how . . ."

Her voice died away and then she added, "I, of course,
will be glad to do everything I can to reinforce her opinion
that being a wife again would be nothing but a dead bore."

Freddie cocked an eyebrow at her. "Told her about
Albert?"

Connie nodded, and he added, "Don't see that she'd
believe you, then. Who would? Here you are panting to get
married, and already promised except for Pa's final blessing, and you start prating about marriage being a dead
bore. No sense to it, Con, can't have thought."

The Earl laughed as he saw the look of chagrin that
came over Miss Wilson's face. "Oh, why did I mention
him," she mourned. "If I had not, it would be the perfect
solution."

Freddie patted her hand. "But you always tell everyone,
Con, generally within five minutes of meeting. Noticed it.
Lord, was there ever anything like lovebirds? I was almost
glad to see the back of Albert when he took himself off to
Vienna, for he himself was becoming a dead bore, always
going on and on about you. Told him finally to cut line. My
own sister, Albert, I said. Assure you I know her excellence; no need to natter on and on about her!"

"This is getting us nowhere at all," the Earl interrupted
sternly, for he could see that Miss Wilson was eager to
question her brother for more details about what Albert
had said he admired about her. "Please bend your wits to
my problem. How am I to keep Lady Spalding away from
Mr. Linwood, and how can I convince her that the best
thing she should do is renounce the emeralds, the title, and
whichever one of us is to become heir, and shut herself up
in a nunnery, since she does not care to remarry?"

"Not a nunnery, Robert," Freddie said firmly. "Not the
type. You can tell that just by looking at her. And furthermore, this not wanting to marry again is all a hum.
She may say that, but you've only to look at her to know
what kind of woman she is."

"And what kind is that?" both Connie and the Earl asked
in unison.

"Warm, vibrant, alive, sensual . . . she should have half

a dozen children and all the loving she can handle." Freddie surprised them by reciting promptly.

"Well, upon my soul!" Robert exclaimed. "Now we have the perfect solution. *You* will court the lady, Freddie, since it is obvious that your admiration for her knows no bounds, and she will be so swept away by your lovemaking that she will forget the emeralds and the title and insist on leaving for Gretna at once. See to it, my boy, with my blessing and my sincere thanks."

"Here, now," Freddie said, his face paling and his blue eyes popping. "I'm not in love with her! Not in love with anybody. Don't even want to be. As for half a dozen children—not my style at all! You have a care there, Robert," he told the Earl, who stood holding his sides, helpless with laughter. "You have a care, or you won't have a friend in the world."

Eventually the Earl's mirth subsided, and he put one booted foot up on the bench and stared out over the lake.

"I do not see any clear way as yet, but perhaps something will occur to me—to all of us. I would appreciate it, Con, if you would stay in Georgie's company as much as possible. I do not like to think of what would happen if that 'cousin' of mine were to get her alone somewhere. I do not think he would be at all gentle in his approach, and I would not have her frightened."

He frowned in thought, and Connie winked at her brother, who was looking a little amazed at the Earl's concern for a lady he claimed so vehemently he did not care for.

"There is something else you can do for me, Con, if you will," he continued, and then he spoke for several minutes, his face earnest and serious as he instructed her in what he wished her to do.

Connie listened carefully, and when he had finished, she nodded her head in agreement, even as she exclaimed, "Why, Robert, how very unethical of you. Never did I think to see the day that you would ask such a dishonest thing of me, and with such a straight face, too. Spare my blushes, m'lord, for this will surely put me beyond the pale if I am ever found out in such subterfuge—"

"Cut line, Con, do," her brother growled. "What's the fuss? Sort of thing you women do all the time, after all."

The Earl took his leave of them then, for they fell into a

hot argument about the wiles and deceits of women in general, as opposed to the nobleness the male sex displayed on each and every occasion, and he could see that it would be some time before they reached any conclusion, if they did so at all.

He would have been surprised if he had known they barely waited until he was out of earshot before they changed the subject.

"Know what, Con?" Freddie asked. "Robert's 'cotched' this time for sure."

"Of course," his sister agreed with a broad smile. "I pray you will not feel you have to bring it to his attention just yet, my dear."

"Lord, no!" Freddie said with a fine display of scorn. "Think I'm such a flat as that?"

The Earl meanwhile continued to stroll along the lakeside, still pondering his problem, when suddenly he heard a female cry, and then the sound of a large splash. His lips tightened as he lengthened his stride and hurried in the direction of the sounds.

David Linwood had eaten a hearty breakfast with the Marquess, while managing to parry any attempts on that gentleman's part to find out what tactics he was prepared to use to get Lady Spalding to choose him as her husband.

"Fine woman, Davey," the Marquess said, spearing a kipper with enthusiasm. "Makes me wish I were twenty years younger, that she does. And since I can tell that you are just such a one as Robert—deuced slow, both of you, to set up your nurseries—I decided to take matters into my own hands and make your marriage to Lady Spalding a condition of the inheritance. You'll see, you'll like marriage, especially to a luscious beauty like Georgie."

"You're a fine one to talk, cousin," David drawled, "when you never married yourself, and had a grand old time of it, from what I hear tell, rakin' your way from one end of England to the other. Why are you so quick to insist I tie myself to one woman, when there are so many of the little beauties to enjoy?"

David had discovered that the Marquess liked to have people about him who stood up to him and spoke their mind, and now, as he had expected, the old gentleman grinned at him, not a bit offended at his plain speaking. He swallowed his kipper and took a long draught of ale before he replied, "Never had to. Robert was born before I was thirty, and two brothers came along to follow him. Presented my Aunt Rose—Robert's mother, you know—with a fine diamond necklet at his birth, for it saved me from *your* fate. But now there are only Robert and yourself, and some distant third something-or-others in Ireland to inherit. I have no intention of letting the direct line die out; *ergo*, Lady Georgie."

David was still thinking of his words as he climbed the stairs two at a time to collect his riding hat and crop, and he was striding along the corridor to his rooms when he heard the voice of Miss Hersham giving some orders to her maid as she prepared to leave her room. Quick as a flash, he retreated to a small alcove and some stairs that led to the floor above. Drat the woman anyway, he thought as he climbed out of sight. It seemed that everywhere he went in the Court, either she or that tiresome Lady Martin lay in wait to pounce on him. He had never spent so much time in his life with older women, and he was sure that at this point he had told them the entire history of the United States several times over. He paused and listened to the patter of the lady's feet as she passed by the stairs, and then he remembered the Waring girl. Now that she was here, if he was not trapped by the old biddies, he kept stumbling over her instead. He shook his head, and then he noticed a smaller set of spiral stairs in the corner of this upper hall, and with some curiosity he went to inspect them. He remembered that Cousin Bertie once told him there was a fine view of the entire estate from the cupola, and he decided to climb up and see. Perhaps that way he would be able to determine the whereabouts of Lady Martin and her bosom bow, as well as the persistent Miss Waring, and make his plans to escape them all accordingly.

When he pulled himself through the trapdoor of the cupola, he discovered that Bertie was right. You could see in every direction for miles. There was an old stool here, and a spyglass rested on one of the windowsills. His lips curled as he picked it up. It was obvious that Cousin Bertie did not use the place merely to survey his domain, for directly under that particular window was the stableyard and dairy, and even as he looked, he saw a pretty housemaid come out of a shed, smiling and patting her hair back in place before she ran back to the house. He was not at all astounded when she was followed shortly thereafter by one of the footmen, still buttoning up his livery. The old roué, he thought as he adjusted the glass to his own eyesight and began a slow sweep of the grounds.

He almost missed Georgie, and if she had not had the misfortune to choose a gown of brilliant yellow that morning, he probably would have, for she still lay asleep on her shawl in the little clearing. But even as the glass swept past her recumbent figure, his mind was registering that splash of colour, and he returned to study it more closely. He whistled soundlessly, all thoughts of the ladies he had come up here to avoid gone from his mind. Lady Spalding! Alone and very far from her locked bedroom door.

He put the glass down and swung back through the trapdoor, and in only a few minutes was walking rapidly towards the end of the lake.

Georgina opened her eyes in some confusion, not sure what had startled her awake. The clearing and the lake were just as they had been when she fell asleep. But then she was sure she felt someone's eyes watching her, and she rose to her feet and whirled to look behind her. Her face paled under the new dusting of freckles she had acquired in the spring sunlight, for there was David Linwood, dressed for riding, standing and staring at her, an unholy smile beginning to curve his lips.

"Time for lesson two? Georgie, Georgie, will you never learn, *belle*?" he drawled, stripping off his gloves as he started towards her.

Georgina backed away towards the water, but then, as if realizing there was no retreat in that direction, she stopped and put up her chin. She was furious that she had fallen asleep, and by her own carelessness was trapped by him, far from help.

"I was not aware that it was unsafe for a guest of the Marquess to take an early-morning walk within sight of the house," she said as evenly as she could. "But I should have remembered your presence. How did you know where to find me?"

"Let that be my secret for now, *belle*," he said, his blue eyes intent on her face. He reached out for her, and she said quickly, "If you touch me, I shall not choose you, sir, and then all your hopes of gaining the inheritance will be lost."

His hands stopped in mid-air, and he appeared to be considering her statement before he reached out again and drew her into his arms.

"I think you are mistaken, Georgie. After I have initiated you into the wonders of lovemakin', I have every confidence that you will choose me. What, an Englishwoman of the nobility to deny the man who has possessed her? Besides, the Earl would hardly want damaged goods, and I cannot see him acceptin' my leavin's."

"I am a widow, not a young virgin," she said, her temper rising at his insulting, arrogant words. "But I see no point in arguing with you. Let me go at once, or I shall tell the Marquess that you forced me against my will."

He leaned down to stare at her, his hands holding her in a cruel grip, his blue eyes bright with his desire.

"Against your will, *belle*? We shall see about that, won't we? Besides, we are not arguin'. You-all will know very well when that occurs, and take care not to provoke me to it again. Let us say rather that we are havin' a discussion of the relative merits of Englishmen and Americans."

"I have no interest in Americans!"

"*No?* It doesn't run in the family, then?" At her look of incomprehension, he explained, "Your aunt never stops demandin' more facts about the States from me! But come, sit down with me on your shawl and I will enlighten you. How very foresighted of you to bring it, *belle*. Now, I have no objection to a few minutes of conversation first, and it is too bad to let you continue in such ignorance, for I assure you, Georgie, America is the country of the future—especially *your* future."

As he spoke, he started to pull her down onto the grass, and she kicked him as hard as she could. In some surprise, he dropped her arm and she backed away, her face white and her voice shaking with temper.

"I have little interest in your country, sir, and none at all in you—you . . . you . . ."

"Boor? Commoner? Uncivilized lout?" he asked, stalking her again, his voice flat and dangerous. "How about foreign devil? Rude ape?"

"Colonial peasant!" Georgina snarled.

He stopped short, his eyes narrowed and his mouth a thin tight line. She noticed his fists clenching and unclenching and thought: Dear God, what have I done? He was beside her in one giant stride, and before she could even gasp, had picked her up in his arms and was walking towards the lake.

"You really should not have said that, *belle*," he told her conversationally, although his voice was taut with anger. "For now I have decided that you need a lesson in deportment even more than you do in lovemakin'."

Georgina found herself flying through the air, and had only a moment to scream in fright before she hit the water of the lake with a loud splash. The water was very cold, for it was after all only May, and she came to the surface sputtering and gasping for breath. It was not very deep here, so although she was an indifferent swimmer, she knew she was in no danger of drowning. She reached up and swept her wet hair from her eyes, and saw David Linwood standing on the shore, his hands on his hips as he laughed heartily at her predicament. She began to half-swim, half-walk out of the lake some little distance from him, but he followed her along the shore, and she realized that wherever she came to land, he would be there waiting for her. She resigned herself to it, for she did not think she could remain in this very cold water much longer. As she reached the shallows, she stumbled over a large rock and went down on her hands and knees again. She had been angry before, but now when she heard his jeering laughter, she was furious, and picking up her soggy skirts, she strode ashore.

"I have heard that ladies of the *haut ton* often dampen their petticoats to add to their allure, but this is ridiculous, *belle*," he said, his eyes going over her dripping figure. Georgie looked down at herself and gasped. The flimsy muslin gown was molded so tightly to her body that every single bit of her showed as plainly as if she had been standing there naked. Why, she realized, even my nipples are plainly visible!

"At least I won't be gettin' a pig in a poke, Georgie!" he drawled next. "Thank heavens you are not knock-kneed or bow-legged, but have lovely long legs . . . er . . . among other things!"

"I hate you!" she hissed at him. "I will make you pay for this. Colonial peasant indeed. No Englishman would ever treat a woman so."

Even as she spoke, she was backing into the water again to hide herself from his appraising eyes. When he saw what she was doing, he said, "No, come out now, Georgie. You will freeze if you do not, for I know the water is cold. When we get home to Virginia, you may swim in much more comfort. No? You will not come out?"

As he spoke, he removed his riding jacket, his stock, and his shirt, and from where she stood, up to her neck in icy water, Georgie could see the fluid movement of the muscles in his naked chest, and the powerful biceps that rippled in his arms. He sat down and pulled off his boots, and when he stood up again and came to the water's edge, he was clad only in his breeches. She stared at the wedge-shaped torso, as deeply tanned as his face, from his broad shoulders to where it narrowed at his slim hips, his whole upper chest covered with crisp curling brown hair, and her shiver had nothing to do with the temperature of the water.

She stood there helplessly as he dived in and began to swim towards her, and only then did she try to escape along the shore. But she had seen how even and long his stroke was, and she knew there was no way to get away from him, and so she was not surprised when his arms came out and pulled her back to him, turning her so she faced him, as he trod water easily. She could feel that naked chest against her breasts, and his rock-hard thighs as he wrapped his legs around hers, and she could also feel the growing hardness in his breeches as he pressed himself even closer to her body.

She tried to scratch his face, and to her surprise, found herself being forced underwater. When he allowed her to come up, she was gasping for air, all the fight gone out of her, and she found herself clinging to his shoulders and spluttering out the water she had swallowed.

"That's more like it, *belle*," he said. "You must not fight me, you know, for it will only cause you pain. I must always win."

Before she really caught her breath, he turned her head and kissed her hard on her open mouth.

His lips were just as she remembered them—hard, insistent, and demanding. Georgina felt herself perilously close to a faint, something she had never done in her life, and knew she could struggle no more. As he lifted his head and smiled down at her in triumph, she sagged against him in defeat. Dimly she heard him chuckle as he began to swim with her back to shore.

"And now, my dearest *belle*, we will get you out of those wet clothes," he drawled. "The sun is warm, and before long I will see to it that you are very warm too."

He was sure he had broken her spirit at last and did not expect any further trouble from her, not now or at any time in the future. Georgina kept her eyes closed. There was no fight left in her, she admitted to herself, and Mr. Linwood could do exactly what he pleased with her. She wondered how she could have been such a fool as to think she could compete with this man when he was so much bigger and stronger, and had no scruples at all about fighting fair.

"Stealing a march on me, *cousin?*" she heard a voice ask from the shore, and her eyes flew open to see the Earl of Amesbury standing there, holding her shawl and watching them in seeming nonchalance. She could not see how his hands were twisted in the shawl in his anger, nor hear in his carefully clipped tones the fury he was feeling.

"What very unusual methods you Americans use in your courting," he added as David carried her up the bank and stood her on her feet. Georgina staggered a little, and he put one strong arm back around her and pulled her once again to his side.

"As you see, m'lord," David drawled, challenging him over Georgina's wet head, "unusual . . . and very effective. I did tell you, did I not, that I had the prior claim?"

Georgina was shivering now, and completely unconscious of the way her gown was molded once again to her body. The Earl stared at her briefly and then stepped forward.

"I really must insist that you let the lady go now, Linwood. She is, after all, a guest of the Marquess'," he said, and there was that in his voice that made the other man comply without question, for the sounds of generations of Hollands giving orders and having them obeyed instantly were in those quiet words.

The Earl shook out Georgina's shawl and wrapped it around her before he picked her up in his arms and prepared to leave the scene.

"I shall tell the others that Lady Spalding has had an unfortunate accident, a tumble into the lake, and that you, *cousin*, went to her rescue. That will explain your breeches, and the lady's soggy self as well. No doubt you will be feted as a hero," the Earl concluded, striding away.

"Till later, *belle* . . . you may count on it!" Georgina heard David call after them, and she shivered again in the Earl's arms. He stared down at her dripping hair, but even the sight of the elegant Lady Spalding looking more like a drowned rat than a lady of fashion could not bring a smile to his cold, furious face.

Without speaking, he took her into the house through a back door, and up the servants' stairs to her room, and Georgina was grateful that the only person who saw her was a very small tweeny, who stood with her mouth agape until the Earl ordered her to fetch Lady Spalding's maid and prepare a hot bath.

Robert opened the door to her room and set her gently on her feet before the fire, and then he ruefully inspected the large patches of damp that now adorned his favourite coat from Weston. Georgina kept her head lowered so the only thing she was able to see were the puddles forming at her feet.

Robert took her chin in his hand and forced her to look up at him. "He did not hurt you, did he?" he asked harshly.

"N-no," she whispered, and then added with something like her old spirit, "unless you call throwing me into the lake and then half-drowning me, until I could struggle no more, hurting me."

She saw the Earl's grey eyes harden. "Mr. Linwood will pay for that, my promise on it. And now I will leave you, Georgie. Get out of those wet clothes as soon as you can, and then, after your bath, try to rest. I will explain everything to the others and see that you are not disturbed until you feel more the thing. And I will not scold you, my girl, not now, about how very unwise it was for you to let yourself be found in such a lonely spot by the likes of my dear *cousin*. The David Linwoods of the world, dear Georgie, although they may be exciting and stir your senses until you cannot help but play with fire, cannot be trusted. You should have remembered that."

He left her then, and when Wiltshire ran in a few moments later, Georgina was standing exactly where he had put her down, but the maid could not tell that the water that was streaming down her face was not from her dripping hair, but rather from her hot tears of distress that she had lost the Earl's good opinion of her forever.

8

Lady Spalding was seen no more that day. The Earl had explained to her aunt, and then later to the other guests at luncheon, what had happened, and he made so light of the incident that no one considered it at all serious. Of Mr. Linwood there was no sign either, for he had returned to the house only to change his clothes before taking his horse out for a long and solitary ride.

Emmaline sighed at his bravery and wished she had thought of falling into the lake so he could save her, and Lord Waring resolved to take the man aside that very evening and shake his hand, for even if he could not like the fellow, his actions in saving the future Lady Waring must be commended. The Marquess stared hard at his nephew with his bright little brown eyes, and wondered what else there was to the story that he was not hearing, even as he resigned himself to wait for Davey's return, for it was plain to see he would get none of the spicy details from Robby! Lady Martin and Miss Hersham exchanged remorseful glances, even as they both resolved to redouble their efforts to watch Mr. Linwood's every move from this time on. Only Connie and Freddie Wilson were concerned, for they had seen the look on Robert's face before he masked it with a polite smile, and they knew that the steely glare in his grey eyes boded no good for the American.

Connie did try to see Georgina late that afternoon, but she found her knock went unanswered, and when she softly tried the door, she discovered it locked. She went away, a frown on her face, to consult with the Earl.

Georgina had been very quiet while Wiltshire exclaimed over her and prepared her hot tub. While she soaked in it, the maid toweled her hair and then brushed it until it was dry, and after putting her into a white lawn nightgown and helping her to bed, she went away to get some food. Georgina could not help being ravenous, for she had missed breakfast and lunch as well. She ate all the hot soup and the biscuits and a little chicken, and drank the wine the cook had sent up as a restorative, and then she told her maid to draw the curtains and leave her alone.

"I will ring when I want you, Wiltshire," she said. "On no account am I to be disturbed until then, by anyone! See to it!"

The maid curtsied and took the tray away, hoping dear Lady Georgie was not sickening for something, for her face was so pale and set, her words so stiff and abrupt.

Georgina climbed wearily out of bed to lock the door after her, and then she fell back in bed, and barely had time to pull the covers over her before she was fast asleep.

Robert heard about Connie's attempt to see her new friend after she ran him to earth in the library, and when she mentioned how very concerned she was becoming for Georgie, since she had been resting some hours now, he patted her hand.

"She will be all right, Con, never fear! In fact, I think you can safely assume that Georgie will appear in the Great Parlour with the rest of us before dinner, as usual."

He went away then, leaving a thoughtful young lady to watch him stride upstairs with a great air of determination.

Georgina came awake in the soft gloom when she heard the sound of a key in her lock. Her own key, she saw with horror, had fallen on the floor, and she sat up in bed, clutching the bedcovers in shaking hands, with her heart pounding, while she watched the door open slowly.

When she saw the Earl bearing a tea tray, her mouth dropped open in astonishment and relief. "How . . . how did you get in here?" she whispered.

He put the tray down on a table and went back to close and lock the door again, and then he came over to her bed. "Mrs. Farrow has the key to every room in the Court, my dear. I have known her since I was breeched, and although Mr. Linwood could not possibly hope to wrest your key from her by any means short of murder, it was an easy matter for me to gain possession of it!" he said, smiling down at her flushed face. "Mrs. Farrow, you see, indeed, all the staff, happen to like me."

For some reason he had the strongest desire to bend down over her as she lay there in bed, and kiss those soft lips, and smooth the tousled chestnut hair away from her forehead and neck. There was one very distracting tress that curled down to her left breast . . . He shook himself mentally and went to throw open the curtains, hoping a little more light would dispel his romantic inclinations. Georgina watched him, her eyes wide.

"But what are you doing in here, Robert?" she asked as he approached the bed again. "I gave orders I was not to be disturbed, and besides, you know it is not at all the thing."

"After the way I saw you this morning, I cannot conceive why it should be at all improper. You have no secrets from me now, my dear!"

He saw her eyes darken with the memory, and sat down on the side of the bed to take her hand, and change the subject by saying, "I knew if I just waited for you to appear, or even sent you a note demanding your attendance, you would not obey me, so I have come to insist you get up and dress for dinner."

"Well, I won't!" she cried, falling back against her pillows. "I cannot, for it would be too embarrassing. I know what everyone must think of me—"

"They think nothing of you at all, except the normal amount of concern for you after your accident," the Earl said, cutting through her exclamations. "I told them you fell in the lake, Mr. Linwood pulled you out, and I carried you back to the Court, and that is the end of the story, although I am afraid I have left it up to you to explain how you, normally so graceful, came to be so clumsy. I am sure your powers of invention are up to the task, for I have never met a woman yet who couldn't tell the most awful fibs without batting an eyelash." Georgina looked as if she might take exception to this, so he hurried on, "The only people who know the truth are yourself and Mr. Linwood— and of course I know as much as I was able to observe from my vantage point on the shore. Come, Georgie. You are not a coward, and even if the ugly truth were known, I would still expect you to get up, put on your prettiest gown, and march down those stairs with your head held high. If you insist on remaining here in bed, it can only excite comment, for everyone knows that a little wetting, even in cold lake water, could not possibly deter you. You are no weak, invalidish woman prone to spells and megrims. Get up!"

He stood up suddenly and wrested the blankets from her hands and with one swift tug pulled them clear away from her. Georgina looked down at her almost transparent nightgown and naked legs and gasped.

"Come on, get up, or I will make you do it!" the Earl said, holding out her dressing gown.

Georgina realized that she had no choice, and knew she would feel more covered wearing the garment he offered, so she did as she was bid, only saying a little querulously, "I do not know why you must give me orders, m'lord. You are as arrogant as David Linwood."

As she tightened the sash of her robe, she could not see the look in the Earl's eyes as he stood behind her, and so did not realize what a narrow escape she had had. One more minute of being forced to stare at her beautiful figure barely covered by the flimsy lawn, and he would have lost his careful control. Now he turned away and went into her dressing room to fling open the wardrobe doors. Georgina padded after him, barefoot.

"For heaven's sake, Robert!" she exclaimed. "What are you doing with my clothes?"

The Earl held out the green satin ball gown for a moment and studied it before he thrust it back into the clothes press. "No, that won't do. For one thing, it's too formal for the country, and for another, it's too revealing. What we need is something dignified but still alluring. Ah! Here's just the thing!"

He took out a gown of black velvet. It was a slim gown, bare of trimmings, and although the front of it would cover her up to her collarbone, the back was cut in a deep V, almost to the waist. Georgina watched him approve it, her hand to her mouth.

"I think you have gone mad!" she said finally as he rummaged through her slippers for a matching pair of velvet sandals. He only smiled at her as he led her back to the bedroom, the clothes he had chosen over his arm.

"Drink your tea, Georgie!" he commanded, leading her back to the wing chair near the fire, and the table where he had set the tray. He poured her out a cup, and pushed the plate of macaroons closer to her, and then he went over to her dressing table and began to inspect her jewelry. Georgina had the sudden thought that they were both participating in a very domestic scene and that Robert Holland was behaving as if they had been married for years. At this thought, she swallowed a larger sip of her tea than she had intended, and had to cough a little.

"Perhaps I missed my calling, and should have been a lady's maid," the Earl remarked as he held up the Spalding pearl set. "Yes, your pearls will complete the picture. They are such chaste, refined jewels, don't you agree?"

Georgina put down her cup with a snap. "I do not know what you think you are about, Robert, but I have had enough. I do not choose to join the others this evening and will send down my excuses. And now I would appreciate it very much if you would go away. You are giving me the headache."

At this cold and determined little speech, the Earl straightened up from the dressing table and came to stand over her. Georgina was suddenly as frightened as she had been that morning with David Linwood, for the Earl's eyes were cold and flinty and his stance was threatening.

"Listen to me, my girl. You will do exactly what I say, if I have to dress you myself. Or perhaps that is what you are waiting for? Have you had such a taste for being treated roughly, that that is what you want from all men? Are you determined to flirt and tease them until they can stand it no longer and gratify you by taking you against your will? Is that what you want from me?"

Georgina caught her breath as he moved the table and pulled her to her feet. He began to tear at the sash of her robe, and pulled away from him, saying, "How dare you? I did not flirt with David, or tease him. He forced me to kiss him."

"Georgie, Georgie!" the Earl said, shaking his head. "Don't you understand that all you have to do is remain perfectly still and you are still teasing? You cannot help it. But come, sit down again and drink your tea while you tell me what really happened this morning. I arrived rather late on the scene."

His voice was light again as he took the chair across from her so he could watch her face, and Georgina sank back into her chair, and looking into the fire, told him of her adventure. When she reached the part where the American had thrown her in the lake, the Earl interrupted to say pensively, "How very strange! I would have thought he had amorous rather than murderous doings on his mind."

"He did, but then I called him a colonial peasant," she explained, her face still averted. The Earl's lips quivered.

"And he, of course, lost his temper as well as any desire he might have had and tossed you overboard, eh? Well, I suppose that was better than the rape he had in his mind when he started, and the rape he certainly would have managed to accomplish if I had not come along."

He saw a single tear roll down her averted cheek and went to draw her to her feet again. In the firelight she looked very lovely, and he was unable to resist reaching out with one long finger to wipe it from her face. "Do not cry, my dear," he said, his deep voice warm and caressing again. "He did not succeed after all. And now, call your maid and dress. I expect you to look your most superb this evening, so Mr. Linwood may have the galling experience of staring at you and regretting his lost opportunity. Besides, it really is too much to let a provincial American best the noble Lady Spalding; that is not to be endured by any patriotic Englishman. You must remember your name and your duty to your country. Besides, I will be by your side. He cannot touch you again, I promise. Will you do it?"

Georgina nodded as if hypnotized, her green eyes intent on his handsome face.

"Good girl!" he said, smiling down at her, and then he flicked her chin with his finger and went to the door. "I shall come back at the second bell to escort you myself," he said.

"That is not necessary, Robert. I would not trouble you," she assured him, a little startled by this attention, and afraid the other guests might make too much of it and think she had chosen the Earl in earnest. He smiled as if he knew her thoughts.

"It is no trouble, dear Georgie, no trouble at all, but my distinct pleasure. I find your charms more appealing every day."

Suddenly aware of their situation, alone in her room, and she clad only in her nightgown and robe, Georgina nodded. If Aunt Bess were to come along right now, she would be writing the announcement for the newspapers as soon as she could reach a quill and an ink pot!

By the time Wiltshire had buttoned her into the black velvet gown and fastened on her pearls, Georgina had not only regained her composure but also was actually looking forward to her encounter with David Linwood in front of the other guests. In reflecting about the matter, she realized that he could hardly admit to the Marquess, to say nothing of the others, what had really happened, and so must go along with the story the Earl had told, and whatever embellishments she cared to add. Applying a light dusting of powder to try to disguise the golden freckles that had resulted from her sleep in the sun, she thought that she must devise a story that would make him seem less the hero of the piece. She watched Wiltshire arrange the severe chignon that she had requested, and when the maid was finished, nodded her head. Yes, it was smooth and elegant—just as she intended to be this evening. She stood before the pier glass and turned slowly, admiring the sophisticated lines of her gown, which clung to every curve of her, yet looked so chaste until she turned her back.

The Earl arrived just as the second bell was sounding, and the admiration in his eyes, and his low bow, told her she had succeeded in her objective.

"Almost too perfect, Georgie," he whispered as he took her arm and led her along the corridor. "Was it really necessary to bludgeon the man so?"

She raised an inquisitive eyebrow, and he laughed at her. "To think that I will have to sit across from him and listen to him gnashing his teeth in frustration all evening. Of course, I flatter myself that it is all my doing that you appear to such advantage. After all, I was your lady's maid tonight."

Georgina raised her brows even higher, and he added as they started down the stairs, "In a manner of speaking, that is."

"I beg you will keep that information to yourself, m'lord," she said with a little smile. "When I think how you bullied me. Disgraceful! It was only when you pointed out that it was my patriotic duty to my country that I relented and decided to appear. However, it is too bad that perhaps you missed your calling, for indeed I could not have chosen a better gown myself."

The Earl smiled at the footman who was holding open the door of the Great Parlour, and then bent over her to whisper, "But why is it only your lovely self who tempts me to the profession? I do not think I would enjoy choosing Miss Hersham's gowns at all."

As they strolled into the room where all the others were assembled, they were both laughing, which is what the Earl had had in mind all along. David Linwood straightened up from where he had been lounging against the mantel, and tried to keep his face expressionless.

"Ah, our lovely Lady of the Lake!" Cousin Bertie cried, rising and hurrying towards them to welcome her. "My dear, you are ravishing . . . ravishing. Those twenty years weigh heavy tonight, alas."

Taking her hand, he led her to the group near the fireplace. Georgina went first to her aunt and Lady Martin, kissing them both, and then Lord Waring was there to take her hand and inquire after her health in his loud, booming voice.

"Dear lady," he said, "I cannot deny that I felt a pang when I heard of your mishap. I have been thanking Mr. Linwood here, and telling him how much it means to me *especially* that you were saved."

"The man's still at it . . . more hair than wit," Cousin Bertie remarked to no one in particular. "Now, wouldn't you think that anyone but a jobbernowl would see he has no chance?"

Georgina took a deep breath and went to David Linwood, holding out her hand and smiling at him. "And I have been very remiss, for I do not believe I had the chance to thank you, sir, for your prompt rescue. Nor the Earl either for taking me back to the Court so swiftly. However, I must tell you, David, there was no need for you to dive in in that impetuous way, for I learned to swim as a child. But then, I must not tell tales. I know how foolish you felt when you discovered I was in no danger at all, but only in water up to my knees."

She turned away from the angry glare of those blue eyes and smiled at the others. "So awkward of me, wasn't it? But as you can see, no harm done."

"But how did it happen, Georgie?" Emmaline asked, sitting on the edge of her chair and still reluctant to give up the picture of Mr. Linwood rescuing her, if only she could discover how to go about it.

Georgina saw Connie's encouraging grin and said lightly,

"Do you know, I am still not quite sure. I was backing up to better observe a pair of hawks flying over the park, and I must have been nearer the lake than I had thought, for all of a sudden, there I was in the water. In a way, I am sorry that David and Robert came along in time to see my mishap, for the whole affair was so farcical, with me floundering about and David leaping in . . . Let us forget it before I am in whoops again."

"Of course, dear," Miss Wilson said. "But no more wettings until we can go in the plunge pool, or I will have a difficult time getting you to try it with me."

Lord Waring then intervened by announcing that he himself, in company with Lord Handford, had used the pool that very afternoon, and pronounced it a beneficial exercise, very refreshing, and in no way injurious to the health if every precaution was taken to dry oneself thoroughly before emerging into the open air again. This discourse took up all the remaining time until dinner was announced. Cousin Bertie insisted on escorting Georgina himself, before David Linwood had a chance to reach her side. Somehow, Miss Waring was standing there expectantly, and he was constrained to do the pretty with her instead.

During one of the courses at dinner, Miss Wilson suddenly put down her fork and said, "David, I have been meaning to ask you, is your plantation anywhere near the lower reaches of the York River?"

He looked a little startled. "Why, no, Miss Wilson. It borders the Rappahannock. But why do you ask?"

"I was in America two years ago, visiting friends, and had forgotten the name of the river where Linderwood is located. These Indian names—so confusing to my English ears! You look so familiar that I am sure I must have met you during my stay there, although surely I would remember! Perhaps it was not an actual meeting, but just that I saw you there somewhere. Now, where could that have been?" She frowned and cut another piece of salmon.

"Whom did you visit, and where in Virginia did you stay?" he demanded. His voice sounded a little harsh, and Georgina looked up in time to see the Earl's intent gaze on his rival's dark face.

"Oh, I was in various and sundry places," Connie replied in a light and careless way. "First of all in Jamestown, where the ship landed, and then I went on a round of visits to a great many plantations. So confusing after a while. Do you know Belle Oaks, David?"

"Of course, who does not?" he said, tossing off his wine and summoning Jenks to refill his glass. "A very famous place indeed, and quite near Linderwood. How came you to know the Griffin-Booths?"

"They are distant cousins to my friend Anne Steed. But enough of this—your pardon, all. There is nothing so boring as listening to another's travelogue." She smiled at the company and then added in a pensive voice, "But I am so *sure* I saw you in America . . . if I could only remember where."

She frowned again, and then turned to her dinner partner, Lord Waring, to ask him to tell her about the plunge pool again. The Earl noticed that Mr. Linwood swallowed his second glass of wine in haste, and that through the rest of the dinner his brooding eyes went often to Connie's face.

After dinner, the ladies adjourned to the Great Parlour again, and Connie was able at last to sit beside Georgina. "Very well done, m'lady," she said in an undertone. "Someday you must tell me what really happened this morning, for although others may believe that farradiddle you told, I am not one of them. As Albert would say, what a hum!"

"I beg you to keep that opinion to yourself, Connie," Georgie said. "Someday I will tell you, if you are very good. But what is this about travelling in America? You must tell me about it, for I am longing to hear."

"And someday, if *you* are very, very good, I will tell you, dear friend," Connie retorted. "But now is not that time. Shall we try the Marquess' piano, or do you prefer to tell Miss Waring about your accident one more time? She is bearing down on us with a determined look in her eyes."

"You play for us, Connie, and I will chat with Emmie. I would not want her to think I have been neglecting her."

Miss Waring settled herself in the seat Connie vacated, and took Georgina's hand. "How glad I am that you are all right, Georgie," she said, her eyes wide. "Teddy was in a fair taking, I can tell you, but I think it was just that he wished he might have been a hero. How romantic—Mr. Linwood carrying you ashore in his arms."

She sighed, and Georgina changed the subject. "Lord Handford seems a nice young man, Emmie. He is obviously smitten with you as well—quite a conquest for someone who once thought of herself as an antidote."

"Oh, William! He is nothing but a boy," Emmie said, shrugging her shoulders. "I don't want him to be smitten, for I must confess that my heart is given to *another*." This last was said in a whisper, as the lady rolled her eyes. Georgina wanted very much to shake her, but she only asked, "Does the gentleman know it, my dear? But that is not a fair question, for you are very young, after all. Well I remember my own early yearnings, all of course for the most unsuitable men. There was Lord Byron—and once I saw Sir Walter Scott and thought I would die happy if he would but notice me. These first crushes have no relation to real life, Emmie, as you will soon discover."

The girl lowered her head and twisted the bracelet on her wrist. "You may make a jest of it, Georgie, but it is not a passing yen, it is real. I shall never love another as long as I live." She looked up suddenly into Georgie's eyes and said with dignity, "I know I have a hopeless passion, for he will never want me, but I cannot help myself. I would do anything . . . *anything*, if I could be with him always!"

Just then the gentlemen joined them, and Cousin Bertie went immediately to Lady Waring's side, and drawing her apart from the others, proceeded to whisper in her ear. Lord Waring looked on in dismay as his mother giggled and smiled, tapped the elderly rake's hand with her fan, and generally made a complete fool of herself, in his opinion. Miss Hersham and Lady Martin rose as one and started to question Mr. Linwood, but this evening he was having none of it.

"May I suggest you apply to Miss Wilson, m'lady? Ma'am? Havin' visited the States so recently, she can tell you her impressions from a feminine point of view, and I am sure you would find her stories much more interestin' than my own so-often-repeated tales."

He bowed, said he was much obliged to them, and took himself over to where Georgina and Emmaline were sitting. The Earl watched him from his place near the fire, but he did not follow him, only continued to chat with Freddie. The two older ladies sat down, heads together, as Connie continued to play a Brahms etude.

"Lady Spaldin', Miss Warin'," David Linwood said, bowing before them. "I believe your brother wants to speak to you, Miss Warin'—or was it Lord Handford? You had best go and inquire."

His voice was abrupt, and Emmaline rose to her feet with alacrity. *She is so besotted,* Georgie thought, *that she will do anything he asks, even if that means she must remove from his vicinity.*

Without asking her permission, David took the seat next to her. "So, dear Georgie, I suppose I must congratulate you. You managed to acquit yourself very well this evenin', and even seized the opportunity to make me look a little silly as well."

Georgina inclined her head at his compliment, and he leaned closer. "You should not have done that, *belle.*"

His voice was harsh, even though he did not speak above a whisper, and Georgina could not help the shiver of terror that ran through her.

"I do not like to be made to look foolish," he continued, "as you will discover to your sorrow, when I come to exact payment for it."

"But you could hardly contradict me, now, could you, sir?" she asked, her eyes going to the Earl's tall figure on the other side of the room. Just knowing he was there made her brave enough to say, "I shall take great care that you have no opportunity to exact payment . . . or repeat this morning's performance."

Suddenly Mr. Linwood leaned back in his seat and smiled, that wolfish smile that turned his blue eyes to fire. "Don't wager on it, m'lady! You really cannot escape me, for I am determined on my course. I suppose you could affiance yourself to Lord Warin', but I cannot see you doin' that just to escape *my* attentions."

"I can accept the Earl!" she said quickly.

"Has he asked you yet?" he riposted, and when she did not answer at once, he laughed out loud. "Even someone with your quick wit and great address might find it difficult to say you would be delighted to be the bride of a man who has never even asked for your hand. No, my dear, as I have known for some time, he does not intend matrimony; what *he* wants is exactly what *I* want."

"You are mistaken. The Earl is nothing at all like you."

"He is a man, isn't he? Do you think because he has a title and pretty manners and a polished approach that he will take you any differently than I would myself? Foolish Georgie!"

Georgina looked up to see her aunt bearing down on them, looking like a small but determined ship of the line, and rose to meet her, saying only over her shoulder, "I have no intention of finding out about it from either of you. Excuse me, sir, my aunt is beckoning to me."

He let her go then, but for the rest of the evening she was aware of his eyes on her, and it added nothing to her enjoyment of the evening, and not even a lighthearted game of whist with the Earl and the Wilsons could take away the cold feeling in the pit of her stomach at his threats. She locked her bedroom door very carefully when she went to bed, and the heavy table was once again pushed into position in front of it.

When she woke the following morning, it was to find that the spell of good weather they had been enjoying had disappeared, for today a fine misty rain was falling. She rang for her chocolate, and then went to unlock her door, wondering what she was to do all day, cooped up as she was in the Court with David and the Earl.

Wiltshire came in with a tray and another note from the Marquess. As Georgina read it, her expression lightened, for here was the perfect solution to her problem. Cousin Bertie begged her to join him in an expedition to the private chapel of some friends of his, where he was planning to make a rubbing from one of the brass memorial plaques. He said he was sure she would find it fascinating, and might even, if she was a good little puss, be allowed to help. He told her to dress warmly in her oldest gown, and set the hour they would leave for eleven.

Georgina asked her maid to bring her a large tray of breakfast, saying she felt a little lazy this rainy day, and then she wrote some letters and read a book until it was time to dress for her engagement with the Marquess.

Wiltshire, at her request, accompanied her to the Great Hall, but she need not have bothered with the precaution, for they met no one, and Cousin Bertie was already waiting for her, attended by a tall and skeletal figure dressed in black, who had a long pale face and red hands. Georgina looked at him inquiringly, and the Marquess said, "My valet, Gudge! Invaluable man, enters into all my pursuits, and a special help with my work!"

Gudge pulled his lank forelock and bowed, before he helped the Marquess into his waterproof cloak and handed him his hat. He followed them from the Court, bearing a large black portmanteau, a roll of material carefully covered with oilskin, three large cushions, and a long white coat. The Marquess carried his cane.

When everything had been disposed in the carriage to Cousin Bertie's satisfaction, Gudge climbed in behind them, and after arranging a rug across his master's and Georgina's knees, sat back facing them, his arms folded as he stared out the window.

"You must tell me, Georgie, exactly what did happen yesterday," the Marquess said almost as soon as the carriage began to bowl down the drive. She looked to the valet, who had drawn his bony knees up almost under his chin as if to efface himself even more, and Cousin Bertie chuckled. "No need to pay any heed to Gudge. Been with me forever, mum as the grave, tell him anything.

"You see," he went on, "I can get nothing from Robby except that fairy tale he told us all, and Davey has been strangely reticent as well. I know you didn't just stumble into the lake—Lord, take me for a flat? No, no, my dear, I am more than two-and-ten. Which one drove you to it, eh? Davey or Robby?"

He saw she was still hesitant to speak in front of his valet, and patted her knee. "That bad, hmm? Well, perhaps you will tell me later. For now I will curb my impatience and tell you something about brass rubbings so you may appreciate what a difficult thing it is to do, and what a valuable work of art when accomplished correctly. Of course, the major English brasses are not here in Upper Littledean. The collection at Cobham, Kent, is your true mecca for fine brass, but for myself, I think my favourite is the memorial plaque dedicated to Sir John d'Aberon at Stoke d'Aberon in Surrey. Do you remember when I did that one, Gudge?"

"A most memorable day, m'lord, and if I may be so bold as to say so, quite your most successful rubbing," the valet said in a high reedy voice, never taking his eyes from the passing scene.

The Marquess went on, "I wish I could show you the original, Georgie. It was crafted in 1277 and is very fine. But today we are only going to Lord Banner's chapel in Grantley Castle. It is quite a distance, but I was sure you would not object to putting a little space between you and the Court today, eh?"

He patted her knee again, and Georgina gave him a grateful smile. The Marquess then prated on at great length, discussing the history of rubbings which began in China centuries ago, and telling her the difference between wet and dry methods, the heelballs made of tallow, beeswax, and lampblack that were employed to transfer the image, and the advantage of thin versus thick paper. In spite of her ignorance on the subject, Georgina found herself fascinated by his enthusiasm, and asked a great many questions, and it did not seem any time at all before they reached their destination and were being ushered into the castle by Lord Banner's butler.

"Family's in town for the Season," Cousin Bertie explained when he saw her looking around for some sign of their host. "Just as well! I can't afford to have my concentration disturbed while I am at work."

Georgina gave her cloak to the butler, and was about to offer to help Gudge with the equipment when she noticed the butler had assigned two footmen to this menial task.

The chapel he showed them to was not large, and it was made entirely of thick grey stone, although there was a small stained-glass rose window behind the altar. The footmen lit several of the flambeaux along the wall before bowing themselves out, and Cousin Bertie bounced down the center aisle to the front of the chapel, where he stopped to admire the brass he had selected as worthy of his art. Georgina could see that some of the memorials were placed high on the walls, and some were even installed under the narrow pews, and she was glad this one was so accessible.

"There, Georgie, isn't that something like? Sir John Banner, dressed in his armour!"

Georgina thought Sir John must have been a pudgy little man before she stooped to read the inscription under the knight's image. At the top, in Latin, were the words "MORS IANVA VITA," and then she read:

Here lieth bvried the body of John Banner, Esqvier, third sonne of William Banner, late of Littledean. He departed ovt of this lyfe beinge vnmarried vppon the thirteenth day of Avgvst in the fower and twentieth yeare of his age and in the yeare of ovr Lord God 1395.

"How sad!" Georgina said. "To die so young!"

"And unmarried!" Cousin Bertie twinkled, as Gudge bustled about them, unpacking the portmanteau and setting out the tools. "You're right, it's sad. Just think what the poor boy missed! But then, they did not make old bones in those days, Georgie."

He took her arm, adding, "The brass must be carefully cleaned before I can begin, and Gudge always takes that as his special task. Let us stroll about the chapel until he is ready for me."

He led her back down the aisle, often pausing to admire another brass memorial or pointing out to her some interesting architectural feature or a fine bit of carving. When they reached the back, he drew her down beside him in a pew.

"Now, Georgie, you must tell me. Which one of my nephies have you chosen for my heir?"

Georgina turned to him and looked straight into those round little brown eyes. "Cousin Bertie, you have put me in an impossible situation, and you know it. I should be very cross with you, for I cannot choose one over the other, and indeed have no desire to choose either. I do not want to marry again."

She looked determined, yet somehow unhappy, and the Marquess took her hands in his. "Dear girl, forgive me when I tell you I cannot believe you, for what a waste that would be. The Hollands need sons, and you could find no better men than Robby and Davey. Perhaps you need more time? Yes, that must be it."

"I do not need more time," she answered in exasperation. "And your nephews have no more desire than I do to be married. What they want from me, sir, and what they have made perfectly clear, does not include holy wedlock."

The Marquess chuckled. "Wouldn't be my nephies if they didn't. But I will tell you a secret, Georgie, if you promise never to let on that I did so. No man wants to marry; every single one of us will try any ploy to avoid it, until there is no other course open to us. It is up to the woman to make a poor, simple man realize that he cannot live without her—or at least thinks he cannot. Now, what do you think of that, puss? You must do the convincing, you see, for if you wait for them to initiate the business, we will be at it forever, and I do not have forever."

Georgina looked down at her hands, held so closely in his, and frowned, and he added, "I am sorry you are unhappy about all this, but I will not change my mind even so, for I know that in the end, you will be the happiest of women, you'll see. Trust old Cousin Bertie, for in this case I do know best."

What Georgina might have replied was lost, for just then Gudge called to them, in his high reedy voice that was so at odds with his gaunt figure, that the stone had been prepared, and the Marquess bustled down the aisle again to don the long white coat his valet was holding in readiness. Georgina was ushered to one of the three cushions placed around the brass plaque, the surface of which was now covered by a thin sheet of fine white paper, carefully aligned and weighted on all sides so it would not shift.

For the next half-hour she knelt and listened as the Marquess issued a stream of orders to his valet, who wielded the heelball with expert strokes so that the knight's image and inscription were transferred to the paper covering it. At one point she was allowed to try it herself, not on the actual brass of course, but on the stone surrounding it. As she worked as carefully as she could, fearful of tearing the thin paper, Gudge added his instructions to those of the Marquess. Suddenly she realized that not once had Cousin Bertie touched the heelball or the paper, and that Gudge had done all the work, and she was hard put to keep her face straight and not chuckle in her amusement. So much for Cousin Bertie's expertise!

"I believe you are finished, sir," Gudge said finally, sitting back on his haunches to wipe his face with a large handkerchief.

"Yes, you are right, Gudge. Now, dear Georgie, this is the part I like the best."

Gudge hurried to remove the weights, and the Marquess leaned over to peel the paper back slowly. He handed the finished rubbing to his valet with a great air of accomplishment, and rose. Georgina was glad to follow his example, for her knees were aching. The Marquess removed his protective coat and dusted his hands before taking her arm again.

"It will be some time before Gudge has packed the equipment, cleaned the plaque, and prepared my rubbing for a safe journey home, my dear, so I think you and I will avail ourselves of Lord Banner's hospitality and repair to the library for a small repast. There is nothing like a hard morning's work to bring on an appetite. Good man, Gudge. Thank you for your assistance."

Georgina stole a glance at the valet's bony face as he bent to his work, but it was carefully expressionless.

After a delicious luncheon accompanied by wines served by the butler, they entered the carriage for the ride home. The Marquess chatted lightly on any number of subjects, for he could see that dear Georgie would not discuss personal matters before a servant, but when he was helping her to alight at Carew Court, he paused for a moment, and looking up into her face, said seriously, "My dear, I beg you will come to me if ever you need advice or assistance, for I am not just a frivolous rake of a man. I have been about the world of a great deal, and I am many years your senior."

Georgina nodded, even as she stared up at the red-brick exterior of the Court, now somewhat dismal-looking in the misty afternoon light. She wondered how she could possibly confess her thoughts even to Cousin Bertie, who she knew would not be the least bit shocked by anything she told him. He went on, as they climbed the shallow steps, "You remember when we first met, I told you that how you feel inside is what is important, not what the world thinks? That is still true, my dear child. You must listen to your heart to find out what is right for you, and then obey what it tells you. Promise me you will do that."

Georgina nodded again and squeezed his arm. Cousin Bertie might be eccentric, and not completely understand her problems, but she would be the first to admit that he was a dear.

9

The rain continued for two more days, sorely trying everyone's patience, for even though the Court was a huge place, it did not seem large enough to be able to avoid those members of the party that one found particularly abrasive. Thus David Linwood was forced to chat with Lady Martin and Miss Hersham for what seemed like endless hours every time he ventured from his room, Georgina was more and more in Emmaline's company so that the young lady might discuss her love for the nameless man she continued to believe she kept a complete secret, and Lord Waring had the bad fortune to discover his mother and the Marquess in the library late one morning, engaged in what he could only call a disgraceful exhibition of immorality, and did.

"Cut line, man!" Cousin Bertie said at last as he straightened his cravat, when Lord Waring spluttered to a close. "Your mama is a grown woman. She can kiss anybody she likes, and so can I! It's the outside of enough to have you in here preaching and prosing to a couple of people who cut their eyeteeth long ago. Come to think of it, it's rude! But then, and forgive me if I give you pain, dear Lavvy, I have never thought the boy had half his share of brains and good sense."

"But it is your age, sir, that offends," Lord Waring boomed. "It's . . . it's disgusting! Mother, you will have the goodness to go to your room. I will speak to you later."

The Marquess drew himself up to his entire five and a half feet. "You will do *what*, you young jackstraw?" He did not look a bit saintly now, and as he advanced on Teddy, m'lord found himself backing to the door of the library in haste before this tiny but furious gentleman.

"How dare you speak to your mother that way?" the Marquess demanded. "Leave us at once, and do not let us see your face again until you have learned your place and a modicum of good manners!"

Lord Waring gulped and nodded, his face very red as he bowed and left the room. The last thing he heard before the door was banged shut behind him was his besotted mother exclaiming, "Darling Bertie! How forceful you are, my love. I have wanted to give Teddy a setdown like that for years." Her son groaned, wondering what he was to do about this impossible situation.

Georgina wondered why Freddie Wilson so often sought her out, and told her amusing stories of town and of the Earl. She did not know that Robert had asked him to keep an eye on her, as well as his sister, but she enjoyed his company and was grateful that it gave her a respite from Emma's constant chitchat and the attentions of David and the Earl.

It was during one afternoon, when Emma came to the library to discover Freddie teaching Georgina to play chess, that Lord Handford seized his opportunity. He found her there, hanging over Georgina's chair, and to both Lady Spalding's and Freddie's relief, took her off to show her the State Bedchamber. Whether he was merely bored with the rain and the inactivity, or whether it was the proximity of that huge bed, he never knew, but he found himself going down on one knee before her to beg her to let him make her his, before he rose to sweep her into his arms to kiss her passionately.

Emma was horrified, for she could not help but feel he was sullying her feelings for David Linwood by even touching her, and she dealt him a resounding slap, with all her not inconsiderable weight behind it. Lord Handford reeled away until he was brought up short by the balustrade surrounding the State Bed, clutching his cheek and looking somewhat dumbfounded at his reception.

"How dare you, sir!" Emmaline cried, her large bosom heaving in her indignation. Lord Handford moaned at the sight. "As if I would ever contemplate marriage to you when my heart is given to *another!*"

In spite of this fine show of anger, the girl was enjoying herself very much. It gave her a feeling of power to deny him, and she had to admit that even though she had no interest in his suit, it was flattering to be chosen by such a wealthy peer, and in her first Season, too. Lord Handford begged her pardon and retreated, wondering, as he did so, why he had been dragged out of London during the Season, if that was the case. After a few hours' reflection, he came to feel very badly used by the Warings, and announced to Teddy in a stiff manner that he intended to take his leave of the Court as soon as the weather cleared. It was not long before Lord Waring had all the facts of the case, and putting his mother's problems from his mind, he sought his sister in her room. He dismissed the maid, and Emmie watched him in the reflection of her dressing-table mirror with horror.

Pacing up and down the carpet in his agitation, he said, "I cannot tell you, Emmaline, how very distressed I am. First Mother's wanton behaviour . . . and now you. What can the world be coming to when a young girl like yourself refuses the most satisfactory offer, and one, I might point out, that I have promoted at a great expense of time and energy, and tells the young man that not only will she refuse to even consider it, but that she loves another instead. What other, Emmaline, tell me that."

He tore at his carefully brushed locks as he spoke, and Emmaline said, in a little voice, that she would really rather not say.

At that, Teddy dragged her to her feet and proceeded to shake her, but Emmaline was made of sturdier stuff than he had imagined. After several minutes of his demanding and her refusing, he came to realize that his sister did indeed mean it when she exclaimed that not even torture could drag the name of her beloved from her lips, and he let her go.

"I believe I am going mad," he said, falling into a chair and burying his face in his hands. His sister watched him in some trepidation, confused by his quieter words of despair. "Here's Mama cuddling with the Marquess every chance she gets, and acting like it's April in December . . . and where is that going to end, Emmie, tell me that . . . and then here are you, flaunting my authority and ruining my life, for how can I ask dear Lady Spalding to marry me until I have your affairs settled?"

"It will do you no good to ask her, Teddy," Emmaline

spoke up, "for she has told me she will never, never accept you."

Lord Waring removed his hands to glare at his sister. "I would advise you to moderate your conversation, sister. You go beyond what is pleasing. What can you know of the matter? If Lady Spalding did indeed make such a statement to you, which I find hard to believe she would do, it was only from modesty. She has such exquisite manners and taste. Of course she is waiting, and impatiently I know, for me to bring up the subject, for she is too much a lady to do otherwise. But now you have denied Lord Handford, and let me tell you, Emmie, he is leaving the Court as soon as it stops raining, so if you were only teasing him, you have lost the main chance. Besides, you are in a fair way of destroying all my chances of happiness."

He groaned in agony, and before he lost complete control of himself, he tottered from her room, a broken man.

Emmaline plumped herself down before her dressing table again, her eyes wide. *She* had defied Teddy, and not only defied him, but bested him as well. Perhaps it needed only a little resolution on her part to attach David Linwood. She could see that dealing with men was nowhere near as difficult as she had imagined. Now, how should she go about it? There must be something . . .

In the Little Parlour, Miss Hersham and Lady Martin were taking a welcome breather, having heard that same Mr. Linwood say he was going to his room to write some letters for the remainder of the afternoon. Both of them were glad of the respite, for it was becoming more and more difficult to ask a question about America that they had not heard the answer to already, time out of mind.

"And you know, Agnes, I am sure he is beginning to suspect something," Miss Hersham told her friend, who was lying back against the sofa, looking exhausted. "He gave me the strangest look this morning when I asked him about the tides, but it was the only thing that came to my mind."

"Do you see any sign that Georgie is coming around, Bess?" Lady Martin asked. "If only there was some hope. But of course, now that Bertie has put her in such an awkward position, how could she show any preference? As for Robert, I could shake him. Treating her with just ordinary civility, and no distinguished attention at all. Where is his famous address now, when we need it? If he would but make a *push* to fix her interest."

Miss Hersham bit into a piece of angel cake. "Perhaps he does not wish to marry her?" she asked, a little timidly.

Lady Martin sat up straighter. "And what has that to say to anything, pray? He is thirty-three; he must begin to look about him with an eye to setting up his nursery. And since it is so, why not a lovely girl like Georgie? Especially since Bertie wants her to be part of the family as well. It seems to me, Bess," she added, her expression darkening, "that Robert is being deliberately difficult."

"Well, *men*, you know!" her friend pointed out.

"Perhaps I should ask him straight out what his intentions are towards Lady Spalding?" his fond aunt asked next. "I know we agreed to wait and let nature take its course, but frankly, Bess, it isn't. Taking its course, I mean."

"I could tax Georgie with it as well, and plead with her to choose Robert. Isn't it a shame that Mr. Linwood does not have bad teeth or an ugly countenance? It is so difficult to say anything to his detriment, when there he stands, so masculine and well-set-up and fascinating."

"You may say he is fascinating, but if I have to listen to him go on about his country one more time, I think I shall go mad!"

"Perhaps we could get Georgie involved in asking him some questions?" Miss Hersham asked, smiling for the first time. "If she found herself bored by him, it might make a difference."

"Bess, you're all about in your head," Lady Martin snapped. "When Mr. Linwood gets Georgie alone, you can be sure it is not to recite the tide tables or discuss his cotton crop with her. He makes love to her—and if only Robert would do the same, we would all of us be much better off."

"I must say I was pleased to see Robert escorting her to dinner the evening after she fell in the lake," Miss Hersham remarked, passing the plate of cakes to Lady Martin. "Didn't they look well together?" She sighed. "Such handsome children they would have."

Lady Martin took a macaroon and said glumly, "By the time they get around to it at the rate they are going, they will both be past the age to do anything more than sop up some weak gruel and totter about on their canes, and you and I will have long before been laid to our rest. But come, Bess, let us put our heads together one more time. There must be something . . ."

That evening at dinner, Connie brought up her trip to Virginia once more. Mr. Linwood did not seem best pleased, although he answered all her questions with aplomb. She remarked again that she still could not recall where she had seen him, but was sure it would come to mind soon. "I have the strangest feeling, David," she said, accepting a helping of *creme à la reine*, "that there was something incongruous about it, as if I would not have expected to see you, the owner of Linderwood, engaged in such an occupation! You are quite sure you do not recall meeting me?"

Mr. Linwood once again denied he had had that pleasure, and changed the subject. The Earl noticed that the American's eyes often went to Georgie's bright chestnut curls throughout the remainder of the meal, but he had been almost subdued for the past few days, and as far as the Earl knew, had made no move to seek her out or try to get her somewhere alone.

Georgina was aware of his glances, and could not help wondering what plot he was hatching now, for she was sure he had not given up his pursuit of her. The Earl was also keeping his distance, and although he was always pleasant, and had a warm smile for her, he did not attempt any closer relationship. She wished it would stop raining, for she was sure it was the weather that was making her so depressed.

Cousin Bertie watched all his guests with glee, not averse to a provocative statement whenever things appeared to be quieting down, for he was enjoying very much indeed the drama he had set in motion. He had had an interview with Lady Martin, however, that had not been at all pleasant. She had raked him over the coals for his ridiculous behaviour, told him he was an old fool for trying to force Georgie to choose one of his nephews, and might just possibly have ruined all her plans for Robert and Georgie in the bargain, and berated him for allowing the Warings to come in the first place. At the end of thirty minutes, her voice was getting hoarse, but she felt she had repaid a lot of debts that had accumulated over the years, and since Bertie just sat and bounced and twinkled at her, felt she had more than conquered the field. When she swept away at last, her head high, he thumbed his nose at her behind her back. Aggie was his cousin and he supposed he loved her, but she could be an awful trial to a man, he thought, going in search of the complaisant and adoring Lady Waring. He had no intention of "moderating his behaviour" or "acting in a suitable manner for a man of his years"—not until age and the gout forced him to it.

On the third day, the sun shone again, and everyone but Lord Handford was quick to take advantage of the cessation of bad weather and go out to the gardens, the rowing boats on the lake, or the stables. Connie and Georgie convinced the head gardener that if a certain part of the lawn was scythed smooth, they could set up a croquet game for everyone to enjoy, while Emmie tried in vain to interest Mr. Linwood in accompanying her to a distant and lonely part of the estate for a sketching expedition, and Cousin Bertie decided to treat his guests to a picnic. He was about to call for Mrs. Farrow to discuss the arrangements, when he saw Lord Handford descending the stairs, followed by his valet and several footmen bearing his trunks.

"You goin' . . . er, Willie?" he asked, skidding to a stop at the foot of the stairs.

"Must thank you for your hospitality, m'lord," Lord Handford managed to get out. "Called back to town . . . must not delay . . . great-aunt on her death bed!"

"Too bad!" Cousin Bertie sympathized. "You'll miss all the fun, and Miss Waring too, of course!" His brown eyes twinkled as the young man coloured up. "Turned you down, eh, Willie? Well, my boy, you may take it from an expert that you have had a narrow escape, and you should be thankful. If I were you, I wouldn't consider marriage for years, at least thirty of 'em. Plenty of time to get leg-shackled, you know; why, look at me. Yes, yes, better be on your way before she changes her mind." He shook his hand and said he was delighted to have met him, and then he bounced away to plan his *al fresco* entertainment.

Either Connie or Freddie kept very close to Georgie's side now the weather had cleared. Freddie went for a ride with her one morning after his sister said she had been most remiss and must spend the time writing to her darling Albert, lest he forget her. But as soon as her brother and her friend had ridden away, she went to find the Earl.

It was a beautiful morning, warm and clear, and Robert was not adverse to putting down his newspaper and going for a stroll with her in the gardens.

"How are things progressing, Robert?" she asked as she took his arm. "I must tell you that the look in Mr. Linwood's eyes when I mention Virginia is beginning to unnerve me a little. Last evening at dinner he looked as if he would like to kill me for mentioning my fictitious trip one more time. Brr!"

"Now, I wonder why?" the Earl mused. "I have heard from my lawyers, and there is no doubt at all that David Linwood is indeed a direct heir of the Marquess, so why would your seeing him in the United States worry him? That was a low blow, dear Connie, for I had such hopes that the lawyers would be able to turn up some evidence that the Linwoods were not related to us after all."

"Should we continue with your plan, then?" Connie asked, stooping to smell some yellow roses. "I am sure there must be some detrimental reason why he is so reluctant to discuss his home." Her handsome face grew sober as she added, "I tell you, though, Robert, I will be very glad to see the back of Mr. Linwood when I leave Carew Court, in spite of all its amenities and the fact that I quite love dear Georgie! I am so pleased to have had this opportunity to become friends with her."

She looked sideways and was not a bit surprised to see Robert smiling to himself. "Yes, she is quite a woman, I agree," he said. "So full of spirit and wit, and so beautiful, but without even an ounce of conceit in her makeup." He paused and seemed to recall himself. "Of course, there are any number of lovely, lively ladies about—right, Con?"

Connie changed the subject. She had no intention of praising anybody else to him but her friend. By the time they had reached the lakeside and strolled back to the Court, the sun was high, and they were both glad to repair to some lawn chairs set in the shade of a large beech tree.

"I think I will ask Georgie to try the plunge pool with me this afternoon," Connie remarked. "I am sure we will enjoy it, and she will be warm after her ride with Freddie. You know how he goes."

"Neck or nothing!" the Earl agreed. "Yes, that is a good idea. I'll tell Cousin Bertie and the servants, so you will not be disturbed. What time should I say?"

Connie set two o'clock for the bathing party and went away to ask Miss Waring if she would care to join them, and Robert lingered under the beech tree, a little drowsy with the heat. He closed his eyes, and suddenly a picture of Georgie swimming naked in the plunge pool came to his mind. He forced himself to rise and stride briskly back to the Court and his newspaper.

The three girls went down to the bathhouse shortly before two, carrying towels and robes. Emmaline was still not certain she would enjoy the pool as much as the others said she would, and hung back as if reluctant.

"Come on, Emmie, do!" Georgie said, running up the marble steps. They entered the small pillared building to find an empty foyer with a changing room on either side.

Connie began to undress at once. "I can hardly wait to try the water," she said, pinning up her long blond hair on top of her head. "It does seem hard to believe that these baths were built mainly for medicinal reasons, does it not? I cannot conceive anything more refreshing on a warm day."

Georgie helped Emmie with the buttons down the back of her gown. "But imagine a cold plunge in January— to do that, you would have to believe it was good for your health."

"At one time, Emmie," Connie continued, "people thought the baths cured headaches and strengthened the constitution. I have even heard they are considered good for impotence."

"Impotence?" Emmie asked, her eyes wide. "What's that?"

"Nothing that you will ever have to worry about catching, Emmie, for fortunately only gentlemen are afflicted with it," Georgie said, shaking her head at a laughing Connie, who was unlacing her sandals. She noticed that although she and Connie both undressed to their lawn shifts, Emmaline donned a bathing costume, complete with long stockings and a mobcap to protect her hair, and she could see the girl was embarrassed by their almost nude state. She made no mention of it as they collected their towels and went back to the foyer and then down a short winding flight of stairs to the pool. This was oval-shaped, as was the marble room containing it, with one large window set high up near the roof for privacy. Connie dropped her towel and robe and ran lightly down the steps to dip one foot into the water.

"I warn you, it is cold," she said as she continued down into the water until it covered her up to her neck and her shift molded itself against her body. "But it feels wonderful. Do come in and see for yourselves."

Georgie followed her, leaving Emmaline to stand indecisively at the top of the steps, staring at the others. She thought Lady Spalding had much the nicer figure, with her little waist and high, round bosom, for Connie was lean and built almost like a boy. Why, she has no shape to speak of, Emmaline thought, and emboldened by her own abundant figure, which she was sure Miss Wilson must be envying, she dropped her towel and crept down the steps.

Georgie barely tested the water before she jumped in, splashing Emmie and causing her to cringe against the side of the steps. "Come in, Emmie," she called as she surfaced, her hair floating behind her. "It is marvelous."

She stroked her way across the pool to the patch of sunlight, and floated on her back near Miss Wilson. They began to talk of other things, and at last overcoming her fear, Emmie joined them, squealing a little when the cold water touched her skin.

For several minutes Connie and Georgie swam back and forth, although Emmie was careful to remain near the steps, where it was shallow. She soon became cold, and when she climbed out of the water, saw that her bathing costume was no protection now, for it clung to her body in revealing folds. Her face turned crimson as she grabbed up her towel and ran to the dressing room.

"Mama is waiting for me, I must leave you!" she called over her shoulder as she fled.

"I do not think I was ever as young as that," Connie remarked. "But perhaps having seven brothers is a sure cure for missishness."

"Poor child," Georgie said, treading water. "I fear we have shocked her with our immodesty."

"But that is so silly," Connie replied. "We all have the same equipment, after all, just in different sizes and shapes. Not that I would not like to have some of Miss Waring's plumpness, for I am sure Albert would prefer it."

Her forehead was puckered in a frown, and Georgie laughed at her and splashed her with a few drops of water.

"Now you are being silly, my dear, for you have an elegant figure, as lean as a racehorse and just as beautiful. Besides, no one looks better in clothes. I am sure your Albert wants you just the way you are."

Connie grinned at her as she swam to the side of the pool. "I do hope so, my friend. Anyway, we plan to have half a dozen children, and by the time the sixth one comes along, I'll probably be as fat as a flawn. At the moment, however, this racehorse has had enough cold water. Are you ready to come out?"

Georgie floated on her back so she could see the piece of sky through the high window. "Not just yet, Connie. I will join you in a little while. This feels so good after that very testing ride Freddie took me on this morning."

Connie hesitated at the top of the stairs, but then she remembered that David Linwood was riding the boundaries of the estate with the Marquess' agent this afternoon, and she knew instinctively that her friend wanted to be alone, so she went on to the dressing room to rub herself dry and to dress. When she was ready to leave, she called back down to the pool, "I'm off, Georgie! Take care, now."

"I will see you shortly, Connie," Georgie replied, and then she heard the door close above her. She closed her eyes as she drifted in the water, only moving her hands and feet enough to keep afloat. It was so good to be alone, to be able to enjoy the cool water and the solitude, and since everyone knew they were using the pool, she was sure she would not be disturbed.

The Earl saw Miss Waring and then Connie come back to the Court from where he stood at the library window, and he wondered what had happened to Lady Spalding. Without thinking further, he went out the French doors and down a side path to the bathhouse. As he opened the door, he told himself he had come because he wanted to be sure she was all right. It was dangerous to swim alone, and the plunge pool was eight feet deep. What if she got a cramp? No one would hear her call.

He reached the top of the steps and, looking down, drew in his breath sharply. He had been sure she would be wearing some sort of bathing costume, but directly below him, facing in the opposite direction, Lady Spalding was floating in the pale green water, her body in the clinging, transparent shift displayed as if for his eyes alone. He could easily see her pink-nippled breasts, so round and perfect above her small waist, and the gentle curves of her hips, as well as the mound covered by a triangle of chestnut hair between her long, slim legs.

"Is that you, Connie?" she called, as if she knew she was being watched. "Did you forget something?"

Suddenly she turned and stared straight up the steps to see the Earl leaning over the railing observing her.

"Robert!" she exclaimed. "What are you doing here, m'lord? You knew we were bathing this afternoon!" She swam to the side of the pool as if to hide herself, but the water was so clear that there was no escape that way, and the Earl was able to enjoy yet another view of the lady, for her wet, flimsy shift was no protection at all.

He came down the steps and picked up her towel. "I was concerned for you, for it is dangerous to swim alone. Besides, what if my dear *cousin* took it into his head to come in on you, almost . . . er, naked, as you are?" He spoke as calmly as he could, although his breath was coming unevenly. When he had seen her coming out of the lake in her wet dress, and later in her nightgown when he threw back the covers to force her to get up, he had been aroused by the beauty of her body, but both those times she had at least been semiclothed. Today she might just as well have been naked, for the fine wet lawn of her shift did not hide her any more than the veiling on one of her bonnets would hide her face. He could even see a small mole high on her left leg. Steeling himself, however, he resolved to do nothing to embarrass her, for he was at fault here, coming in on her as he had, and so he held out her towel and said, "Have you had enough? I see I am destined to be a bath attendant, as well as a lady's maid, just like those horrid old women who drive the bathing carts into the sea at Brighton."

In spite of his casual words and indifferent tone of voice, Georgie was embarrassed, but since she knew the water was no protection, she hurried up the steps to reach for her towel, only to find he insisted on wrapping it around her himself. She noticed his grey eyes were blazing with a dangerous light, and hurried into speech.

"You are very bold, m'lord!" she said, feeling a little less exposed now that the large towel was covering her body. "I do not think I have ever stayed in a house where gentlemen wander in and out of your room, throw you out of bed and threaten to dress you, and surprise you in your bath as well! Surely Cousin Bertie is not the only eccentric Holland, and it is too bad of you!"

Her words died away and she tried to smile, but there was no answering smile on the Earl's handsome face. They stared at each other for a long moment, and then, as if he could not help himself, he reached out and took her towel away before he folded her in his arms and whispered, "You are a witch—a lovely water-witch!"

Georgie looked up into his face, her heart beating rapidly as he bent his head and kissed her.

He was not gentle, but his compelling force was completely unlike the American's practiced skill. Georgie found herself returning his kisses, at first tentatively and then without reserve, and she realized that she was surrendering to him in a way that she had fought against with David Linwood. She wondered if she were becoming abandoned and immoral, but then she realized the truth. In spite of all her protestations to the contrary, she had fallen in love with Robert Holland. Now his hands caressed her back and her hips, drawing her closer to him still, and she moaned a little against his mouth.

Finally Robert raised his head and stared down at her again, her green eyes hidden by her lashes, and her soft mouth half open and trembling. "You are so very beautiful," he whispered. "Forgive me, but I could not resist the temptation."

Georgie did not know what to reply. Her legs felt weak, as if they would not hold her up if he took his arms away, and she realized that she wanted him to go on kissing her, to carry her up the steps, to . . . The earl just touched her full lower lip with his mouth, and then, holding her to him with one strong arm, he reached out with his other hand and began to unbutton her shift.

"I cannot imagine why you and Miss Wilson left Lady Spalding here alone, Emmie!" Teddy Waring's deep bass voice boomed just outside the bathhouse. "She might be in danger of drowning! It was the height of imprudence, and I shall not rest until I know that she is safe!"

Georgie's mouth fell open and she stared at the Earl in horror.

"Damn the man!" he whispered, and after one quick glance showed there was no place to hide in the pool room, he hurried her up the stairs. "Quick, Georgie! Go into the dressing room, and I will hide in the other one until you have both gone. I would not ruin your reputation."

"What reputation can I have left, m'lord?" Georgie asked, a little bitterly, all thoughts of love gone from her mind, but she did what he told her, and when Emmaline came into the building and called to her, she was able to say in a normal voice, "Is that you, Emmie? Be a dear and help me, would you? These buttons are impossible."

From where he was pressed against the nearer wall, the Earl could hear them both clearly as they chatted while Georgie dried herself and dressed, then wrapped another towel around her wet hair.

"Please forgive me, Georgie," Miss Waring said. "Teddy is so angry that I went off and left you alone. He is waiting to escort you back to the Court. But after all, Miss Wilson was with you . . . Oh, isn't she funny, Georgie? She has no bottom or bosom, in fact, no shape at all!"

"I do not wish to discuss it, Emmie," Georgie replied, aware the Earl was listening.

"Well, I have never seen any almost naked women before this afternoon," Emmie persisted, "and I never realized they could be so different. Now, Miss Wilson is too thin, and I'm too fat, but you're perfect. No wonder Teddy is mad for you and that the Marquess wants you to marry into the family, and I'd be willing to wager that the Earl and David think your figure is perfect too."

"Hand me that sandal, will you, my dear?" Georgie interrupted this hymn of praise. "Do you like this shade of blue, Emmie? I thought it a little too vivid after I purchased it." Without waiting for an answer she continued, "Come, I'm ready now, and we must not keep Teddy waiting any longer."

The Earl heard them leave and the outer door close, but he remained where he was, leaning against the wall and chuckling for a moment at the innocent conversation he had just listened to with such enjoyment. But then his eyes narrowed as he remembered Georgie's kiss, and how she had felt in his arms, wet and slippery and warm, with only that flimsy shift between them. If Teddy Waring had not come along, he knew what would have happened. He wondered why he felt so uneasy about it now, and why he was almost relieved that it had not happened. In London he had promised himself the pleasure of an affair with the lady, so why, when he was so close to achieving this goal, did he have the feeling that he did not want her that way, so casually, as if she were just any beautiful woman who had captured his fancy. It was very confusing and not at all his customary response.

He was not the only one who was confused. Georgie spent the remainder of the afternoon in her room, pretending to read a book, although she stared with unseeing eyes at the pages before her.

She admitted she had been attracted to David Linwood in the beginning, and even in her fear of him she had felt a stirring of answering desire. Yet here was the Earl raising even stronger feelings in her breast, feelings she knew she must call love. He did not frighten her like David did, and she wanted to believe he would never hurt her, even though she also knew that if Teddy had not come along, Robert would have taken her right there in the bathhouse. She had seen the desire in his eyes, but she had not seen any answering gleam of love for her. Obviously, David was right. Robert Holland had no more intention of marrying her than he did. She was a widow, and therefore fair game, and the way he had treated her showed he had no respect for her and thought her only another light woman who would welcome a dalliance for a brief period before she faded out of his life.

Georgie got up to pace the bedroom. She knew she was not loose or casual, and she had more than her share of moral standards, although they appeared to be crumbling away at a rapid rate during her stay at Carew Court. Of course the Earl was certain to think her wanton after the way she had responded to his embrace. And her near-nakedness, too, and the fact that she had not screamed or fainted or had a spell, which surely a good woman would have done. She had the sudden and irrelevant thought that the Earl had seen more of her already than her young husband ever had, visiting her only in the dark, and she blushed a little.

That evening she was very subdued, so quiet in fact that Cousin Bertie was quick to notice. "I do hope you are not sickening with something, my dear Georgie," he said with a little frown. "The plunge pool is supposed to be refreshing and invigorating."

"I am sure Georgie found it most stimulating, Bertie," the Earl interposed, trying to spare her an answer. As he saw her colour rise a little at his words, he cursed himself and added, "Perhaps she is tired. This warm weather, the ride I know she took with Freddie this morning, and her swim this afternoon—she has had a busy day!"

He closed his mouth abruptly. No matter what he said, she could take it in a way he did not intend.

Bertie's little brown eyes darted from the Earl's face and then back to Georgie's, and he smiled. "Or perhaps she is quiet because she is making up her mind which one of my nephies she will marry?" he asked, waving his wineglass at his butler.

"Bertie!" Lady Martin scolded in a long-suffering voice, knowing he would not attend to her at all.

The Earl turned aside to ask Miss Waring how she had enjoyed the pool, and in doing so he missed the level look that David gave him. Georgie also felt his eyes on her, and when she looked up, it was to find his dark face harsh and serious, his eyes probing her face as if he would look into her mind. She stared back as levelly as she could, but she was the first to lower her eyes.

Lord Waring cleared his throat and began to speak in his booming bass. "I must beg an immediate interview with you, m'lord, for I cannot in good conscience remain silent any longer, and I know that if you will allow me but a short time, I can make all clear, and although I am sorry to have to bring this matter to your attention, your words leave me no choice, for—"

"Amazin', ain't it, how the boy can carry on with never a pause or a period?" Bertie interrupted. "Cut line, Teddy. Glad to give you all the time you need, as long as you promise not to prose on and on about my darling Lavvy and me."

"Sir!" Lord Waring said, his face turning red. "I beg of you! We are in company. The ladies!"

Cousin Bertie twinkled at him but he said no more, and dinner continued with no more contretemps, for Miss Hersham and Lady Martin began to discuss the current London Season.

Only David Linwood rejoined the ladies in the Great Parlour, and he came purposely to Georgie's side. She looked around, but her aunt was talking to Lady Waring, and Connie and Lady Martin had their heads together as well. Of Teddy and Cousin Bertie there was no sign, and she had heard Freddie challenging the Earl to a game of billiards at dinner.

"So, my dear *belle*, now perhaps you will tell me what happened this afternoon at the plunge pool?" he asked, his voice quiet but nonetheless compelling for that.

"What do you mean, sir?" Georgie asked, keeping her eyes steady on his face. "And I should like to ask what business is it of yours? I do not have to account to you for my actions."

"*Belle!*" he replied, shaking a finger at her. "Do not provoke me or try to change the subject. Even a ninny-hammer could see that somethin' happened, somethin' that involved the Earl and your lovely self. I see I shall have to keep you away from the Rappahannock when we get back to Virginia, for when you are allowed to be in close proximity to bodies of water, the results tend to be provocative. Did the Earl find you there— alone? Did he try to make love to you?"

Georgie's heart was beating faster now, but still she tried to act normally, and she raised her eyebrows at his bold words.

Mr. Linwood leaned closer, his blue eyes narrowed in anger. "Did he succeed?"

He reached out and grasped her arm, and Georgie tried to shake it off. "Take your hands off me," she hissed. "Here, at least, I am safe from any such attentions."

"Your pardon, *belle*," David said in a deceptive mild voice. "I was overcome by the thought of you in another man's arms, for that I *will* not tolerate."

"You do not own me," Georgie was quick to reply.

"Not yet, that is true. But no one must touch you but myself, do you hear? I would not hesitate to kill the man who did." His voice was flat and his southern drawl even more pronounced than usual, but Georgie shivered at those cold words, even as she rose.

"Excuse me, sir. I do not care to continue this conversation, for it is not only absurd but also insulting."

She turned to leave him as he got to his feet leisurely and said, "Take care, *belle*! His blood would be on your head, for what I said was no idle threat. I have killed many times before this, and for less reason."

Georgie pretended she had not heard him as she made her way to Emmie's side. The girl had not taken her eyes from David since he came into the room, and she wished she could tell her that he was not only a rapist, but a confessed killer besides. Perhaps she should give the hint to Teddy? Just then he entered the room in the wake of the Marquess, and it was apparent that his interview had not gone well.

Cousin Bertie was chortling with glee, and smiling and shaking his head, while Teddy was looking extremely angry and discomforted. He came to her side and was brusque as he ordered his sister to take herself elsewhere, for he wished to be private with dear Lady Spalding. Emmie moved away to the sofa where Mr. Linwood was still seated watching the others.

"I am glad that you and I are not even distantly related to that terrible old man," he began, his colour high. "It is impossible to talk to him in a rational manner, for he refuses to hear anything that does not agree with his own conception of reality. I assure you, my dear Lady Spalding, I feel for you especially, placed in this awkward situation, but I can also assure you, all will be well. We must stand firm and not waver, and we shall win through."

He nodded his head as Georgie replied, "I will not pretend to misunderstand you, m'lord, but believe me when I say that you presume too much, on too little authority. I have told you over and over that I do not care to marry again, and yet you continue to think it is only womanly modesty that makes me say so. You are wrong. I mean what I say."

Lord Waring stared at her for a moment, and Georgie thought she saw a tiny flicker of doubt in his eyes for the first time, but then he said, "My dear lady, you must allow me to know your mind better than you do yourself. I do understand why you speak as you do, but it is not in my power to make all clear to you at this time. You must be patient."

Georgie was furious, for she felt he was being deliberately obtuse, and she rose and curtsied. "Please excuse me, m'lord. I have the headache and would retire."

He bounded to his feet and took her arm. "Of course you do. In this company, how could you not be constantly unwell? I myself do not feel my usual degree of cheerful confidence. I look forward to the day we can leave, for I see that you do not find the air at Carew Court any more salubrious than I do. Now I will take you to your aunt so you might make your good-nights, and then I will escort you to your room."

Georgie opened her mouth to deny him, but when she saw Mr. Linwood rising and looking her way, she decided to accept Teddy's escort, for with him she would be safe, albeit bored and in danger of incurring a real headache.

She overslept the next morning, and when she went to the breakfast room and found Connie there alone, she was not sorry. After they had eaten as much of the lavish buffet spread for the guests as they wanted, and had had a comfortable coze over the coffee cups, Connie suggested a game of croquet.

"I am sure we will both be better off for it, my dear, if you have no plans to ride this morning. All those biscuits and honey. The coddled eggs, sausage, and bacon. And neither one of us should have succumbed to the strawberries or the blueberry conserve, either."

Georgie laughed and agreed, and arm in arm the two friends made their way to the croquet field. The head gardener had done a wonderful job, for the short grass was as smooth as velvet. He had set up the wires and posts for them, and in a short time they were enjoying a spirited game. Connie won the first handily, but was swiftly routed by Georgie in the second, and they had just commenced a third and deciding game when Robert and Freddie came along.

Georgie hoped the Earl would not put her off her stroke. She had not spoken to him alone since their meeting at the pool, but she had been very conscious of him at dinner the evening before. Freddie called impartial encouragement to both ladies, while the Earl lounged in a lawn chair to watch, his eyes never leaving Georgie's face, which glowed in the sunshine under her wide-brimmed straw hat. She was wearing a soft morning gown of sea-green muslin trimmed with matching ribbons, and in the gentle breeze it swayed with her movements. He found himself remembering how she had looked in the plunge pool the day before, and was glad when Cousin Bertie came out with Lady Waring on his arm, so he could rise to welcome them. They were closely followed by Lord Waring and his sister, for

Teddy was more determined than ever to chaperon his mother's every move until the happy day they left Carew Court.

There was no sound but the hum of the bees busy in the flower gardens, the cooing of the doves in the cote nearby, and the songs of the wild birds from the home woods. Suddenly there was an abrupt and alien interruption to the quiet country morning—the sharp, loud report of a gun. Georgina froze in horror, wondering for a moment what it was, and then she ran to Connie, who had bent down to retie her sandal string while waiting for her turn to play. Connie's face was white and frightened, and Georgie was glad to see the Earl hurrying towards them. Without speaking, Connie pointed to the beech tree just beyond where she was standing. There was a fresh scar in the bark that showed the path the bullet had taken.

The Earl put an arm around both ladies and drew them back to where the others were waiting in some agitation, his eyes busy all the while searching the windows of the Court. Not a curtain fluttered, nor was there any movement there that he could see on the entire East Front.

"I say!" Lord Waring exclaimed. "That was a near thing! A poacher, do you think, m'lord?"

Freddie Wilson, who had put his arms around his shivering sister, looked up, and would have spoken, had he not caught Robert's eye.

"It is possible, of course," the Earl said smoothly. "May I suggest you have the keepers out, Bertie? We cannot have the ladies frightened this way."

The Marquess' little eyes were popping, and he looked very much as if he had something he wished to say, but one glance at his nephew's stern, angry face deterred him.

"Of course, at once, my boy. Come, everyone. Perhaps it would be better to quit this location until the men have had a chance to look around. I am so sorry that such a thing should have happened to you, Connie, my dear girl."

Connie tried to make light of it, but Georgie saw her face was still pale and strained, and when she looked to the Earl, she was shocked, for she had never seen him look so coldly furious. He seemed like a loaded duelling pistol himself, one so finely tuned that a single jar would fire the hair trigger.

As the party came around the North Front, they saw

David Linwood standing beside Bodkins, the head groom. He seemed a little surprised at the size of the group, as his eyes went from one to the other.

"You have been here some time, sir?" the Earl asked in a dangerous voice.

"As you say, *cousin*," the American replied. "Was there some particular reason for your question?"

"Now, now, boys," the Marquess interrupted. "Davey, Connie has just been frightened by an errant bullet from some poacher, and Robby was just trying to discover if perhaps you noticed anything unusual. Bodkins, did anyone come this way?"

The head groom shook his head. "Not for the last half-hour, m'lord," he said, doffing his cap. "Mr. Linwood and I have been walking his horse all that time, for he felt the animal favoured his left hock while out riding yesterday. Perhaps there was someone, but we did not notice him, sir, for to be truthful, our attention was all on the horse."

The Marquess nodded and looked relieved, and Georgie saw that the Earl appeared very thoughtful as he ushered them all before him into the Great Hall. Everyone was talking at once: Emmie and her mother exclaiming, Teddy pontificating on the evils of poachers, and Freddie and Georgie soothing Connie. The Marquess took them all to his library and called for Jenks to bring some wine. It was not long before Lady Martin and Miss Hersham had been informed of the near-miss, and they joined the others to beg for information and exclaim over the unusual incident. The Earl drank his wine without speaking, and then, with a jerk of his head summoning Freddie to follow him, he left the room.

10

The Earl stopped in the Great Hall and spent several minutes talking to the butler, who nodded his head and promised to start his investigations immediately, and then he left the Court again, Freddie close on his heels. David Linwood and the head groom had disappeared, and Robert frowned, his eyes narrowed in thought as he stared at the empty drive. "I would not have had this happen for the world, my friend," he said as they went down the front steps and turned towards the croquet court.

"I know, Robert, I know. But Connie was not hurt, thank God, and she's a sensible thing, not given to faints or hysterics. But why was the shot fired at her? And don't tell *me* any silly tales about poachers, man! At this hour? On the lawn within sight of the Court? Bah!"

"Of course it was no poacher, Freddie. I agreed with Teddy Waring only to calm the others."

They walked down the lawn until they reached the beech tree, and the Earl put his hand over the hole the bullet had torn in the bark before he turned and stared up the slight rise to the mansion.

"It had to have been fired from one of the upper floors of the Court. Observe the path it took, and the angle it entered the tree. It could not have come from the woods or the gardens. But why Connie?"

They looked at each other in silence, and then Freddie turned to stare at the bullet hole again, his fair-complexioned face frowning.

"See here, Robert! The bullet entered the tree over six feet from the ground. It was not fired to injure her, for even if she had not stooped at just that moment, it would still have passed harmlessly over her head. Con's tall, but she's not that tall."

The Earl's expression lightened a little. "You're right. I was about to insist that you and Con leave today, for I would not put her into further danger, but perhaps it will not be necessary." He touched the bullet hole again and mused, "We can assume, then, unless a terrible marksman fired the shot, that he just meant to frighten her. But why? Who among us has any reason for doing that, and what purpose would it serve?"

Freddie kicked at a tuft of grass with the toe of his polished boot. "Perhaps he was hoping she might take it into her head to leave the house party? Most women would be packing their portmanteaus and calling for their coaches as soon as they could do without their vinaigrettes and hartshorn."

The two friends stared at each other in silence, each knowing the other's thoughts.

"You have no proof, Robert, no proof at all," Freddie said finally. "Besides, he was with Bodkins all the time, and you know your cousin's head groom could never be bribed by Mr. Linwood, for everyone knows the servants are all most firmly on your side in this struggle for the inheritance. We must rule the dangerous Mr. Linwood out."

"What you say is true," the Earl admitted, staring down to the sunlit woods, his expression somber as the slight breeze ruffled his black hair, "although regrettable! How neat and tidy and satisfying it would be if it were he. And yet . . ."

He appeared lost in thought, and Freddie picked up one of the croquet mallets the girls had dropped and sent his sister's ball through the nearest wicket.

At length the Earl sighed and recalled himself to his surroundings. By this time Freddie was lining up the shot that would see the ball home and win his imaginary game, and the Earl strolled to meet him, his eyes once again going over the East Front.

"Game!" Freddie exclaimed.

"You are very nonchalant, my friend, to be playing here so casually. Come away," the Earl remarked, taking Freddie's arm to stroll down to the lake. Going back to the discussion they had been having, he said, "I agree with you that the bullet was fired to frighten Connie and no other. Perhaps Jenks will be able to find out where all the servants were in the Court at the time, although Bertie keeps such a crowd of them, I think it unlikely. For the time being, I suggest Con stay indoors, for although I do not think the incident will be repeated, it is better to be on the safe side."

Freddie agreed, and after going over all the ramifications of the morning's events, and still coming to no satisfactory conclusion, he changed the subject to other topics. Robert followed his lead, but he was still preoccupied and taut with anger. After one sideways glance at his face, Freddie was glad there was no possibility that he would ever be an enemy of Robert Holland's.

Of course the keepers found no trace of poachers, as Bertie reported to the others as they took their seats at the dinner table.

"I have been to see the bullet hole," David Linwood drawled. "It could not have been fired by a poacher, cousin, unless he was poachin' inside the Court." He grinned his wolfish grin and stared at Georgie, adding, "Of course there are poachers and poachers, and not all of them are after an easy rabbit for the pot."

There was a moment of silence, and then Connie said in a firm voice, "Do let us stop talking about it. It is becoming a dead bore, and if I am determined to forget it and put it behind me, then so must you all. Cousin Bertie, I am most anxious to inspect your brass rubbings while I am here. Georgie was telling me about your visit to Grantley Castle, and the process sounds fascinating."

Conversation became general then, although Georgie wondered why she was feeling so low this evening. She chatted with Freddie Wilson, ignored David's knowing glances, and told Emmie her gown of deep rose was vastly becoming, but all the while her thoughts were on the Earl. She knew he was upset that Connie had been frightened, even though the shot had just been a warning, but since that was the case, why was he ignoring her this way? She had not spoken to him alone since they had been together at the plunge pool, and that evening, even though she had dressed carefully in one of her prettiest gowns, he paid her no more attention than he did Miss Hersham, perhaps even less, for she saw him talking to her aunt at some length.

Later, when Georgie addressed a remark to him, he did not even hear her, and looked right through her until Freddie brought his attention back to the company with a jesting remark.

Georgie felt a little ache under her heart, for she was sure she knew the reason Robert was so distant. He was not averse to an affair, if all the dibs were in tune, but he did not want her enough to put himself to any trouble over it. If she were available, he would oblige her; otherwise she was not worth the trouble of seeking out, even to continue what they had begun in the bathhouse. It was a lowering thought, but having come to this conclusion, Georgie was determined he would never know how she felt.

David Linwood was pleased to see her sudden coolness to the Earl, and decided to try his luck one more time with the lady. Perhaps he had been a mite too rash in his approach? These highborn Englishwomen had to be wooed to be won, and after all, Lady Spalding was no little tavern wench to be tumbled into bed within five minutes of meeting. As well as the Earl, he too became lost in his thoughts after the ladies quit the Dining Chamber, and the Marquess did not hesitate to call both his nephews to order for their wool-gathering.

"See here, you two, pay attention. Poor Freddie and I are having enough trouble trying to talk to Teddy here while you two moon about like two halflings. Not that we have to think very hard to guess what they are imagining, eh, Freddie?"

He dug the Earl in the ribs and chortled at David. "The glorious and gorgeous Georgina, of course!"

Robert quirked an eyebrow at his obstreperous relative as Lord Waring shook his head in despair. "My apologies, Cousin Bertie. In this case, however, you are wrong. I had a very interesting letter from town this afternoon, and I am most anxious to receive a reply to one I sent a few days ago as well, which accounts for my preoccupation."

He was not looking at David as he spoke, but Freddie Wilson saw the way the American leaned forward in his chair, and how his strong fingers tightened on the stem of his glass.

After the men rose to go and join the ladies, David paused to have a few words with the Marquess. The Earl saw him bending over the little man and talking to him in a quick, earnest voice, gesticulating all the while, and he also saw Bertie nodding and chuckling and obviously agreeing with the American's request. Freddie called to him just then, and he turned away, still wondering what that had been all about.

Neither Bertie nor David came back to the Great Parlour, and Georgie was about to join a table for cards when Jenks came and told her that the Marquess wished her to join him in the library for a few minutes. Georgie looked up in surprise and saw Teddy's angry red face. She felt like laughing at his obvious indignation that Cousin Bertie might be planning to get up to his tricks with her too, or coerce her into naming his heir, as she excused herself from the card game and followed Jenks. He opened the door of the library and bowed, and Georgie smiled as she walked in.

But there was no Cousin Bertie in the library, indeed there appeared to be no one there at all. She went forward a few steps and stared about her in bewilderment, and then she heard the door close behind her, and whirled to see David Linwood, his grin as white in that tanned, rugged face as his spotless cravat.

"What are you doing here? Where is the Marquess?" she demanded, determined to hold her ground this time.

"Come, *belle*, a few moments of your time is all I ask, if you please. Bertie agreed that I might see you alone, after I told him how difficult it was to speak to you without a crowd around. Come, sit down with me by the fire."

Georgie had never heard such a quiet, gentle note in his voice before, and since he did not appear to be dangerous at the moment, she nodded her head and moved to the chair he indicated. He could hardly attack her with the butler within call, after all. David took the seat across from her, and without offering her refreshment, raised his snifter of brandy in her direction in a silent toast.

"What did you want to see me about, David?" she asked, still not entirely at her ease.

"I wanted to ask you to make me Bertie's heir by agreein' to marry me," he said in a conversational tone of voice. Georgie's eyes widened as he went on, "I can see I have gone about it the wrong way, but it is a little late for me to drop to my knees before you and stun you with my polished periods and vows of worshipful devotion. That is your fault, Georgie, for you are enough to drive a man wild, and you caused me to . . . er . . . forget my manners. I beg your pardon, ma'am."

He smiled at her, but whereas once she might have been deceived by his polite words, now they put her even more on her guard. She had seen the way his eyes flashed when he looked at her, and how he had admired the low neck of her evening gown.

"We would make quite a team, you know," he added when she did not answer him immediately. "I can guarantee that your life would never be dull." He put back his head and laughed out loud for a moment, and then, still chuckling, he went on, "A number of other things, of course, but never dull! My promise on it! And you will like America; you have the spirit for it. It is a land of opportunity for those with the guts to grab it, and I am such a man, my sweet."

"But what of Carew Court?" Georgie couldn't help asking.

David swallowed the last of his brandy and went to refill his snifter. "What of it?" he asked, an insolent tone creeping into his voice. "I am not English, I am American. What care I for a mouldering old pile in this quiet countryside? Or for a worthless title? Marquess of Carew—who cares for that? Tell you what, *belle*, I'll be generous and let the Earl have it. All I need is the emeralds and gold—and your bewitching self, of course!"

"What would you do with the Holland Treasure then, David?" she asked, already suspecting his answer.

"Why, break it up and sell the emeralds separately, for the best price I can get, and melt down the gold to sell as well. With the money such a treasure would bring, we can make a fresh start in the States—anywhere we want."

He sipped his brandy as he sat down again across from her, and leaned back to stretch his powerful legs to the fire. He did not seem to care that in the presence of a lady, his whole posture was very rude. "Perhaps we will not return to Linderwood after all—in fact, I am sure we will not. I am tired of the place, and I can say truthfully I have not missed it at all during my stay in England." He smiled to himself and then added, "We will make a fresh start somewhere else, perhaps farther west."

Georgie had never heard of a man who could walk away from his home that way, as if it were of no more account than a worn-out coat. The lands his ancestors had cleared and settled and worked so hard to bring to successful fruition, perhaps even died for—how was it possible for him to be so careless of such an inheritance? She was still pondering this strange attitude when he asked, "Well, Georgie, are you game?"

She looked up at him and felt a moment's regret. The firelight was playing over that sharp, craggy face with its knowing grin, and the light that blazed in his blue eyes was pure deviltry. His brown hair was slightly disarranged, and a few locks fell over his dark forehead, making him look very impetuous and reckless. She knew he was a man she would never forget, but she also knew she did not love him. Even now, when he had made himself agreeable and easy, she did not trust him, and she had no desire to marry him.

She remembered too that for all his gentlemanly words tonight, he had not once said he loved her, and she knew she had made the right decision. David Linwood was not capable of love—not for his home, his country, or another human being.

She rose to her feet and stared down at him where he sprawled in his chair, still grinning lazily at her, sure of her answer, and she felt a little spark of fear again. The words of refusal she had been about to speak died on her lips.

"I cannot say, just like that, David," she murmured instead. "You must give me time to think, for it is such an important decision. To leave my country, my home . . ."

"Oh, you ladies," he drawled. "Very well, sweetheart, you shall have your thinkin' time, but as you are well aware, I am not the most patient of men. I will give you until tomorrow night at this time, and then I will expect your answer. You know the only answer I want to hear, don't you, *belle*?"

He stood up then and stretched before he came towards her. Georgie stood very still and steeled herself, but he only bowed and raised her hand to his hard lips to kiss it softly, as if he mocked society's rules but would abide by them—for now.

"Tomorrow night will be time enough for kissin', my

dear, among other things!" He laughed, and tucking her hand in his arm, walked with her to the door. "You have seen enough of me to realize how impatient that side of me is as well. There will be no need for you to speak. Just give me the key to your room and I will have my answer."

He chuckled again as he opened the door to the library, and Georgie was relieved to see Jenks waiting there to escort her back to the Great Parlour. She had not been alone then after all with David, for in spite of Bertie's carelessness, he had seen she was protected.

As she rejoined the others and went to sit beside her aunt before Teddy could come over and demand to know what she had been doing, she was deep in thought. What words, what excuse, could she use to say no? He would be furious, and she was not even sure he would not try to hurt her if she dared to refuse him. Should she insist that her aunt and the Marquess be present? It would be unusual, but she did not think that even Jenks on guard would deter him when he heard her decline the honour of becoming his wife. She did not hear Miss Hersham's whispered questions or see Teddy's red face, and she also missed the speculative look the Earl gave her from where he sat facing her at the card table. He had noted the American's absence, as well as his cousin's, and suspected the meeting that had just taken place. Since the lady looked so grave and thoughtful, and since she had returned to the Parlour alone, he surmised she had not accepted Linwood's suit, and he was surprised at the feeling of relief and happiness that he felt. Connie exchanged a triumphant glance with her brother, and they both smiled, leading Lady Martin to imagine there was hardly any need to play out this hand, since they appeared to hold all the cards.

Late the following morning, a travelling chaise arrived at Carew Court, and a middle-aged man got down, tossing the reins to one of the grooms who had come running to hold his horse. He was a man of medium height, quietly dressed in brown, and as he climbed the steps, he looked about him with interest, his lips pursed in a whistle of astonishment for the grandeur he was facing.

He did not appear to be intimidated by it, however, for he gave his name and his card to Jenks with a careless air of assurance, saying he was sure the Earl would receive him. The butler bowed and ushered him into the small gold

salon at the side of the Great Hall, and offered him refreshments while he waited for the Earl to be summoned.
The gentleman accepted a glass of Madeira, and strolled
about inspecting the salon until Robert Holland appeared a
few minutes later.

"Mr. Fredericks!" he said, coming in with his hand extended. "Now, this I had not hoped for, that you would
come all the way from London yourself in response to my
letter! Let me introduce myself—Robert Holland, Earl of
Amesbury."

"Joshua Fredericks of Virginia, at your service, suh,"
the older man replied with a twinkle in his eye. "Your
letter was mighty intriguin' and I felt it best to come and
see for myself. You see, suh, I happen to know that my
good friend David Linwood of Linderwood Plantation is
safe at home in Virginia, for I left him there only a few
weeks ago. And since he was so ill at the time, I find it
hard to believe he could recover in time to take a faster
ship than mine, especially since you wrote that your Mr.
Linwood has been in England for some weeks. Quite a
mystery, don't you agree, suh?"

The Earl agreed and begged his visitor to be seated.
There was no exchange of pleasantries or discussion of the
weather and Mr. Frederick's journey, for Robert was too
elated at the man's news, and the Virginian had no objection to getting right to the point of his visit.

"What does this man who calls himself Linwood look
like?" he asked next.

"He is very tall and has a heavy, muscular build, with
brown hair, bright blue eyes, and a deep tan," Robert
replied. "A hawkish man to look at, who gives the impression of barely leashed power and a great deal of restless
energy. I would put his age at about thirty—perhaps a
little more or less."

Mr. Fredericks held up both his hands. "Then I know
who he is, indeed, I suspected as soon as I received your
letter, which is one of the reasons I came to you so promptly. I would very much like to see this impostor exposed,
suh!"

The American's face had reddened with anger and he
paused for a moment before he continued. "The man you
have here at Carew Court is Bartholomew Forrest. He
was Mr. Linwood's overseer, but he left the plantation

under a cloud some time ago. I heard he had left the country and gone to Jamaica, which would account for his dark tan. No one had any idea he meant to try to impersonate David. That gentleman is my age and slightly built with grey hair, you see—not at all like your Mr. Linwood."

"Perhaps if you could observe him when he was not aware of it?" the Earl asked. "I would like to be sure I am on firm ground before I accuse him."

"Of course," the American agreed, and after several more minutes of discussion Mr. Fredericks was handed over into Jenks's care, and taken to a bedroom on the North Front side of the Court, where Robert promised to parade "Mr. Linwood" sometime that afternoon. He begged his guest to make himself comfortable, ordered him some luncheon, and took himself off to find his rival, feeling better than he had for weeks.

As the Earl regained the Great Hall, he ran into Connie and Georgie coming out of the Marquess' library, where they had spent the morning, each immersed in a book. He smiled and bowed and was as polite as ever, but Georgie noticed his air of suppressed excitement and the speed with which he took his leave of them, and her heart sank. She had spent another restless night wondering how she was to deal with David Linwood, and in spite of her good intentions, had thought an equal amount of time of the Earl as well. And here he was, barely taking time to be civil before he turned away from her and disappeared. She sniffed and put up her chin, and Connie remarked, "My, Robert has something of vast importance on his mind today, doesn't he? I wonder if he has discovered some clue to the identity of the man who fired at me? I have never seen him so remiss in his manners as he was just then."

"I am sure I do not know," Georgie said airily, quite as if she was sure she did not care as well. "It is certainly no concern of *mine* how he behaves."

"Well, *men*, you know, Georgie," Connie said in gentle reproof for her careless words. "They can be so exasperating at times, but as Albert has pointed out, so can the fairer sex. We must make allowances until we discover the reason."

Georgie sniffed again, and went away to change her aqua morning gown for a riding habit. She and the Wilsons had made arrangements to ride to the church at Upper Littledean, where Bertie said there were several brass memorial plaques they should not miss seeing.

The ride in the fresh air and her companions' amusing conversation lifted Georgie's spirits, and when they returned later that afternoon, she had managed to put both Mr. Linwood and the Earl out of her mind. As the threesome cantered up the curving drive to the front of the Court, however, she saw David striding towards them from the stables, and the Earl coming down the steps to meet them as well, and her spirits sank.

Mr. Linwood arrived before the Earl had a chance to come and lift her from the saddle, and his hands caressed her back and he held her close to him for a moment after he set her on the ground. "Well, Georgie, have you decided to end my suspense, sweetheart?" he asked in a whisper, his eyes daring her to answer him.

Georgie shook her head and indicated the others with her crop, and David chuckled. From where the Earl was standing with Connie, it looked a very intimate exchange, and his expression darkened that this impostor should touch her after all he had learned of the man from Mr. Fredericks. Then he saw that "Linwood" was facing the North Front, so his face would be clearly visible to Mr. Fredericks in the blue bedchamber. He watched the American tuck Georgie's hand in his arm and pull her close so he could lean down and whisper again, and he also saw how she paled a little in reaction to his words, and he almost forgot his careful plan to go and tear her away from the man.

Before he could act so impulsively, Connie exclaimed, "Georgie, my dear, I think you have forgotten our appointment with Miss Hersham and Lady Martin. You remember we promised to take tea with them in the Little Parlour?"

Georgie pulled away from Mr. Linwood and came to Connie's side, trying to hide her relief at this timely intervention.

"So we did—you must excuse me, David," she said, nodding her head in dismissal as she prepared to climb the steps.

"Only for now, *belle*. I will see you this evening, when I trust you will be quicker to remember you have an appointment to keep with me."

Georgie turned at the top of the steps and stared down at his mocking face for a moment. She noticed that the Earl and Freddie were exchanging a few quiet words as the grooms led the horses away, and then she followed Connie into the Court.

"Now, my dear, I think it is time that you confide in me. What was that all about?" Connie asked quietly, stripping off her riding gloves and handing them and her crop to a waiting footman. Georgie followed suit, and then, making up her mind, she took Connie's arm and led her in the direction of the Little Parlour, where she knew her aunt and Lady Martin were often to be found at this time of day, gossiping over a cup of tea or perhaps doing needlepoint.

"Yes, it is more than time to ask your help, Con, as well as my aunt's and Lady Martin's," she admitted, feeling better immediately she made this decision. "I am at my wits' end and do not know what to do."

Connie smiled and knocked on the Parlour door. "Well, if we three cannot help you, there is no help to be had, my dear. Come, let us go in and join them, and you can tell us everything. I was beginning to think you would never confess, for I have been waiting this age to find out about Mr. Linwood, especially what he asked you last evening and how you replied."

After a fresh pot of tea was brought, and more cups, and Lady Martin had urged the girls to try the watercress sandwiches, Connie came right to the point.

"Georgie wants to ask our advice, m'lady, ma'am," she said. The others sat forward in eager anticipation and Aunt Bess straightened her cap, her anxious eyes on her niece's face. "Yes, my dear Georgie?" she prompted.

"Mr. Linwood has asked me to marry him," Georgie said baldly, with no preliminary explanations. "And I do not want to, but I do not know how to tell him so, for he can be such a dangerous man. I admit I am afraid of him, but I cannot marry him, I simply cannot."

"Oh no, never!" Miss Hersham breathed.

"It does not bear thinking about!" Lady Martin agreed.

"*Especially* not now," Connie added, causing both older ladies to stare at her. She smiled and nodded to them, and they exchanged puzzled glances, wondering what dear Miss Wilson had in her mind.

"But how am I to refuse him? He has warned me that he

will accept only one answer, and I know how violent he can be when he is angry."

She shuddered as she waited to hear their advice.

"You must tell him in *my* company, my dear," Miss Hersham said, a militant light coming into her eyes that that bold American had dared to frighten her niece.

"And perhaps I should be there as well," Lady Martin added. "There's safety in numbers, you know, and never fear, Georgie, *we'll* deal with him."

Connie had a vision of the three of them advancing to meet Mr. Linwood in perfect step, her tall friend flanked by the two little grey-haired ladies, and wished she might be there to see his expression, even as she suggested, "Would it not be simpler to tell Cousin Bertie you have no desire for the gentleman's hand, and let him deal with it? I realize it is not customary to refuse an offer via another, but in this case . . ."

Georgie frowned. "But then Cousin Bertie will assume I have refused David because I really want to accept Robert's offer." She essayed a tiny, brittle laugh. "I can assure you that is not the case. Far, far from it, in fact! Even if he did offer, which I have to tell you he has not, I would refuse him."

She turned her head to stare out at the gardens, and with only her elegant profile in view, she did not hear Miss Hersham's soft moan, or notice Lady Martin's disappointed frown, nor did she see Connie's eyes brimming with amusement.

"Of course you would refuse, my dear," this lady agreed in a soothing voice. "He is such an arrogant man, so careless and unaccommodating. I fear Robert is destined to end his days as a bachelor, like the Marquess, if he does not mend his ways, for who would have him?"

The other three ladies sat in silence for a moment, running over a large list of candidates known to be eager for the position, and then Miss Hersham asked, trying to hide the chagrin in her voice that she felt on learning the Earl's suit had not prospered, "When were you supposed to give Mr. Linwood your answer, Georgie?"

"After dinner this evening," Georgie said, sipping her tea, her eyes dark and worried.

"Very well," Aunt Bess said as she folded her tapestry and put it away. "You and I and Lady Martin shall all of us join the gentleman in the library after dinner. We will insist that Jenks remain within call, and the door be left ajar."

"That's a good plan, Bess," Lady Martin agreed. "Being a foreigner, he probably won't know it is unusual, and will take it as common practice."

Connie thought he would rather think them all mad, but she said no more as she bit into another sandwich, for her mind was busy with new plans to bring the Earl and Georgie together at last. She had to admit she had seldom seen a more difficult pair, for although she knew they were both in love with the other, they adamantly refused to confess it. She was not discouraged, however, which would have come as no surprise to her fiancé. As Sir Albert Adams had often remarked, when Con put her mind to something, there was no holding her.

11

The Earl had pondered whether he should tell Cousin
Bertie, or at least Freddie, of the plan he had conceived for
this evening, but in the end he decided not to, for he
wanted the denouement to come as a complete surprise to
everyone, a conceit he was to regret bitterly in only a
short time. Now, however, with only a curt nod for
"Linwood," he took his leave of him and Freddie and went
into the Court and up the stairs to the Blue Bedchamber to
consult with Mr. Fredericks and make their final plans.

For him, the hours until dinner dragged by, but for
Georgie they flew. Even with the support of Lady Martin
and Aunt Bess beside her, she knew she was in for a
difficult time, and she also realized that it would be completely out of character for David to let the matter drop
there and accept her refusal with a good grace. No, she
thought, staring out of her window at the green moors as
Wiltshire prepared her bath, he is more apt to come here
tonight, break down my door, and beat me for daring to
cross him.

She showed no interest in what she would wear that
evening, and her maid shook her head over this unusual
happenstance as she laid out a gown of sea-green silk and
matching slippers, with a sarsenet stole embroidered with
a gold design to drape over the lady's bare shoulders.
Georgie recalled herself when it came time to arrange her
hair, and because she decided the chignon that she had at
first requested made her look positively haggard this evening and must be changed to a softer, more flowing arrangement, she was very late. She almost flew down the
stairs, smiling at Jenks as he opened the doors of the Great
Parlour for her.

She was the last to arrive, for inside, all the other guests and Cousin Bertie were grouped in their customary circle around the fireplace. David Linwood was standing before the blaze, and his eyes went immediately to her face as she entered the room. A small grin played over his harsh features, as if he sensed her discomfort. The Earl and Freddie were talking together by the drinks table, and Connie sat with Lady Waring and Emmaline on a sofa a little removed from the others. Cousin Bertie had chosen his usual high-backed wing chair with its matching footstool, but he bounced up to come and kiss Georgie's hand and compliment her on her gown, much to Teddy's disgust. Georgie could hear him snorting in the background from where he stood beside Lady Martin and Miss Hersham.

"Sounds like a bull we once had," Bertie remarked to no one in particular. "Had to have him put down, for the silly animal didn't seem to have the least idea what was required of him. Too bad we can't do that in this case as well."

"*Bertie!*" Lady Martin exclaimed, just as she always did, while David Linwood laughed right out loud.

Georgina saw Jenks come into the room with his stately tread and go to the Earl's side. Robert looked around the room and smiled before he nodded his head, and the butler bowed and withdrew. She wondered at the Earl's air of repressed excitement, but she had no time to ponder it, for David was beckoning to her, and Bertie giggled as he gave her a little push in his direction.

"My dear, I have a great suspicion that we are to be treated to some exciting news this evening," he said, standing on his tiptoes to whisper in her ear. "Go and see what Davey wants; I abdicate my rights, as always, for one of my nephies."

Georgie moved forward until she was facing Mr. Linwood.

"Well, Georgie?" he asked softly.

"I shall tell you my decision in the library after dinner, sir," she whispered, raising her chin to stare at him with a straight look. "You cannot expect me to answer you in a room as crowded as this is."

He grinned at her. "It might be a mite awkward, true, for although we would be able to accept the numerous congratulations that would be tended, I would have no opportunity to take you in my arms until . . . er . . . later. As you wish, *belle;* I shall try to curb my impatience until then. You have your key with you?"

Georgie ignored this comment as she moved away from him, and as she did so, the doors opened and Jenks stood on the threshold. His large frame partially obscured the middle-aged man who followed him.

"Mr. Joshua Fredericks of Virginia, m'lord," Jenks announced in stentorian tones. The guests looked at the door and then at each other, and Georgie heard David utter a startled oath.

The gentleman who entered the room was not dressed for evening, but wore a plain brown riding suit that was hardly in the first stare of fashion. Everyone was quiet at the appearance of this unexpected guest, and the Marquess looked around to see the Earl nodding his head, as if to say he would explain everything in good time, before he went to greet the guest.

"Milords, miladies," the stranger said with a courteous bow for the company. "And Bart Forrest too. What a surprise to see you here, suh, dressed as fine as ninepence. Quite a change from your usual attire in the fields of Virginia. Well, well, we all wondered what became of you after you were forced to flee the United States, but no one ever suspected you would turn up in England impersonatin' Mr. David Linwood of Linderwood Plantation."

Georgie had her back to David, but she saw Miss Hersham go pale and grasp Lady Martin's hands, and she heard Emmie's cry of surprise.

"Everyone stay right where they are," she heard David say, his drawl harsh and brutal as he gave the order. "Most especially you, Robert. Georgie, come back here to me!"

She turned to face him and could not restrain a gasp when she saw the pistol he was holding and pointing at the others, and she did not think she could move.

"You heard me, *belle.* Come here or I fire! Now, who would it be? Your aunt? Robert Holland? How satisfyin' *that* would be! Perhaps the Marquess or Miss Wilson?"

Georgie forced her reluctant feet to move until she stood by his side, and he reached out and put his free arm around her waist, dragging her close to him.

" 'Pon . . . 'pon my soul!" Bertie exclaimed, too shocked for once to even bounce in his chair. "Davey? What is the meaning of this? And who is this strange man?"

"Not 'Davey,' m'lord. The gentleman was correct, for my real name is Bartholomew Forrest. I suppose it was you, m'lord"—and here he turned to sneer at the Earl— "who discovered my true identity. Well, I took a mad chance, and although I had every hope of a successful conclusion, I see it is not to be. However, all is not lost. I shall take Lady Spaldin' when I go; that will ensure your good conduct until I have left England, and since I understand the lady is as wealthy as she is beautiful, I shall not repine that I lost the major share."

"Oh, Davey . . . I mean Bartholomew . . . take me instead!" Emmie pleaded, leaning forward and wringing her hands in her eagerness. "I have much more money than she does!"

"*Emmaline Waring!*" her brother shouted. "Have you taken leave of your senses?"

"No, I have not," the girl replied, never taking her eyes from Forrest's startled face. "I love you so, Dav . . . I mean Bartholomew. Everything I have will be yours. I don't care if you are an impostor! Please take me!"

Forrest looked at her as if bemused, and then his glance dropped to the chestnut curls and lovely figure of Lady Spalding, held so close in his arm. "I think not, Miss Warin'. Even such wealth as you boast cannot make me give up this prize, for Georgie and I have a private matter to settle, don't we, *belle?* Besides, and you must forgive me for being rude, you are hardly temptin' enough to make me change my mind."

Emmie moaned and sank back in her seat to cover her face with her handkerchief, while her mother stared at her with horror, leaving Connie to put her arms around the girl and try to comfort her. Teddy finally appeared to have been struck dumb with shock at Emmie's immodest behaviour.

"But I don't understand!" Bertie wailed. "Won't someone please tell me what is going on?"

"It's an ugly story, m'lord," the older American called Mr. Fredericks said, speaking for the first time since he had entered the room. "I will be glad to explain it, but first let me say how sorry I am it has come to this, but of course neither the Earl nor I expected the man to carry a loaded pistol to dinner."

"I am always prepared, Josh, always thinkin'," the impostor said, and Georgie could hear the grim humour in his voice.

"Be that as it may. This gentleman was askin' for an explanation. If I may?" He waited until Bart Forrest nodded his head and said, "I suppose we have the time, and you have been kind to me, 'Cousin Bertie,' so it is only fair that you know how close you came to bein' cheated. Go on, then, Josh."

Mr. Fredericks continued, eyeing the pistol with contemptuous eyes, while Emmie sobbed softly in the background. " 'Tis like this, m'lord. Forrest here was David Linwood's overseer on the plantation. What you here in England call an estate agent, I suppose. He always was uppity and thought too well of himself by half, and the way he treated the slaves was a disgrace. I knew it was only a matter of time before David got rid of him, but before he could do so, he fell ill and did not have the strength to supervise Linderwood or his overseer. Soon after that, Miss Cecily Linderwood fell in love with Forrest and behind her father's back allowed him the freedom of the big house."

"Yes, Cece was very kind indeed," Forrest drawled, and the older man's face reddened at his impudent grin. "She allowed me more than the freedom of the house, you know."

"So we discovered after you left with all David's private papers and identification and a great deal of money besides. Tell me, Forrest, did you have any intention of returnin' for the girl? She waited faithfully for so long, sure you would come back for her. Why, even on her deathbed she maintained that you would not fail her."

"Cece is dead?" Forrest asked, as if he were not much interested. "I'm not surprised. She was a whining, puling babe with no more starch to her than a boll of cotton!"

Mr. Fredericks glared at him. "She died havin' your stillborn son, suh! Everyone thought she died of a broken heart and the shame of havin' a babe out of wedlock."

"Oh dear, the poor thing!" Emmie cried, lowering her handkerchief to stare at the monster she now discovered to be standing before the fireplace.

"Poor thing indeed," he mocked her. "Haven't I just been tellin' you so? No, of course I never intended to return for her after she served her purpose. The world's full of women; did weak, silly little Cece Linwood think to hold *me*? Ha!"

Georgie tried to keep from shivering. From where she stood held tightly to the man's side, she could not see his face, but she could see the expressions of the others', and there was not one face that was not filled with disgust and horrified disapproval. She saw the Earl move slightly, and prayed he would not try anything foolish. Connie must have caught the movement too, out of the corner of her eye, for she spoke up to ask, "But why was that shot fired at me? And who fired it, if you were with the head groom all the time?"

"Miss Wilson, ma'am. The travellin' lady," he drawled. "After you kept goin' on and on about your trip to the States and how sure you were that you had met me there, I knew I had to get rid of you. I never intended murder, I only meant to frighten you so you would leave the Court. The evenin' before you were shot at, you remarked that you had seen me someplace where you would not expect the owner of Linderwood to be. I was sure you must have spotted me stripped to the waist in the fields, and that eventually you would remember it and tell the Marquess. And so you had to go. My valet fired the gun from the cupola, but he was so frightened that he might hit you, the shot went wide. Must have been that it was the first time he ever fired at a woman that disturbed his aim, for Wilks is generally a superior marksman." Forrest laughed at this failing in his servant, and the Earl moved a step closer.

"Stand very still, m'lord!" the American said, drawing a bead on him. "It would give me such pleasure to have an excuse to shoot *you*, above all else."

"But how did you expect to inherit?" the Marquess asked as the two men glared at each other, their hatred an almost palpable thing in the heavy silence. "Even if Georgie did choose you as the heir tonight, as you said she was going to do, eventually the deception would all have come out, and then where would you be?"

"I am sorry to have to tell you this, suh, but Carew Court and the title were not in my schemes. By the time the truth was known, I planned to be on the high seas with

only the Holland Treasure and Lady Georgie in my possession. I never wanted your worthless title or this small
farm."

"*Small farm?* Carew Court?" the Marquess repeated in
a stunned voice. "How dare you!"

"In America this would perhaps do for an indentured
servant recently released from his bond," Forrest explained,
and Cousin Bertie subsided, his little brown eyes popping
and his mouth hanging open in amazement.

Mr. Fredericks spoke up again. "I do apologize, milords,
miladies! You are not to suppose that all Americans are
like Bart Forrest here. He is a disgrace to our country,
and I am ashamed he is a Virginian to boot."

"Shut up, you old fool!" Forrest snarled, his arm tighten-
ing on Georgie's waist until she thought she must cry out
with the pressure. "Where would your precious country be
without men like me to do your dirty work? Manage your
slaves . . . fight your wars . . . take care of the details
that you plantation owners won't soil your hands on?"

Mr. Fredericks subsided before his ferocious glare, and
Forrest continued, "And now I think I have delayed long
enough. I fear that Lady Spaldin' and I must decline to
grace your table this evenin', suh," he said to the still-
speechless Marquess. "If you will be so good as to ring for
Jenks and have the horses saddled, I will tell my man to
begin packin' and have him inform Georgie's maid what
will be required as well." He watched the Marquess pull
the bell rope and said to his captive, "Not anythin' too
fancy, *belle*. Where we are goin', you won't be needin' silks
and laces—in fact, you won't be needin' anything at all for
quite a spell!"

He laughed, a low coarse chuckle, and Georgie's eyes
flew to the Earl's face. Although she had meant to plead
with her eyes that he do something—anything!—she stilled
her fearful expression, for the look on his face was murderous. She would never have believed that Robert Holland could look like that, so poised and deadly and
determined. He will get himself killed any moment now,
she thought wildly, and I cannot bear it! Better to go
with this Bart Forrest, if only to be sure Robert would be
safe.

She looked to the others, but there was no help there.

Teddy still stood frozen beside Lady Martin and Aunt Bess, who had fallen into each other's arms for support, and Emmie was holding Connie's hand tightly while her mother cowered back in her seat. Mr. Fredericks' whole posture showed he knew there was nothing he could do at the present time, and Freddie had a desperate look on his face, as if he wanted to help her but did not know how to go about it.

Her gaze went last to the Marquess, and she was surprised to see him wink at her. Just then Jenks appeared, and although he paused for a brief moment at the sight of the gun, not a muscle moved in his face. "You rang, sir?" he asked the Marquess.

"You will order three horses saddled at once, Jenks," Bart Forrest said. "Lady Georgie's mare, and Captain, the Earl's roan, as well as my own gelding. Then you will tell my man Wilks to pack some saddlebags with the gear we will need. He is also to have this lady's maid assemble some sensible clothes and a warm cloak for her. At once, man! And I warn you, do not alert the other servants or try anything at all that would put the lady—and especially your precious Earl—in danger."

Jenks did not turn in his direction but continued to watch the Marquess. "M'lord?" he asked again, awaiting his master's orders.

Cousin Bertie waved a hand. "Do as he says, Jenks, and do nothing to jeopardize the others. The man is dangerous and he means it when he says he will shoot."

"Certainly, m'lord," the butler said before he bowed and backed away, never once allowing himself to look in the American's direction. It was as if he did not exist, and Georgie could not help feeling proud of him as he left the room, his step as measured as it had been when he entered.

"But come, Davey . . . er, Bart. No, it's too late for that, can't expect me to change your name at this late date," the Marquess complained, squirming in his chair. "Perhaps we can come to some more amiable arrangement?"

"What could be more amiable than possessin' Georgie?" Forrest asked, hugging her to him again and darting a triumphant glance at the Earl's rigid face.

"Now, Davey, you said yourself the world is full of

women. Even as lovely as she is, is Georgie worth as much to you as the Holland Emeralds?"

Forrest stood very still, his taunting of the Earl forgotten. "The Holland Emeralds, suh?" he asked.

"I am suggesting an exchange, Davey. Give Georgie her freedom and leave her here, and you may take the treasure with you instead. There is no wealth in England to compare with it, certainly not Georgie's little portion! I have no doubt you will break up the crown and stomacher, but I am willing to sacrifice them for her life."

"What's to stop me from takin' the treasure and the lady as well?" Bart Forrest sneered.

"You would never get them," the Marquess said easily. "Think, man. Fickles is on guard right now. He is paid well to be sure the emeralds are safe, and he will give them up to no one but myself. You might shoot him, but he would be just as likely to shoot you first. Of course, after you gave me your word that the exchange was agreeable to you, you might take Georgie anyway, but somehow I do not believe it of you. You may be a sad rogue, but there's some sense of honour in you, I trust."

"Nay, milord!" Mr. Fredericks spoke up in alarm. "There's no honour in him at all. You cannot trust him to keep his word."

Georgie felt the man beside her stiffen. "Now, there you are wrong, suh," he said in his harsh voice. "When I give my word, I keep it. You do not approve of me, and I agree that to such fops and weaklin's as you all are, I am a dangerous man. I have had to be! For Bart Forrest there was no high-and-mighty title, no inherited wealth, no easy life. I have had to scratch and whop and kill whoever got in my way, to be sure I would survive, and survive in style. I may be a poor shareholder's son who wanted more from the world than I could get honestly, but my word is my bond."

He paused, and Georgie could feel his quick breathing stirring her hair, and then he released her and gave her a push. She staggered away from him, hitting her hip against a corner of a table that lay in her path, and she was quick to grasp it and hold on so she should not fall. She backed away from the fireplace, her green eyes never leaving Forrest's face.

"You have a deal, m'lord," he said, and then he bowed to Georgie. "Your pardon, ma'am, but the Marquess is right. There are too many beautiful women in the world, most of 'em more easy goin' and passionate than you are, for me to turn down such a plum. A fair exchange—the emeralds for the lady. My hand on it, suh."

He strode forward and held out his free hand, and after a moment's hesitation the Marquess shook it.

Forrest backed up again quickly to the fireplace, moving the pistol in a slow circle to catch everyone's eye. "We will all remain right here," he said, his voice flat and dangerous again, "and be very still while Bertie goes to the vault and fetches the treasure. No tricks, now, Bertie!"

The Marquess pulled himself from his chair and straightened to his entire five feet, four and three-quarter inches. "Certainly not, my boy. Do you take me for a flat?"

He harumphed and marched down the Great Parlour to unlock the door that led to the vault. Georgie sank down into a chair, relieved as she had never been in her entire life, although she had certainly not expected the Marquess to give up the Holland fortune for her. It was too much, but she could not help but be grateful, because for the last half-hour, the veneer of gentility that the American had assumed to play his part as Bertie's heir had dropped away, and she could hear in his drawling, hateful confession the kind of man he was.

Bart Forrest leaned back at his ease against the mantel, but this casual pose fooled no one, for the pistol he held so steady in his right hand remained pointed at the guests.

No one spoke, and there was no sound in the room but the cheerful crackling of the fire. Although they could hear nothing of the Marquess' progress, everyone pictured him climbing the stairs, knocking on the door of the vault, and confronting Fickles with his outrageous request. Georgie was not sure even now that the Bow Street Runner would give up his charge, even to his employer, no matter how good the cause, and she said a silent prayer that the Marquess would be able to convince the giant red-headed guard. She caught Connie's eye for a moment, and saw the encouraging little smile the girl gave her, and she herself tried to appear calm when she turned her gaze to Aunt

Bess, who was so white she looked as if she were about to faint.

"Mr. Forrest," she surprised herself by saying, "could my aunt and Lady Martin be seated? They have been standing throughout, and neither of them looks at all well."

Forrest inclined his head, and both ladies sank gratefully onto a nearby sofa as he asked, "No questions for me this evenin', ladies? This is your last chance to hear more of the States."

Miss Hersham seemed to wilt even more, but Lady Martin stiffened her back and glared at the impostor. "We *never* had any interest in your country, you blackguard. It was only to keep you away from Georgie."

There was a stifled exclamation from Miss Hersham, and Georgie drew in her breath as Forrest laughed out loud. "So that was why you were so very attentive. How distressin' to find that it was not my fascinatin' conversation that made you seek my company so often. Well, it has no doubt been educational for you, although it seldom kept me away from Georgie; right, *belle?*"

Just then the door at the far end of the room opened, and the Marquess entered, followed by a furious Fickles, who was burdened by the Holland Treasure. His face was red, and the muscles of his huge arms bulged with his effort, and if looks could kill, Mr. Forrest would have instantly fallen to the hearth rug.

"I have had Fickles bring the treasure, Davey, for I could not carry it myself. His pistols and indeed all his weapons are still in the vault room. Would you care to search him to make sure?" the Marquess asked as the guard put the treasure on a heavy table.

"That will not be necessary, m'lord," Forrest told him.

"Thank you for trusting me, my boy." The Marquess beamed.

"It is not so much trust as it is preservation, suh. While I am busy searchin' his person, no doubt the Earl and his crony there would try to jump me. No, no, I am much more interested in a speedy escape."

The door of the Parlour opened and Jenks came back, followed by a servant Georgie had never seen.

"Everything has been prepared as you ordered, m'lord," the butler reported to the Marquess.

"Excellent, Jenks," Bertie said, his tone very light and carefree for a man who was about to lose a fortune, and Georgie noticed the Earl's speculative look.

"Wilks?" Bart Forrest asked, never taking his eyes from his captives.

"All's ready, suh," the man said. Georgie saw he was dressed for riding and that he too held a pistol in his hand. "The horses are at the door, and the bags are packed, including the lady's . . . but, Bart, what's this foolishness to be takin' a woman? She'll only hold us up!"

Jenks had never looked so disapproving as he did now, hearing the American servant speak in such a familiar way to his master, and daring to criticize him as well, and for a moment his impassive facade slipped.

"Plans have changed, Wilks," Forrest said. "Instead of the lady, we'll put the Holland Treasure on one of the horses. See to it, man, and use the gelding as packhorse, since he's the strengthiest beast we have. You take the lady's mare, and I'll ride the roan."

"Now, this is somethin' like!" Wilks crowed as he picked up the treasure and staggered to the door.

Forrest said, "Have Jenks accompany him, Bertie, and again, no tricks. I shall be right here watchin' you all."

The Marquess nodded to his butler, who left the room in the wake of the struggling Wilks.

It seemed a very long time before Jenks returned alone to report the treasure was secured, and Georgie was uncomfortable, for she could see the way Bart Forrest was staring at her, his eyes speculative. Suppose he was not to be trusted, as Mr. Fredericks had warned them? Suppose he still insisted that she come with him?

Her hands felt icy as she clasped them together in her lap, and she could feel the chills of apprehension that washed over her body. Go, *go!* she screamed inwardly, trying to keep her face expressionless. Why don't you *go?*

Forrest straightened up from the mantel. "I thank you, m'lord, for your treasure, as well as your hospitality," he said with a little bow to the Marquess, and then he beckoned to Georgie. "Come, *belle.*"

"No, no," Miss Hersham wailed. "You promised!"

The Marquess frowned, his little eyes narrowed and his lips pursed, while behind him, Mr. Fredericks snorted as if to say: I told you so. Georgie could see the tension building again in the Earl's face, and rose in despair, her shoulders drooping.

She was surprised to hear Bart Forrest laughing. "Do not fear, Miss Hersham, ma'am. I gave my word to the Marquess, and I will keep it. But I am not so foolish as to attempt to ride down that long, long drive without a hostage, for I would surely be shot from ambush. Acquit me of such madness! The lady will accompany us to the gates. If I reach them safely, she will be free."

The Marquess's face was red now. "But, Davey, I give you my word. There are no ambushers."

Bart Forrest smiled at him. "Perhaps *you* gave no such order, suh, but how much would you wager that your butler has not spread the word, and all unbeknownst to you, the drive is thick with guns? No, it shall be as I say. The lady comes with us until we are safely away, and no one is to leave this room until she returns. Come, *belle*."

He held out his left hand, and in order to avoid touching him, she walked before him to the door. Behind her, she heard Teddy Waring exclaiming, and then Lady Martin saying, "But she'll catch her death of cold, Bertie. She must have a wrap.

Georgie heard Mr. Forrest snort in derision as he put the pistol tight against her spine, and the footmen who were standing to attention along the walls of the Great Hall stiffened and remained very, very still.

They reached the massive front door and passed through it and down the steps. Wilks was there, already mounted, and she saw his head swivel for a quick glance to be sure it was Forrest behind him before he turned back to keep the moonlit drive under surveillance. The pistol was withdrawn from her back for a moment, and then Forrest handed her the shawl which had been lying on top of her discarded bag.

"Wrap up in this, *belle*." His voice was light now that he had almost pulled off his coup. "Can't have it said that a southern gentleman was not always the soul of chivalry."

He tossed her up before the saddle of the Earl's horse, and mounted behind her, to tuck one arm around her and catch up the reins.

"I'll go first, Wilks; then you come behind, leadin' the

packhorse. We won't travel above a walk—I want all those grooms and keepers to see I have Lady Spaldin'. The moonlight will help us."

"Aye, suh!" came the cheerful reply, and the small cavalcade started off. At least I am spared his conversation, Georgie thought, as she saw him constantly moving his head from side to side to listen carefully. There might have been men waiting for him, hidden in the beech forest, but there was no sign of them, and in a little while the entrance to Carew Court was reached. The gatehouse was dark and shuttered, and no smoke came from its chimney.

"I dunno as I like the looks of that, Bart," Wilks muttered as he followed Forrest through the gates to the road. They continued on for quite a distance, and just when Georgie was sure he was taking her away with him after all, in spite of what he had told Aunt Bess, Forrest halted his horse on an empty stretch of road.

"Down you go, *belle!*" he said, loosening his grip on her waist. She slid to the ground and backed away, and in the moonlight he saw her green eyes flashing with her hatred of him, and he checked and dismounted, handing his reins to Wilks.

Georgie tried to run then, but he was too quick for her, and caught her and pulled her close to him, one big hand capturing both her hands and holding them behind her.

"A kiss in partin', *belle?*" he drawled, and suited his actions to his words. Georgie struggled as those hard lips ground against hers and his hot tongue explored her mouth. She felt a trickle of blood from her lower lip as he raised his head, and then he reached out to take off her shawl. "Why not?" he mused, as if to himself. "There's always time for *that.*"

The shawl was pulled away and Georgie felt a hand fumbling with the skirt of her gown, and then she heard the servant exclaim, "Have you gone mad, Bart? To be dallyin' with a wench when we've got the gold to get away. Give over, man! They'll be after us in a moment. When we have this treasure safe, we'll both have time for all the wenches we want, now and forever."

Forrest paused, and then he nodded, and Georgie closed her eyes for a moment in gratitude for the man's greed before he pushed her away.

"Go back, *belle*, and marry your highborn Earl, but you'll never be able to forget Bart Forrest, I'll wager," he taunted as he swung one powerful leg over his horse's back. "Wilks! We ride!"

Georgie stumbled back as he spurred his horse and laughed, and she stood there unmoving until they were out of sight. Only then did she reach down and pick up her shawl and start her long trudge back to the Court.

12

The Earl did not waste a moment after Bart Forrest took
Georgie away at gunpoint. Ignoring his order that everyone was to stay in the Great Parlour, and the horrified
exclamations of the others, he ran to the Hall and issued a
stream of orders, the effect of which had the butler and the
footmen scurrying in every direction. A chaise was to be
driven to the gates to pick up the lady when she was
released, the fastest horses in the stables were to be saddled, and the best riders among the grooms, as well as the
canniest trackers of the Marquess' keepers, were ordered
to make ready to go after the thieves as soon as it was safe
to do so. The gun room was unlocked, and the necessary
weapons loaded and checked, with extra ammunition issued to the Earl's small but efficient army.

Robert was cold and precise and determined, in spite of
his fury, and he was obeyed without question. The Marquess came to the door of the Great Parlour to ask what he
was doing, and was told crisply that everything was in
hand and that he should go back and reassure the others,
and Miss Hersham in particular, that her niece would be
restored to her in good time. Bertie opened his mouth to
protest this tame role, but one look at Robert's handsome
face, set now in stern, implacable lines, and he shrugged
his shoulders and rejoined the others.

Robert paced the Hall after all was in train. He would
have liked to ride to the gates with the others, but he did
not dare put Georgie in jeopardy by disregarding Forrest's
orders in such a flagrant manner. He beat one fist against
the other as he paced, and the footmen stared straight
ahead, not daring to move a muscle.

If she were hurt, if that devil did not keep his word and

release her, he knew he would never rest until he himself had hunted him down and shot him for the vermin he was. It seemed that an endless amount of time passed before he heard the chaise returning, and he brushed by Jenks in his hurry to be sure the lady had been restored to them safely.

Robert himself opened the door of the chaise, and as Georgie held out her hand to him, his eyes flew to her face and his expression darkened even more as he spotted the trickle of blood on her lower lip, clearly visible in the moonlight and the light of the flambeaux flanking the doorway of the Court.

"Why is your lip bleeding, Georgie?" he asked, his deep voice harsh with his rage.

"Do not regard it, Robert, and do not mention it to the others," she whispered. "It was just Mr. Forrest's charming way of bidding me good-bye."

The Earl handed her from the chaise and gave her his handkerchief, and as they went up the shallow steps, she wiped away the blood. His arm was tight around her waist to support her, and Georgie felt a curious lightness of relief to be held in such a strong, competent grasp.

"The man has even more to answer for than I thought," he said in that unfamiliar harsh voice. "When I find him, and I *will* find him, I shall add that insult to all his other crimes. Mr. Forrest does not have much time left in this world."

Georgie shivered at his tone. "I would so much rather just forget him, Robert. I am so very tired after all these alarms. But what a terrible disappointment for the Marquess, to be tricked in such a way."

She missed the Earl's change of expression as he stiffened and removed his arm, for although he had put in the back of his mind Bertie's remark earlier that Georgie planned to choose his rival as her husband and the heir, he had not forgotten it.

"A terrible disappointment for you too, m'lady," he said formally. "But I am afraid you must come and reassure your aunt and Cousin Bertie that you took no hurt from your adventure."

Georgie stared at him, but before she could ask him what he meant, Aunt Bess was there, closely followed by the others, all exclaiming and talking at once.

"Dear aunt." Georgie smiled at the tears in Miss Hersham's

eyes, trying to forget the Earl's sarcastic comment. "Please do not fuss over me now. It is all over, and I am quite all right."

"Georgie, dear girl, I would never have had this happen—and at Carew Court too—for the world," the Marquess said next, taking her hand to peer up into her face. "Come and sit down, and we will get you some brandy as a restorative. Jenks! Jenks!"

"What happened, Georgie? Did he get away?" Emmie asked, and then, when she felt the others staring at her, she drew back, blushing a fiery red.

Connie moved forward to lead Georgie to a sofa near the fire. "Not another word until she has had a sip of brandy," she ordered.

Everyone took a seat again except the Earl, and as Jenks began to serve the drinks, he stepped forward. "Now that I have seen Lady Spalding restored to us safely," he said, not meeting her eyes, "I shall join the men who are already searching for Forrest and his servant."

"I'll ride with you, Robert!" Freddie volunteered eagerly.

"And I!" Mr. Fredericks chimed in. "I know his ways; perhaps I can help, suh!"

"Oh, why bother? Let 'im go!" the Marquess said in an airy voice.

"Let him go? Are you mad, Bertie?" Lady Martin asked, almost upsetting her sherry glass in her astonishment. "That devil has the Holland Treasure. We must recover it at once."

The others looked at the Marquess with varying degrees of disbelief, and Bertie chuckled, well pleased to hold center stage again.

"But he doesn't, Aggie." He giggled. "And since Georgie is unharmed, and no one else was hurt, why not let him escape? I find I still have a fondness for the boy, even if he is such a great rogue."

"He doesn't have the treasure, cousin?" Robert asked, coming forward to lean against the table where the gold and emeralds had rested just a short time ago. "What do you mean?"

"Those frippery things he took away with him were only paste copies of the real treasure," Bertie crowed. "Thank heaven he was so busy guarding us, he didn't have time to inspect them too closely! Now, don't you think it punishment enough when he discovers that what he has stolen is worthless, and that he has lost the Lady Georgie as well? Why, it is enough to make you feel sorry for the man."

After everyone's first startled exclamations, he explained, "You see, after I took you all up to the vault to see the treasure, I got to thinking about whether that had been a wise idea, and so Fickles and I exchanged the crown and stomacher with some paste copies I had made several years ago. You'll never be able to guess where the real ones have been hidden all the time, never."

He bounced up and down in the chair in his excitement. "Does anyone care to hazard a guess? No? Well, I was really very, very clever," he congratulated himself as the company remained silent. "I put 'em under the bed in the State Bedroom!"

He laughed out loud, and Georgie couldn't help smiling, he was so pleased with himself. "So there was never any danger of your losing them, then? And here I was just about to thank you fervently and with all my heart for giving up such wealth to save me. Never have I been so deceived. I fear you are a great rogue too, sir."

She shook her head at the Marquess and he hurried to assure her that of course he would have done anything in his power to help her, he had not meant she was not worth more than paste jewels, and other like sentiments, until he ran down and had to take a reviving sip of wine.

"But *why*, m'lord?" Freddie asked, his fair face frowning in thought. "Whatever made you move them in the first place?"

The Marquess looked around, his little brown eyes darting from one to the other, and for the first time he looked a little self-conscious, as if he would really prefer not to say. After a last peek at Lord Waring, he confessed, "It seemed to me that the treasure was in some danger after that night. You see, I have never really trusted Teddy. These naturals, without all their wits—you can never tell what notion they'll get into their brain boxes, and yet some of 'em can be deuced clever. Look how he behaves so normally most of the time!"

"*Bertie!*" Lady Martin cried, clasping her hands to her heart.

"I *say!*" Teddy exclaimed, putting down his wineglass with a ringing snap. "I have never been so insulted in my entire life! I beg to be excused. Lady Spalding, I will call on you when you return to town. I know that a woman of your superior understanding realizes that not even my devotion to you and care for your welfare makes it possible for me to remain at Carew Court and be maligned this way. Mother! Emmie! We will retire, and you may be assured, sir, that we will be on our way back to town the first thing in the morning."

"That's all right," Bertie said easily. "Thought you'd never go. Are you sure you want to accompany him, Lavvy? Delighted to welcome *you* for a long visit, you know."

Teddy's face was almost purple as he shepherded his female relatives before him. "Not another instant more than we have to, will any Waring remain in your house, sir."

"Don't follow you, Teddy," the Marquess complained. "Can't see what you've got to be so hoity-toity about. Here's your sister throwing herself at Bart Forrest— you really should take the gel in hand, you know, my boy. Wild to a fault, and bad ton besides—and here's yourself, making a cake of yourself over Lady Georgie when it's as plain as the nose on your face that she wouldn't have you even if you did have all your wits."

He raised his voice to be sure he was heard as the Warings reached the door. "But don't worry, Teddy. My lips are sealed, and I daresay I can persuade the others to keep mum about it, too. No need to fear that ugly gossip will result, and not a word will leak out about your unfortunate condition either. Here, I say, Waring—can't go away mad, you know."

But by this time the indignant Lord Waring had left the room, and the Marquess looked around as if amazed at such singular behaviour. Connie and Freddie were trying hard not to laugh out loud, Mr. Fredericks was looking amused if mystified, and the two older ladies were shaking their heads in reproof at the Marquess, in perfect unison. Georgie leaned back in her chair, her husky chuckle escaping her lips, and the Earl, for the first time that evening, had an answering smile for her as he strolled over to his cousin and told him he was not only very bad and had outrageous manners, he was a disgrace to his name as well.

"Got rid of him, didn't I?" Bertie asked innocently, which

was too much for the Wilsons, who dissolved in helpless laughter in each other's arms just as Jenks appeared in the doorway and cleared his throat.

"Dinner is served, m'lord," he said in a majestic, carrying voice, just as he did every evening. It was the final straw, and everyone was laughing as they all rose to follow the butler up the stairs to the Dining Chamber, Bertie assuring Mr. Fredericks that there was no need for him to change his clothes, for as the exposer of the impostor and the saviour of the Holland name, he was more than welcome to join them, dressed any way he chose.

At these words, Robert's face became stiff and formal again, although only Georgie noticed it. She wondered why Robert did not seem at all pleased, even though everything had turned out well in the end, and wondered if it had anything to do with his sarcastic remark to her in the Hall. But then, she told herself as she took her seat at the dinner table, she had always found the Earl a difficult man to understand.

By the time she came down the next morning, Mr. Fredericks had gone back to town, leaving only a short time after the Warings had taken coach. Connie and Lady Martin relayed this news in the breakfast room, both of them smiling with good humour. For herself, Georgie had the headache. They also told her that the men from the estate had been unable to find any trace of Bart Forrest and his man, although they had searched through the night in an ever-increasing area. She learned the Earl had ridden early to Upper Littledean to apprise the justice there that there were two felons loose in his district, and to make arrangements to have the nearest ports watched, and word brought to him the instant either man was spotted. Bertie might wish Mr. Forrest to escape; it was clear that Robert Holland did not have such a forgiving nature.

But somehow Georgie did not think they would catch Bart Forrest. He was too clever, and by virtue of his early training in America, too adept at evasion in the woods and countryside. She wondered briefly if he would dare to circle back here for the real treasure, feeling chilled at the possibility until she realized that Mr. Forrest, although he would be in a towering rage at the way he had been tricked, would know he could gain nothing further at the Court, for he would be arrested and tried for impersonating another man and for stealing if he ever set foot here again. The Earl would see to it, if he didn't just shoot him down first.

Connie poured herself another cup of coffee, as Lady Martin chatted to a silent and unresponsive Georgie, wondering what on earth was wrong with her friend. She was to ponder many times in the next few days, not only with regards to Georgie, but to Robert as well. "What can be wrong with those two, Freddie?" she asked her brother after they returned from a canter on the moors one afternoon. "Why doesn't Robert *do* something now that the fascinating American has been vanquished and the stage is set for him to sweep in and carry all before him? Why does he insist on treating Georgie so formally, with that stiff expression on his face? I shall be forced to take steps before long, and ask him plainly what the problem is!"

"Don't do it, Con," her brother advised. "Won't thank you for it. See his point, though. If he offers for Georgie now, or even shows warmer feelings, what's to stop her from thinking he's only after the title and the treasure? Didn't try to fix her interest before, did he? Can't do it now without looking like a bounder."

"Oh, *men!*" Connie said in exasperation as she slid off her mount and stalked into the house.

The Earl was indeed in a quandary. His uncle had flatly forbidden him to go after Forrest, saying he had no desire to lose his only real heir in a thankless cause, for he had no wish to prosecute the impostor, no matter how hot for revenge Robert was. The Earl tightened his lips and resigned himself to letting his rival escape, although it went very much against the grain with him. Balked of action and the satisfaction such a pursuit would engender, he became so quiet and forbidding that Lady Martin felt he must be coming down with something, and begged him to try some of her latest remedies.

But if he felt sick, it was due more to a feeling of terrible guilt that the whole affair had happened because of his mismanagement. If only he had told the others so they might have been prepared, if only he had not underestimated his opponent, none of this would have happened. But no, he had to surprise them with his brilliant detective work, and in doing so he put everyone—and especially

Georgie!—in danger. No wonder she had not chosen him—a man so incompetent and so insufferably proud!

The four younger members of the house party were thrown very much in each other's company now, a situation that both Georgie and Robert found uncomfortable in their present states. Georgie especially was confused. Why was Robert behaving this way? Why did he frown every time he looked at her, and treat her with barely civil indifference? She loved him—indeed, she had known she loved him ever since the episode at the plunge pool, but there was no way she could let him know, especially when he showed her so plainly that he did not care a snap of his fingers for her. She decided that he would never learn of her love, but although she knew the easiest thing to do would be to leave Carew Court, she could not make herself take that final step.

In spite of her brother's warning, Connie gently tried to find out the reasons for the Earl's bad mood, but since she had forgotten the Marquess' revealing remark that Georgie was about to choose David Linwood as her husband the very night he was exposed, she did not realize Robert was brooding about it, and he did not enlighten her.

One evening, when Bertie was going over his plans for the picnic, which he had now decided would be held in the evening three days ahead, when there would be a full moon, Robert announced that he had been called back to town on a matter of business that could not be postponed. There was a startled silence, and as Lady Martin and Miss Hersham exchanged glances, Georgie clasped her hands tightly in her lap and lowered her eyes. The Marquess was indignant at this defection, but in spite of all his entreaties, the Earl insisted that his business could not wait and that he must leave no later than the day after tomorrow.

Lady Martin and Miss Hersham spent all the next morning together in serious conference, but neither lady came up with a feasible plan to get the Earl and Georgie together in the time they had left. It was only by the merest chance that Miss Hersham stumbled onto the solution.

Robert found her that afternoon, wandering through the gardens, and offered her his arm.

"Thank you, m'lord," she said in a chastened voice. "How peaceful it is here at the Court, now that that horrible American is gone. I wonder you can bear to leave it." She paused, but the Earl made no reply, so she said, "I must tell you I was never so glad of anything in my entire life as I was that night when we found out that he was an impostor."

"Even though you knew Lady Spalding was about to choose him for her husband, ma'am?" Robert could not help asking. Miss Hersham widened her blue eyes to stare at him.

"Choose *him*? Oh no, my dear sir, you have it all wrong! It is true that he asked her to marry him, but she told me—and Lady Martin and Connie besides—that she would never consider it. No, no, Georgie had no intention of marrying the American—none at all."

Robert Holland stopped dead on the gravel path and took both her hands in his. "But how is this possible?" he asked, his deep voice shaken. "Why . . . why, Bertie said . . ."

"Oh, Bertie!" Miss Hersham exclaimed in a dismissing tone. "What did *he* know of the matter, pray? He was only going by what Mr. Linwood told him." She sniffed her scorn. "The man was so conceited, he could not believe that Georgie would refuse him; besides, he thought her too afraid of him to defy him."

"I see," Robert said, nodding his head, his expression brighter than it had been in days. "So *that* is why . . . Of course! You must excuse me, ma'am. There is something of the utmost importance that I have to take care of right now!"

His usually polished bow was sketchy as he left her to hurry back to the Court.

" 'Pon my soul!" Miss Hersham said, plumping herself down on a convenient bench, but from the smile on her face it was plain that his discourteous manner had not offended her at all.

At that moment, Connie and Georgie were drifting in one of the rowing boats on the lake, each equipped with a book and several pillows for comfort. Connie noticed that although Georgie held her book open before her, her gaze was intent on the far side of the lake. After she gave a particularly heavy sigh, Connie closed her own book and sat up to ask, "What is the matter, my dear? It is obvious that Mrs. Underwood's latest gothic tale is boring you, but is there any special reason for that?"

Georgie hesitated, her brows drawn together in a little frown, and Connie added, "You can tell me, Georgie. Believe me when I say I only want to help." She reached out and took her friend's hand, and Georgie decided to confide in her.

"Connie, how did Sir Albert propose to you?" she asked, and for a moment Connie was stunned by the question, for it was not at all what she had expected. "I mean," Georgie went on, "when did you both know you loved each other? You see, my father arranged my marriage, and I had very little to do with it but to say 'yes' at the proper time. I feel so ignorant!"

Connie squeezed her hand, her mind working rapidly. "Georgie, must I confess? Well, only to you, dear friend. He did not propose to me, I proposed to him."

At Georgie's questioning look of disbelief, she nodded her head and laughed. "You see, half the time, gentlemen are not aware they are in love until it is pointed out to them. I gave Albert several opportunities and all kinds of encouragement, but nothing at all happened. And then, when I learned he was about to go to Vienna on this diplomatic mission, I knew I had to act at once. Put any man several hundred miles away, amidst the most beautiful women in Europe, and it would take more than a fond remembrance for his friend's younger sister to restrain him."

She chuckled again and added in a matter-of-fact way, "I waited until we were together one evening in the garden of my father's home, and then I told him I would miss him, for I had come to care for him as for no other man . . . oh dear, this is hard to tell! . . . and then I cried because he was going away!"

Georgie was entranced, and for a moment she forgot her own reluctant, bad-tempered Earl.

"What did he do?" she asked, her eyes wide with interest.

"What could he do?" practical Connie replied, "especially when I threw myself in his arms and begged him to kiss me good-bye. We were engaged in five minutes."

She chuckled at the memory, and Georgie joined in for a moment, but then her laughter died away and she was lost in thought again. Connie took up the oars to row them back to shore, adding, "It was simply that Albert had not made the connection as yet. Until that time he thought of me as Freddie's sister and as a friend. Of course *I* knew he loved me." She rowed in silence for a moment and then said in a soft voice, "As Robert loves you, dear Georgie, and does not know it yet. You too must act before he leaves for London."

Georgie stared at her as she continued, "You do love him, don't you, my dear?" She nodded, unable to speak past the tears in her throat. "Then you must take the initiative. It will work, Georgie, believe me it will work, and this is no time for missishness."

Georgie was very quiet as Connie rowed them back to the landing, and she excused herself shortly thereafter, leaving Connie with the good feeling that she had done two dear people a very special favour.

As Georgie wandered through the garden, she came upon her aunt, who was still seated on the bench where Robert had left her, smiling a little as she dreamed of the future. As Georgie sat down beside her, she decided that she would help Robert Holland further by speaking plainly to her niece.

"I have just been having the most interesting conversation with the Earl, my dear. Do you know, he thought you had decided to accept Mr. Linwood's proposal all this time?" She saw the light come into Georgie's eyes and added, "You may be sure I corrected him smartly." Then she said, "Georgie, did you ever wonder why I never married?" Georgie turned to stare at her and saw that her eyes were downcast and her cheeks a little flushed.

"Of course I have wondered, aunt, for I know you had a great many offers, and my mother said she could never understand why someone as lovely as you, who would have made such a splendid wife and mother, remained single."

"Well, dear, it was not because I did not care to marry," Miss Hersham explained. "I did fall in love with a wonderful man in my second Season, and he loved me in return."

"Whatever happened?" Georgie asked, somewhat surprised at all the revelations she was being treated to this sunny afternoon.

"He was already married, my dear," Aunt Bess said, her eyes growing sad with her memories. "His wife was a terrible woman who had married him for his title and his fortune when he was very young, and who at that time ignored him and treated him with contempt. He offered to divorce her for me, but I . . . I would not allow it, and so it came to nothing." She sighed, and then she turned slightly on the bench and looked straight into Georgie's eyes. "I was very foolish, my dear. Even if I could not face the scandal of divorce, we could have had some happiness together, but I was too cowardly, too conventional to take such a step. I have regretted it bitterly for many years, for after Roger, there could never be another man for me."

"Oh, Aunt Bess!" Georgie exclaimed. "How sad."

"Yes, it was sad. He is dead now, and I cannot even see him from a distance anymore." She wiped her damp eyes and then said in a low yet strong voice, "Do not let that happen to you, Georgie. Do not let love escape you for a scruple or false pride, for I would not have you suffer the lonely long years that I have had to bear."

Her niece put her arms around her and hugged her, and for a long time they sat there together before Georgie rose and asked to be excused.

"There is something I must ask the Marquess about before the first dressing bell rings, aunt. Thank you for telling me your secret. It means a great deal to me to know about it."

"I am glad, my dear," Miss Hersham said simply. "By the way, you will find the Marquess in the greenhouse. I saw him going that way a little while ago."

As Georgie made her way to the greenhouse, the Earl was finishing his search of the Court, but the elusive Lady Spalding was not to be found anywhere. He repaired to the library after telling Jenks to let him know when the lady returned, and poured himself a glass of wine before he sank down into one of the leather chairs to think. Now, how could he convince her that he loved her? How could he make her see his behaviour was only the result of his false interpretation of the events that had occurred?

The Marquess was puttering around some of his exotic plants, attended by his patient and long-suffering head gardener, who looked delighted to see Lady Spalding and bowed himself away with alacrity when she asked if she might speak privately with the Marquess.

"Of course, dear Georgie. Let me just dispose of this trowel," Bertie said, leading her to a wrought-iron bench. "Mind now, Duncan, I will see you tomorrow about the care of these plants. You are using too little water, any idiot can see that," he called after the rapidly retreating gardener.

"Now, my dear, how may I help you?" he asked, his brown eyes twinkling and his head tipped to one side in interest.

"Cousin Bertie," Georgie began bravely, "you told me once that if I ever needed your advice, you would be happy to give it, and now I do. Need your advice, that is."

"Certainly, delighted to be of service," the Marquess said, bouncing up and down on the bench. "It's Robert, ain't it? You'll never know, Georgie, how close I've come to putting a flea in that boy's ear. Disgraceful the way he's been treating you, when it's as plain as plain can be you are both in love with each other."

Georgie, who had been steeling herself for a very unusual confession, stared at him openmouthed. "However did you know?" she asked.

"Lord, child, you can't live to be two-and-sixty without seeing all the signs," he scoffed. "But since the episode with Dav—Bart Forrest, I mean—Robert has been barely civil. Of course he is embarrassed, first because he put you into danger in the first place, and second because he believes you really preferred the American. Then too, he is afraid you will think he is after the title and the treasure."

He shook his head. "I am afraid that it is all up to you, dear girl, as I told you once before. You must convince him it is no such thing. But with this stupid plan of his to go up to town, you will have to move at once. Now, let's see. It had better be tonight. There's no time like the present, eh, puss?" He chortled and patted her knee. "Shall I ask him to meet me in the library? Then, instead of old Bertie, you will be there in my place." He crowed and clapped his hands, and Georgie begged him not to be so obvious, suddenly afraid of what she was going to have to say to the Earl.

"No, Bertie, please." she pleaded. "Let me do it my own way, for I do not want him to think we are all in league against him."

The Marquess agreed so reluctantly that Georgie extracted a further promise from him. "And no heavy hints, no winks and chuckles at dinner, mind," she warned him.

"My dear girl," Bertie said in his stiffest, grandest manner, bouncing to his feet as he did so, "as if I would let the cat out of the bag that way. Give over, Georgie. I am more than two-and-ten you know."

Georgie rose and dropped him a curtsy before she took his arm and hugged it. "Indeed I do, sir, but I also know your sense of humour. You must promise me, now. No shenanigans."

"Oh, very well," he grumbled, resigned to playing a passive role instead of the elderly cupid he had intended.

As they walked back to the Court, he suggested that perhaps a rare champagne might put the Earl in the proper frame of mind, and perhaps a special toast? Or did Georgie wish to wear the Holland Treasure this evening, for surely that would convince even a man of only moderate understanding, which of course the Earl was not, of her intentions? Georgie was adamant in her refusal to consider any of these proposals, although she was still arguing about the merits of the champagne as they walked upstairs.

Jenks went to the library to inform the Earl that Lady Spalding had just come in in company with the Marquess, and was even now going to her room to dress for dinner. Robert noticed the time, and resigned himself to a further wait as he went upstairs himself.

Georgie chose to wear the black velvet gown again, the one Robert had selected for her after the American threw her into the lake. As she came into the Great Parlour, she saw by his expression that he remembered, for he smiled at her warmly. Much encouraged, she turned to chat with the Wilsons, which allowed the Earl time to admire the creamy expanse of skin that the low back of the gown exposed, and he lost the thread of his conversation with his cousin in imagining how it would feel if he could run his hand up and down it in a caress. Like satin, he mused, or the softest velvet; the Marquess bounced and twinkled as he sipped his wine, not at all displeased in this case to be ignored.

There was an air of excitement that evening, and the conversation sparkled. Lady Martin and Miss Hersham were all smiles, Connie and Freddie looked quietly pleased, and Bertie beamed, his bald pate shining in the candlelight as he regaled his guests with amusing stories of the ton in years gone by. When dinner was announced, he had Robert take Lady Spalding in, and insisted on seating her beside him. At this, Georgie frowned, and gave a warning shake of her head to the irrepressible Marquess, which Robert was quick to note. His spirits plummeted again with his disappointment. So Bertie was pushing him at her, and the lady obviously did not care for it, or want his attentions. Although he was still polite, he became cool and distant then, and although Georgie and the others often addressed a remark to him, he had sunk into abstraction. How surprised he would have been if he had known that all the others at the table wished for nothing so much as to be able to shake him as hard as they could.

After dinner, the Marquess bustled Freddie and the Earl away from the table after only a single glass of port. Robert raised his brows at this, and again when the Marquess insisted he rejoin the ladies alone while they played billiards.

As the Earl was traversing the Great Hall, Jenks came to tell him that a man of Mr. Forrest's description had been spotted in Portsmouth by a gentleman currently waiting to see him in the gold salon. Diverted from his original destination, Robert joined him there, and it was a very long time before he returned to the Parlour. By the man's description, it had indeed been Bart Forrest, accompanied by the man Wilks, but he had slipped from the Earl's grasp once again, for he had taken ship to the Indies a few days before. Robert rewarded his informer and then sat on after the man bowed himself out, pondering the vagaries of fate that had denied him his revenge.

By the time he roused himself to return to the others, the ladies were concluding a rather listless game of cards as the tea tray was brought in and the Marquess and Freddie came to join them. Robert reported the news he had received, and everyone discussed it over the teacups, so there was no further opportunity for privacy before they all went up to bed. The Earl wondered why Bertie looked so annoyed and peevish when he bid the others good night. He had wanted Forrest to escape, hadn't he? And why were his aunt and Miss Hersham sniffing and looking so grim? Only the Wilsons seemed at ease, as of course did Lady Georgie. He could not resist lifting her hand and kissing it as she bade him good night, and the sparkle in her green eyes as she smiled at him made his heart turn over.

Sometime later, the Earl sat in a chair beside his bedroom fire, which gave off the only light in the room. He had removed his evening coat and cravat and unbuttoned his shirt for comfort. It was very late now, and the house was quiet, and although he knew he should get some sleep in preparation for his journey to town on the morrow, somehow he did not feel like going to bed just yet. He stared into the glowing red-and-gold flames, but he saw only Georgie's hair, for it was the exact same shade in sunlight or candlelight.

There was a decanter of wine beside him on a small table, and he poured himself a glass. Well, it was finished. He had waited all this time, but she had not spoken to him, and when in desperation he had told them he was returning to town, she had made no move to stop him, although her green eyes had flown to his face for one brief moment when he made the announcement. And tonight, when Bertie had placed her at his side at dinner, she had frowned and shaken her head. What could be clearer than that? What more proof did he need? Lady Spalding might not have wanted the American for a husband, but she didn't want him either!

He sighed, twirling the glass slowly between his long white fingers. It was obvious that Lady Spalding had nothing but a casual liking for him after all, and what a setdown that was. The elusive Earl of Amesbury had finally found his bride, only to discover she did not care for him above half. He had been so sure, that day in the bathhouse, that she wanted him as much as he wanted her, but she had shown no sign of it since then. Now of course his hands were tied. If he told her he loved her, after everything that had happened and all the chances he had had previously, she would believe it was because of the emeralds and the title, and she would always doubt him. No, it was too awkward, and there was no way he could convince her he loved her for herself, the title be damned; no way he could *make* her love him. If only the Marquess had taken her in dislike, he thought, or Forrest stolen the real treasure, it would have been so much easier. He sighed again, and then he heard a small sound at the door.

He turned his head lazily. Mice at Carew Court? How he would roast Bertie. Then his eyes narrowed and he rose to his feet, setting his glass down with great care, but never taking his eyes from the door.

As if his thoughts had conjured her up, Lady Spalding stood there, framed in the open doorway and dressed only in a silk nightgown and matching robe, with her feet bare and her long chestnut hair streaming down her back. She looked very beautiful. When she saw him staring at her, she put one finger to her lips, although he had not spoken and felt incapable of doing so in any case. He watched her close the door quietly behind her and turn the key in the lock.

Then she stood there, just inside the door, and twisted her hands before her as if her courage had suddenly deserted her, and she made no move to come towards him, nor did she speak.

"Good evening, Georgie," he said softly, just as if he were used to welcoming her to his room so attired and so late at night, every day of the week. "Come in, and let me give you a glass of wine while you tell me why I am honoured by this visit and in what way I might serve you."

Georgie moved forward, never taking her green eyes from his handsome face with its steady, intent grey eyes as she looked for some clue to his feelings. She saw the strong column of his throat above his open shirt, and the triangle of short curly black hair on his chest, and she felt a stiffening of resolve. Yes, she would do it.

"I have come to ask something of you, Robert," she said, and then she paused.

"Yes?" he asked encouragingly as he poured the wine and went to draw her towards the fireside. As he touched her hand and felt it trembling a little, his good resolutions almost failed him, and all he wanted to do was take her in his arms and let those words of love escape his lips at last. Instead, he forced himself to help her to a seat opposite his before he turned away to regain his composure.

Looking back to her after a moment, he saw her holding her wineglass with two hands like a child, her eyes troubled and confused.

"Yes?" he asked again. "What did you want to ask me?"

Suddenly she put up her chin, and with a great air of resolution set the glass down on the table untasted.

"I have talked to my aunt and to Connie, and I asked Cousin Bertie as well, and in effect they have all advised me to do the same thing." The Earl's eyebrows rose, but he did not interrupt her.

"Robert, I do not know how you feel about me, and I know there is to be no question of marriage—oh, pray do not think I have come to trap you into that, I beg you!"

She held out an imploring hand to him where he leaned against the back of the wing chair so he might watch her better.

"No, I do not think that, Georgie," he said when he was able to speak. "But, and you must forgive my bluntness, what *have* you come for? I have to know, you see."

She looked away for a moment and then her eyes came back to his face as she said, "I have come to ask you to make love to me."

The Earl tried to keep his face impassive. "Why?" he asked.

"Why?" she repeated, as if that was the last thing she had expected him to ask her. "Why, because I am in love with you, and I do not think I could bear it if you just went away and I never knew what it was like to be with you. So I thought that perhaps you would be so kind as to . . ."

"Kind?" the Earl asked, his voice wondering. "My dearest Georgie, I have wanted and loved you forever, but there was no way I could tell you after Bertie put my fate in your hands. Besides, there was the handsome Mr. Linwood, and for a long time I was sure you preferred him to me."

Georgie did not lie. "At the first I did. You were right, Robert, it was exciting to play with fire, but you see, it did not take me very long to discover that I was more afraid of him than I was in love with him. I do not think it is possible for a woman to love a man like that. Be fascinated by him, perhaps, but not love him. The only man I can love is you."

He went to her then and drew her to her feet, but when he would have put his arms around her to kiss her, she drew back again.

"No, wait. I have another confession to make, Robert."

He raised one black eyebrow, and she whispered, "I am so afraid you will be disappointed! You see, I am not very good at it—lovemaking, I mean."

The Earl stared down at her face and lowered eyes, thinking he had never seen anything so lovely as the way her heavy lashes trembled against her cheeks. "Forgive me, sweetheart, but did you and John Spalding have a marriage of convenience?" he asked.

"Oh, no, I know how it is done," she told him, a delicate colour washing over her face, "but David told me when he kissed me that I didn't have the least idea how to go on, and I am afraid he is right. I am woefully green, Robert, just as you said. John made love to me many times, but I cannot understand what all the fuss is about. Do I shock you?"

The Earl drew her into his arms at last and held her close to him for a moment. "No, my dear love, I am not shocked, nor will I be disappointed," he said in his deep warm voice which held an undertone of laughter, as his lips moved against her hair. "Come to bed now, and I will be delighted to show you what all the fuss is about!"

And so he did, slowly and carefully and with great loving tenderness, and when Georgie did not think she could bear those warm caressing hands and lips touching every part of her for even one more second before she would have to explode, he took possession of her and in only a short while she realized that the act of love could be a glorious, consuming abandonment that was totally unlike anything she had ever experienced, or even imagined she could feel.

When she woke, she was puzzled about her whereabouts for only a moment. There was a thin grey light coming through the curtains that told her dawn was not far away. Slowly she turned her head on the pillow so she could see the Earl's sleeping face beside her. He looked younger and completely relaxed in sleep, and Georgie studied the aristocratic planes of his face, his black eyebrows and strong nose, and the chiseled lips that had given her so much pleasure. Both his arms were around her, one hand cupping her breast.

Georgie smiled and snuggled closer to him, and as if he had been waiting for her to wake, he raised himself on his elbow to smile down at her. Georgie reached up to caress his lean cheek, and he turned his head to place a kiss in the palm of her hand.

"Well, m'lady?" he asked.

"Well indeed, m'lord," she replied, her green eyes glowing.

"And you understand now, dear love, what 'all the fuss is about'?" he asked, his hand beginning to caress that soft breast. She gasped as she felt her nipple harden and thrust upward as if seeking even closer contact with that hand.

"I never knew I could feel like that," she told him in

innocent surprise, and then she added, "But still, I cannot help but wonder . . ."

"Hmmm?" he asked, bending to kiss the tip of each of her breasts, and she drew in her breath as she asked, "I wonder if it goes on. What I mean is, dear Robert, perhaps it ceases to be so marvelous after the first time?"

He buried his face in the hollow of her neck for a moment, and when he raised his head, she saw he was laughing at her.

"Minx! Baggage! Witch!" he said. "I see there is nothing for it but to find out."

Georgie drew him down into her arms again and covered his face with kisses. "If you please, m'lord," she said. "But I warn you, I am afraid I will need a great many demonstrations before I am completely convinced."

The Earl meant to return Georgie to her room, but somehow the time slipped away. Neither one of them thought of convention or what the household would say if they were discovered as they made love and then dozed before waking again to the further delights of each other's arms. Sometimes they talked—of their misunderstandings and the adventures they had shared these past two months, and of the future they would spend together. Before they knew it, it was broad daylight and there was a knock on the door. The Earl's face darkened for a moment in annoyance, but Georgie just smiled up at him, so confident that it drew an answering smile as he put his hand over her mouth in warning.

"Yes?" he called. "Is that you, Townsley? I'll ring when I want you, man!"

"Your pardon, m'lord," a strange voice replied. " 'Tis Gudge. I'm the Marquess' valet, sir. He desired me to deliver this tray to you, m'lord."

The Earl pushed Georgie out of bed, and snatching up her robe, she fled to the dressing room as Robert put on his own robe and went to open the door to take the tray. She came back when she heard him laughing, for on the tray were a large bouquet of roses, two glasses, and a bucket of iced vintage champagne.

"Trust Bertie, my love!" he said, handing her the roses with an elegant bow before he opened the champagne and poured them each a glass. "He'll not take no for an answer this time, and neither will I! Besides, it is of the utmost

mportance that we make haste and marry at once in order
o give Bertie his heir. I have just discovered that besides
he sadly deceived Miss Linwood, there is another child at
hat Virginia plantation, a *Master* Linwood, age twelve."

"Why should that trouble us, Robert?" Georgie asked.
"I'm sure that Bertie has had his fill of Americans, and has
oo much regard for you to dispossess you for a mere
child."

The Earl sipped his champagne, and eyeing her over the
rim of the glass he asked morosely, "Even though his name
s Bertram James St. Denis Linwood, Georgie, dear heart?"

Gudge, who was lingering in the hall outside, on orders
from his master, heard the sudden peal of Lady Spalding's
laughter from behind the Earl's bedroom door, and nodding to himself as he also heard how abruptly it stopped,
he went away to report this very good news to the Marquess of Carew.

About the Author

Barbara Hazard was born, raised, and educated in New England, and although she has lived in New York for the past twenty years, she still considers herself a Yankee. She has studied music for many years, in addition to her formal training in art. Recently, she has had two one-man shows and exhibited in many group shows. She added the writing of Regencies to her many talents in 1978, but her other hobbies include listening to classical music, reading, quilting, cross-country skiing, and paddle tennis.